9/7

1-80

Too many people say "oh, well, now
then".

THERE'S A REASON FOR EVERYTHING

BY THE SAME AUTHOR:

THERE'S A
REASON FOR EVERYTHING

by

E. R. PUNSHON

LONDON
VICTOR GOLLANCZ LTD

NOTE

Every character in this book is entirely fictitious
and no reference whatever is intended to any
living person

First published July 1945
Second impression (first cheap edition) 1948

PRINTED IN GREAT BRITAIN BY PURNELL AND SONS, LTD. (T.U.)
PAULTON (SOMERSET) AND LONDON

CONTENTS

AEI

CHAPTER I

ASSORTED

Newly appointed deputy Chief Constable Bobby Owen, feeling both a trifle unemployed and a trifle grand, sat in his big new office on the first floor of the Wychshire county police headquarters, while below, on the ground floor, in Bobby's old office, reigned Inspector Payne, new head of the Wychshire C.I.D., and so dealing with all that routine work which, as Deputy Chief Constable, Bobby had now relinquished to Payne's care. It was a loss he was inclined occasionally to regret because of the close relationship into which it had brought him both with events and with his men. Now Payne only let him know those more important events he thought worthy of troubling the remote dignity of a Deputy Chief.

Even promotion, Bobby reflected with some surprise, has its thorns, and though, as Chief Constable's private secretary, the position he had previously doubled with that of head of the Wychshire C.I.D., he had long acted in practice as deputy, now his position was official, and due etiquette had to be observed. And Payne, jealous of his own new dignity, was taking care that it was so observed, and that no superior got away with any poaching on his preserves.

One letter this morning he had, however, allowed to be passed on for Bobby's information and direction. Because it was so unimportant, Bobby suspected, though certainly a little out of the way. It was from a Dr. Clem Jones, of Wessex and Mercia University, and was to the effect that he and two or three friends and colleagues had received permission from Mr. Ivor de Tallebois to investigate the rumours of renewed hauntings at Nonpareil, the ancient seat of the Tallebois family, though it is true that there seemed some doubt as to the exact connection of the present de Tallebois, whose great-grandfather had done well—even exceedingly well—supplying, or, as the unkind said, not supplying, food and clothing to the British armies during the Crimean war, with the original owners of Nonpareil. However, this was a detail of small interest, and in no way diminished the size and importance of that ancient and historic building, where it was often said more murders, torturings, crimes, had been committed than in any other in England, excepting the Tower of London itself.

No wonder, then, that it was provided with a choice assortment of ghosts, all well authenticated by numerous accounts of eye-witnesses. The particular stories Dr. Jones and his friends wished to investigate were first the tale of the cavalier, Sir Thomas de Tallebois, who, in the reign of Charles the First, had taken refuge from pursuing Roundheads in the great cellars of the building, and had there been inadvertently locked in, to die of starvation, he, his wife and children together. Their groans and lamentations were said still to be heard once every year on the returning anniversary of the tragedy. The other tale was that of the twin brothers who, rivals in love, had fought a duel to the death in one of the upper rooms. With some apparent lack of justice, however, it was not their ghosts that had been doomed to haunt the scene of the duel, but that of their presumably innocent mother, who was often to be seen wringing her hands in despair as she fled along the corridors leading to this room. After each of these visits, it was believed, a fresh blood-stain always appeared on the floor of the room, gradually fading away and then reappearing after each renewed visit.

Dr. Jones had apparently thought it well to inform the police of his impending visit in case of their attention being attracted by rumours of unusual proceedings at Nonpareil, closed for the duration, and, indeed, considering its enormous size and total lack of all modern amenities, never likely to be occupied again. Midwych Corporation, for example, had already refused, with some haste, an offer of it as a free gift. Bobby supposed that it was, in fact, possible that undesirable rumours might become current if strangers were observed in the vicinity of so lonely a building so long deserted. In time of war the fewer rumours to gain currency, the better. He marked the letter 'Ack. C', which meant that it was to be acknowledged under formula C—the most polite and flowery of the three in use—and decided it was time for lunch.

So he descended to the ground floor, and looked in at his own old room, though well knowing that Inspector Payne would soon make him aware that while Deputy Chief Constables might have time to spare, C.I.D. inspectors had none. However, to-day Payne seemed in a more chatty mood, admitted he, too, had been thinking of lunch and there was an odd report sent in by the sergeant-in-charge at Lone-some, a small, half village, half suburb dormitory, just outside the Midwych city limits. It seemed the new man there, Constable Reed, known to his superiors as Broken Reed, since his first name was Brodie and he, an old pensioner recalled to war-time duty, was much troubled by rheumatism, a fact whereof he seldom failed to remind the world in general and the Deputy Chief Constable in particular.

Payne, indeed, so far unbent as to allow Bobby to have a look at the report, if only to admire the dexterity with which a reference to the pangs of rheumatism had been brought in. Leaving the recurrent rheumatic theme apart, it was to the effect that while Constable Reed and Major Hardman, of The Tulips, were 'passing the time of day'—so said the report, though it seemed the time was ten at night—they had both heard what sounded like a shot coming from the direction of Wychwood forest, on the outskirts of which, between the forest and Lonesome village proper, stood Major Hardman's pleasant detached villa, known as The Tulips.

Shots are not rare in country districts. But the hour was late, and Constable Reed had felt it his duty to investigate. As he found nothing in any way suspicious, and neither saw nor heard anything further, he would probably not have troubled to report the incident had not Major Hardman shown a certain uneasiness about a young nephew of his who had recently appeared in the neighbourhood on his discharge from the army as medically unfit.

The young man was, it seemed, not much approved of either by his uncle or by his sister, Miss Frances Hardman, who kept house for the Major. This unpopularity with his relatives seemed to have some justification, for already he had created a disturbance at the nearby Horse and Groom, wherefrom it had been necessary to eject him with some vigour. Why Major Hardman associated his young nephew with the shot heard did not appear, except for a vague reference by Reed in the course of his report to 'threatening language', though by whom or against whom was not very clear.

"Nothing to take action on," Payne had decided, and Bobby agreed.

"Who is Major Hardman?" he asked idly.

"Retired business man from London," Payne explained. "Came up here to be out of the way of the bombing—not so much out of the way either, but that was the idea. Lives in a fair-sized house, The Tulips, between Lonesome village and the forest. Wears an Old Etonian tie, and is over fifty, so is exempt from national service. Bad health, too. Does fire-watching, though. Reed reports he is a quiet, pleasant-spoken gentleman, keeps very much to himself. The niece keeps house for him. She has registered, of course, but has not been directed to any employment, as she has to look after an elderly uncle in poor health, and, anyhow, does a lot for the W.V.S. The young man thrown out of the Horse and Groom is her twin, and it seems they are as like as two peas. Only for the young lady having a permanent wave and the boy a smudge of a moustache, Reed says you would never be able to tell one from t'other."

"Couldn't you, though?" asked Bobby thoughtfully.

"Oh, it's the way with twins sometimes," Payne explained, a little proud of his knowledge. "Depends on which they are. I mean, if they were always meant to be two, then they are just ordinary brother and sister, and no more like each other than any other brother and sister. But if they were meant to be one and then somehow split up to make two, then they are always dead spits of each other."

"I see," said Bobby, still more thoughtfully, trying to remember what he had once read about twins. "Yes, I have an idea I read about

9

all that somewhere. Well, anyhow, nothing to bother about, unless the young man starts trouble."

Therewith Bobby departed to get his lunch at the Midwych Union, a club to which most of the Midwych celebrities belonged, and whereto his recent promotion to Deputy Chief Constable had secured his election. Returning after one of those meals of deadly monotony over which heart-broken chefs weep daily wartime tears, Bobby, entering head-quarters, met Payne bustling out. Payne stopped to speak.

"Reed has just 'phoned in," he said. "I asked his sergeant to find out what was the threatening language used at the Horse and Groom. It seems the young man's uncle—Major Hardman—gave him a five-pound note, and told him he wouldn't get another farthing till he found himself a decent job, preferably as far away from Midwych as possible. At the Horse and Groom they say the language he used about the Major fair blistered the paint—and that's a bit of a tribute from the Horse and Groom, where they know quite a lot of language. Reed was sufficiently impressed to have a look along the footpath that's a short cut starting from near the 'bus stop on the main road and then through Wychwood forest to Lonesome. It saves a lot. Comes out by the new bungalows there."

"Find anything?" Bobby asked.

"He found a cartridge recently fired from a point three two automatic. A lady's shoe, size four, and a good deal worn. And a five-pound note, identified by Major Hardman by the number as the one he gave his nephew. You remember there was heavy rain later in the night till well on in the morning, so there was no chance of finding footsteps or any-thing like that."

"An odd assortment," Bobby said, "a very odd assortment. Have to wait and see if there are any developments, I suppose."

Payne agreed, and went off on his errand, while Bobby continued on his way to his room on the first floor.

CHAPTER II

LEGENDS

THAT EVENING THERE was to be a meeting between the heads of the Midwych city civil defence authorities and those of the out-side districts. In a recent raid a certain lack of co-operation was thought to have been shown, and the meeting was to discuss ways and means of putting this right. Bobby was to attend and speak, since a good deal of general official responsibility was his now that he was Deputy Chief

Constable. His wife, Olive, was also to be present, as one of the representatives of the organization outside the town boundaries. Bobby had suggested that a really dutiful wife would get someone else to take her place and herself stay at home, rather than see her husband make an ass of himself—as Bobby was always gloomily sure would be his fate whenever he had to speak in public. Olive, however, had pointed out that to see a husband making an ass of himself was no novelty to any wife; that, in any case, she would rather know the worst at once; and then had added the consoling reflection that on the whole sometimes he did not do so badly. Nor did she know why the prospect of speaking in public should invariably reduce him to a state of anguished panic. Hadn't he, she asked, faced worse things? and Bobby said, No, because there was nothing worse than speaking in public.

The meeting was to begin at a comparatively early hour on account of blackout conditions and the possibility of another raid. Accordingly Olive appeared in good time, demanding to be taken out to tea. Bobby protested that was impossible. They must have their tea sent up from the canteen. He explained he had just written out an entirely new version of his proposed speech, and he had to learn it by heart. Olive asked to look at it, and, when he handed it over, put it in her handbag, snapped the handbag fastening to with great firmness, and told him that his old speech was good enough, that the fewer versions he burdened his somewhat limited intelligence with, the better; and that, anyway, she wanted her tea, and Not from the canteen, where it was intended for the most He-like of He-men, and not for poor weak, fragile, feminine constitutions like her own.

"What about this stuffy old club of yours?" she demanded. "Or is it one of those places where they daren't let a woman in because it isn't fit to be seen?"

Bobby tried to stall, but soon realized that Olive had made up her mind, and that that being so, further argument was useless. To the Union club accordingly they adjourned, since a newly-elected revolutionary—practically Bolshevik—committee had recently ordained that members might entertain women friends in the smaller and less convenient tearoom—the one that had suffered bomb damage—between the hours of four and six. And what these changes would end in was a matter of somewhat gloomy speculation among the older and more staid members.

However, Olive had to admit that the service might have been worse, and that the anchovy toast was, at any rate, tolerable. Cakes, of course, in war time, are always wartime cakes, but she did wonder why women were not allowed in the bigger, brighter tearoom, since all the service there was now by women attendants.

"But then men always are so illogical," she admitted, and did not stress the point.

They had nearly finished their tea when a member who knew Bobby, the one, in fact, who had proposed his election, brought up a Mr. Parkinson, a tall, thin man with thin, ascetic features, so thin, indeed, that Olive was at once convinced he must be a bachelor with no one to look after him and see he had proper meals. So she at once ordered a fresh supply of anchovy toast and made sure, too, that he ate it.

It appeared that Mr. Parkinson was the colleague to whom in his letter Dr. Clem Jones had referred as his companion in the contemplated Nonpareil investigation. This had begun the previous night, and the member who was Bobby's friend had thought the story of what had been seen and heard might interest Bobby. So Bobby said politely that he was sure it would, inwardly prepared to be bored, reflected that anyhow he would soon have to leave for his meeting, and settled down to listen.

"Some odd things happened," explained Mr. Parkinson, looking slightly embarrassed and also grateful for the newly-arrived anchovy toast in which he seemed inclined to seek refuge. "Dr. Jones was extremely interested—excited. I am meeting him there again to-night." Mr. Parkinson paused, and laughed uneasily. "Not too willingly," he said. "The more I think of what happened last night the less I like it."

"What was it?" Bobby asked.

"First of all, we thought we heard footsteps. Empty houses are always full of noises, of course—especially old houses. But what we heard did sound like footsteps. I remember in the last war, when I was on sentry duty, how exactly the sound of dry leaves blown by the wind seemed like footsteps. But this was indoors."

"Rats, perhaps," suggested Bobby for the sake of saying something.

"I thought of that," Mr. Parkinson answered. "Dr. Jones didn't think so. He was quite emphatic. Even before that we had been—I don't know how to put it . . ." He paused to turn his attention to the anchovy toast, and with such effect that Olive thought it well to order a fresh supply. "There was a sort of feeling," he went on, when his mouth was comparatively empty again. "I can't describe it—a presence, someone, something, watching. Yet the caretaker had assured us that he was in the building nearly every day, and he had never seen or heard anything unusual. A surly sort of man, the caretaker, I mean. Not very civil, either. He made difficulties about admitting us in spite of the letter from Mr. de Tallebois we showed him. All other letters had been from the agents, he said, and he wanted to know how he was to tell the letter we showed really came from Mr. de Tallebois. However, he let us in at last. Do you know the Nonpareil legend?"

"Well, there are several, aren't there?" Bobby remarked. "I think there's one about some people during the Cromwellian civil war getting locked up by accident in the cellars and starving to death."

"I hadn't heard about that," Mr. Parkinson said. "I meant the story about twin brothers having murdered each other in one of the rooms of the corridor leading to the old picture gallery."

"That was a duel, wasn't it?" Bobby asked. "They were both in love with the same girl, and so they had it out together, and managed to kill each other. Isn't the story that their mother's ghost is still to be seen in the corridor trying to find the room where they were fighting, and knocking at the door to be let in?"

Mr. Parkinson nodded, and pushed aside the freshly arrived anchovy toast Olive was now offering him. He seemed to have lost his appetite. He said:

"The story goes that on the floor of the room where it happened there appears at intervals a fresh bloodstain."

"Oh, does it?" asked Bobby smilingly. "Did you see it?"

"Yes," said Mr. Parkinson, and Bobby sat upright with a jerk.

CHAPTER III

HEIRLOOMS

"ARE YOU SURE?" Bobby asked after a moment's pause. "Were you and Dr. Jones actually in the room? You saw it yourselves?"

"Yes," said Mr. Parkinson again. Then he said: "Jones saw it first. He called me. We examined it closely. I touched it. It was fresh. Jones drew a chalk mark, an outline round it. Unluckily we had no camera— at least, we had a camera but no film. We hadn't been able to get any— none in the shops we tried. So we couldn't take photographs. But that there was a stain of fresh blood on the floor of the room, where the twin de Tallebois brothers are said to have killed each other three hundred years ago, is an absolute fact."

Bobby hardly knew why his thoughts returned at once to that tale he had listened to earlier in the day of the shot heard in Wychwood, by the lonely and rough path that led past the new bungalows erected there immediately before the outbreak of the war; and to the odd assortment, the cartridge case, the lady's shoe, size four, the five-pound note originally in the possession of Major Hardman's nephew, all found thereby. Could there be any connection, he asked himself? Nonpareil was at least two miles distant. He said:

"What time was this?"

"About twelve—midnight. I don't know exactly. We had meant to be there earlier, but we got delayed with one thing and another, finding the way, arguing with the extremely unpleasant caretaker. I should say it was nearly eleven before we were inside the house. We had a look round the ground floor. It was then we felt—as I said, I can't describe it. A feeling we were not alone, a feeling that there was a presence, a watching, hostile presence. Then we went upstairs. There's an enormous double central stair rising from the inner hall."

"You had torches, I suppose?" Bobby said.

"Oh, yes, both of us. It was when we were going up the stairs we heard—well, it sounded like footsteps, very low, cautious. Rats, I said it might be. Jones wouldn't have it. We went on to the murder room."

"You knew which it was?"

"Jones did. He knows all about Nonpareil, and its history. He is some sort of distant connection of the family, I gathered. Through his grandmother he said, I think."

"Oh, yes," said Bobby when Mr. Parkinson paused to help himself afresh to more anchovy toast.

"It shook me a little," said Mr. Parkinson, and Bobby wondered if this referred to the footsteps or to the just-mentioned grandmotherly connection.

"You remember the legend?" Mr. Parkinson asked. "The story is that the appearance of the bloodstain is a sign of an approaching death in the de Tallebois family."

"I didn't know that," said Bobby, and he looked thoughtful.

"I didn't like it, I was—disturbed," said Mr. Parkinson, suddenly, and once again, seeking refuge in the anchovy toast.

"Did Dr. Jones seem worried at all?" Bobby asked.

"Oh, no. Interested and excited rather. Well, nervous perhaps. He did just mention the story in a joking way."

"Did you take any further action? I mean, make any further search?"

"Yes. Yes. But we found nothing, saw nothing. At least—Jones said it was nonsense, nerves."

"What was?"

"Well, as we were leaving the picture gallery I thought I saw one of the statues move. Jones said it was just the shadows. But I was clearly under the impression that when we first went in, the pedestal second from the door was vacant and all of those farther on were occupied. As we were leaving I happened to look back and certainly then the pedestals near the door all had their statues, and one of the others seemed vacant."

"Statues do not change places," said Bobby.

"No, they don't, do they?" agreed Mr. Parkinson, and looked quite cheered up, as if this were a most novel and encouraging statement.

"Your torches were giving a good light?"

"Excellent. The windows are boarded up so the blackout wasn't affected. Naturally it seemed darker still when we switched off or where the light from the torches didn't reach."

"Yes. Yes. Of course, it would be that way," agreed Bobby absently. "What is the picture gallery like? Furniture, curtains? Anything besides the statues? I understood the house had been completely emptied."

"I think that's so, except for the statues and, I believe, for a certain amount of rubbish in the cellars that's never been got rid of."

"About the picture gallery?"

"It's long, lofty, narrow. About a hundred feet long I should say, more or less. Doors at both ends, and one in the middle. Windows at one side. Niches between the windows. That's where the statues stand."

"Do you know why they have been left?"

"Jones told me they are quite valueless, and yet they are all listed as heirlooms. So they can't be got rid of. Of course, the courts would give permission. But it would be troublesome and expensive to get it —permission, I mean. The things have an odd history. Until recently they were supposed to be of very considerable value, artistic and historical as well. Examples of ancient Greek art and one or two attributed to great Italian artists like Michelangelo and della Robbia, I think. They are all certainly antiques. At any rate they would be admitted into America duty free as over a hundred years old. In the eighteenth century, when everyone made the grand tour and when people like the Earl of Carlisle were making really fine collections, the de Tallebois of the time wanted to show he was a cognoscenti, too, as they were called. Unfortunately he had no qualification except money, neither taste nor knowledge. Not unnaturally he was as a sheep to the shearer. Astute Italians weren't going to miss a chance like that. Many people seem to think faking works of art is a modern industry, but they knew all about it two hundred years ago. There's a description of how Mr. de Tallebois himself presided over the recovery from the site of a buried Roman villa of a statue of Hermes with an inscription saying that it was dedicated to the gods by Praxiteles. Unfortunately, neither the lettering nor the language is in the style of the fourth century B.C. Eighteenth-century Greek in fact. The statue had evidently been buried beforehand, all ready to be found when Mr. de Tallebois was there to see. And in one of his own letters he tells very proudly how his agent told him of a story that Michelangelo's portrait statue of the Pope, Julius the Second, placed over the gate of San Petronio and believed to have been destroyed later on, had really been rescued at the last moment, and was in existence on a farm near Rome. Mr. de Tallebois tells how, in spite of his agent's reluctance, he insisted on going to look, spent a day or two in the search, and finally discovered the statue. The farmer at first refused to sell because the statue was of a saint, and if he sold it he would have bad luck. In the end Mr. de Tallebois, to secure the statue, had to buy the farm as well—at a price that probably made several Italian families rich for life. For his share the agent got the farm as a free gift, Mr. de Tallebois probably having no wish to become an Italian farmer. Unluckily the statue is in marble and of poor workmanship, and the Michelangelo statue was in bronze—it was melted down for cannon, which wouldn't happen with marble. Much the same applies to the other pieces of sculpture, though for many years the de Tallebois family clung to the belief that their collection was of enormous value from every point of view. But when death duties came in they had to think again. If the collection was still valued at a good many thousand pounds, there would be appropriate duty to pay. So they got expert opinion, which was that the whole lot were crude eighteenth-century fakes, and had better be sold to make lime. But they are still listed as heirlooms, and can't be touched. In time of course they will be quietly dropped, and no more heard of. There seems, though, to be still some lingering hope somewhere that one or other of them may be of value. Jones had heard that another expert had asked permission only the other day to examine them—a Mr. Marmaduke Clavering, an Honourable, I believe, a son of Lord Grandlieu."

Bobby sniffed. He didn't think much of Honourables. But for the grace of God and for the accident of his father being the younger of twins he might have been an 'Honourable' himself. Bad enough as it was—having an impecunious peer for uncle.

"What was his verdict?" Bobby asked, his voice expressing all the contempt he felt for the opinion of any expert who was also an Honourable by right of birth.

"I don't think Jones had heard—probably the same, though."

"Can you say anything more about why you thought one statue moved?"

"No. No. It was my impression. I hardly know. All the statues are covered with dust sheets. It gave them a very ghostly appearance. Jones pointed that out."

"Did you move the dust sheets?"

"Oh, yes. Yes. We were very much on the alert. We missed nothing."

"How many of the things are there in all?"

"Thirteen. I am quite clear about that. I happened to remark that it was an unlucky number. Jones insisted there were only twelve."

"Are they all single statues? Any groups among them?"

"Mostly they are single statues. There were two busts I think, two or three. Two large groups, one of a goddess reclining by a stag, a barefaced copy of Goujon's work in the Louvre, but supposed to be an original work of the school of Phidias—a modest touch that 'school of'. Another is a group showing a river god with attendants, a big, clumsy thing."

"Very interesting," Bobby said. "Thank you very much. You mean to join Dr. Jones at Nonpareil to-night?"

"Yes. At least I shall if I can get there. I am trying to arrange for a taxi, but it seems difficult. The friend I'm staying with has a car but no petrol. I don't cycle and it's too far to walk."

"I could give you a lift," Bobby said unexpectedly. "I think I should like a look at this bloodstain. Interesting. Do you think Dr. Jones would mind?"

"I'm sure he would," Mr. Parkinson answered with emphasis.

"Pity," said Bobby. "I suppose, like most experts, he hates having blundering amateurs messing about. How I sympathize! There's a meeting to-night I'm bound to attend, and there's no knowing how long it will last. Much longer than it ought to or need, I expect. If you care to wait for me here, I'll look you up as soon as I can. I'll have a car."

Olive lifted both hands in resigned dismay.

"Talk about mobile women," she sighed. "Why haven't I a static husband?"

CHAPTER IV

ESCAPE

THE MEETING, AS is the way of such meetings, did, in fact, last much longer than was in any way necessary—or, for that matter, desirable. So it was getting late before Bobby was able to pick up Mr. Parkinson whom he found waiting for him, not at the Union Club, but outside the hall where the meeting had been held. Parkinson, it seemed, had remembered some small piece of business or another he had wished to attend to, and, having done so, instead of returning to the Union Club, he had come on here to wait. Olive had already departed for home in the company of her own special contingent of Civil Defence workers, and with enough reorganization work on hand to keep her and them all busy for some considerable time to come. With him Bobby had brought Inspector Payne; and Parkinson, when introduced, murmured:

"The Deputy Chief Constable and a police inspector. Jones will feel like murder."

He was still chuckling happily at the thought as they started off. Bobby was driving, since, in the general shortage of man power, no constable could be conveniently spared to act as chauffeur. In the darkness, for night had fallen now, Bobby managed to take a wrong turning; so that it was eleven before they reached the entrance to Nonpareil, where huge stone griffins crowned gate posts even more gigantic. Then, to gain admittance, for the gates were locked, they had to rouse the caretaker from his bed in the lodge he occupied. It was a task that took some minutes, for it seemed that he slept soundly.

When he appeared he showed himself a short, thick-set, bullet-headed, scowling individual, with a cast in one eye and black, broken teeth that lent him no attractive appearance, even apart from his scowl. But then many people would be apt to show a scowling countenance on being summoned from a warm bed and a first sound sleep to attend to strangers on an errand that seemed most unnecessary.

"The gentleman's gone," he protested. "Gone long ago. I'm letting no strangers in this time o' night. So what's the odds?"

He tried to bang to his door, but failed, for Bobby's foot was there first. Excusable, perhaps, this show of temper, Bobby thought, and was about to declare his identity and produce his official card, when abruptly the man's manner changed. Where, before, it had been hostile, truculent indeed, it became subdued, conciliatory. He was even muttering words of excuse as he produced the key giving admittance to Nonpareil. The change of tone was so sudden and so marked that Mr. Parkinson spoke of it as they walked on towards the building—their car they left outside, since the approach by the drive was short and to admit the car would have meant opening the great iron gates, a lengthy and trouble-some business.

"Our caretaker friend was beginning to think he might get reported for insolence," Parkinson was saying. "I suppose it struck him he might lose his job if he wasn't careful."

"It might be that," agreed Bobby. "I don't know. He certainly changed his tone in a great hurry."

"Nowadays," grumbled Payne, whose temper was not good, for he put little faith in all this talk of perambulating statues and bloodstains appearing where no bloodstain could be, and would much rather have been on his way to supper and bed than where he was in actual fact, "nowadays, it isn't the worker who is afraid of losing a job, it's the job that's scared stiff of losing the man."

"Do you know his name?" Bobby asked Parkinson.

"The caretaker's?" Parkinson said. "Bailey, I think. I think that's how the letter was addressed. And I think I heard his wife call him Alf."

"Bailey?" repeated Bobby. "Alf Bailey? Can't remember anyone of that name. Mean anything to you, Payne?"

"Not a thing," answered Payne. "I'll inquire, shall I?"

"Might as well ask our people here if they know anything," Bobby agreed. "You can never know too much in our job, Mr. Parkinson."

"I suppose not," agreed Mr. Parkinson. "A most unpleasant man. A thoroughly criminal type of countenance in my opinion. But perhaps I am prejudiced. He was anything but civil when Jones and I were here before. In fact, Jones threatened to complain to his employer."

By this time they had entered the enormous shadow thrown by the great mass of the building now close before them. There was only a thin crescent of a moon, but the night was clear, with strongly-shining stars, so that till now progress had not been too difficult. But here, in the shadow of the building, the darkness was intense; and on the paved path they were following, their footsteps sounded heavily. Guided by Parkinson, they made their way round to the east wing where was the small side door to which Bailey had given them the key. All other entrances had been carefully secured by bolt and bar and lock and every window in the place—the number ran well into three figures—had been boarded up. Closing behind them the small door whereby they entered they found themselves in a narrow passage. It led them to the inner hall, into which they emerged through what once had been the serving door, and to the well of the great double stairway, one of the features of the building with its marble steps and its fine gilt iron railings, that rose in a majestic sweep to the gallery above.

There in the old days, when Nonpareil had been the centre of county society, when an invitation to its balls or banquets had been a proof of social standing and importance, when at times even Royalty itself had been entertained, had stood host and hostess to receive their guests ascending that great stairway in a double stream of rank and fashion, a blaze of light from many hundreds of candles shining upon every jewel and ornament and glittering order, upon the colourful dresses of the women, on the often even more colourful uniforms of the men. Now all was dark and silent and alone; and what made Bobby act as he did he never knew, what faint warning reached him, what almost unheard sound told him to beware, what obscure instinct made him know death was near. Abruptly he pushed Payne aside, caught Parkinson, instinctively resisting, by the arm and pulled him back, as, almost simultaneously, something huge, black, heavy, crashed down with such a reverberating roar in the stillness of the quiet house as though itself had crashed about their ears.

Bobby had overbalanced himself. At least he supposed so, at any rate he was flat on the floor of the hall. He scrambled to his feet, flashing his torch, which he still held. Payne, overthrown by Bobby's unexpected push, was on his knees, looking very bewildered. Parkinson was prone and motionless. Round about them lay the shattered fragments of a stone bust—of a Roman emperor apparently. Had Bobby's action been less prompt, had the thing fallen a foot or two more to one side, one or more of them must inevitably have been killed. The air was full of dust, the tessellated flooring of the hall was badly broken where it

19

had taken the full impact of the falling bust. Still on his knees, Payne said:

"What was it? What happened?"

"Murder try on, apparently," Bobby answered grimly. "Look after Parkinson. He's hurt."

While he was still speaking, Bobby was racing up the stairs, and as he was doing so was telling himself he was wasting his efforts. Whoever was responsible, whether it had been a deliberate attempt at murder or merely meant as a diversion to cover escape, had certainly already got away. Easy enough to run down the other side of the double stairs —or that side up which Bobby was now racing, for that matter— while they themselves were all three still prostrate on the hall floor, still bewildered and put out of action by the suddenness of the attack.

When he reached the gallery on which abutted the two wings of the stairway he stood and listened. The house seemed very still and silent, more so by reason of the contrast with the recent crash, whereof the last reverberating echo had now died away. Bobby could almost have fancied that like a living thing holding its breath it waited expectant and eager to know the result of what it itself had done. There were sounds though from below where he had left Parkinson, with Payne to look after him. Bobby threw the light of his torch down on them where they stood. To Bobby's relief, Parkinson was on his feet again, and so he was alive and not too seriously hurt.

"Payne?" Bobby called. "Payne? Mr. Parkinson? Are you all right?"

"Yes, I think so," Mr. Parkinson answered. "What happened?"

"Will you be all right by yourself?" Bobby asked. "Payne, is Mr. Parkinson fit to be left?"

"Yes, sir, I think so," Payne answered. "Bruised a bit, but no bones broken, I think."

"Then leave him and come up here," Bobby said.

"I'm not being left," said Mr. Parkinson with dignity. "I'm not lost luggage," and he followed Payne up the stairs with sufficient speed to show he was not seriously hurt. When they reached the gallery he said to Bobby: "What happened? Who was it?"

"Someone trying to explain we weren't wanted here," Bobby answered.

"Surely Jones wouldn't . . ." began Parkinson, still a trifle dazed. "I knew he would be annoyed, but surely . . ."

"Rather a drastic way of showing annoyance," Bobby suggested. "I hardly think it's Dr. Jones. But let's have a look at you first, and then we'll have a look round."

Mr. Parkinson's shoulder was badly bruised by the glancing blow it had received, and in his fall he had hurt his left side. Bobby had a small pocket first-aid case with him, but Parkinson wanted to refuse treatment,

20

declaring stoutly that he was perfectly all right, and all he wanted to know was what Jones had been up to.

"Can he have moved the bust for examination or some reason and let it overbalance?" he asked.

"I shouldn't think so," Bobby answered, as he persisted in administering a little elementary treatment to the bruised shoulder. "Didn't the caretaker say Dr. Jones had left some time ago?"

"I forgot that," admitted Parkinson. Then he said: "There's been no other living creature in here, none."

"Well, someone was here," Bobby said, helping Parkinson readjust his coat and shirt. "Ghosts don't throw busts about."

"Poltergeists do," Parkinson told him. "Is there a poltergeist history here?"

Bobby did not answer this, as he did not feel competent to discuss the manners and the habitat of the poltergeist. Nor, for that matter, did he think the moment appropriate.

"That thing weighed fifty pounds or more," put in Payne. "Hefty sort of ghost needed to throw that about."

"Can you show us the room where you saw the bloodstain?" Bobby asked.

"I think so," Parkinson answered. To Payne he said rebukingly: "You can't measure super-normal phenomena by avoirdupois weight." Payne grunted. To Bobby, Parkinson continued: "It's this corridor to the right through here, the third or fourth door, I think. Anyhow, I can easily identify it. We took precautions. Necessary in psychical research."

He led them through a vast reception-room, then into a broad corridor, from which several doors opened on each side. Before two successive doors he paused, examining each in turn by the light of his torch. "This is it," he announced the second time. "You see? We placed threads in position across the crack of the door. Undisturbed, you notice," he pointed out with modest pride. "A most effective precaution." Then he showed a small paper wad fixed between the doorpost and the door, so that it would fall if the door were opened. Still gently proud, he said: "We take every care, one has to in these matters of super-normal phenomena. Absolutely impossible for any one to have been here during our absence."

He opened the door as he spoke. Within was a large, empty room, the windows boarded up, the darkness complete.

"It's in the middle of the floor between the fireplace and the westerly window," Mr. Parkinson said, throwing the beam from the torch he held on the spot mentioned. The rays from Bobby's torch, from Payne's, followed, questing, searching. Payne said sharply:

"There's nothing there."

"It's vanished," Parkinson said bewilderedly. "It's gone."

CHAPTER V

SCULPTURE

THE LIGHT FROM the three torches all directed on the floor between the fireplace and the windows did show, however, a roughly oval chalk outline, but an outline that outlined nothing save bare boards, as bare and clear of mark or stain as any other portion of the floor. Looking very disturbed, Mr. Parkinson said:

"It was there. Now it's vanished clean away. Impossible. Normally, that is."

"The impossible doesn't happen, normally or abnormally," remarked Bobby.

"There's something going on round here," said Payne slowly, "that I don't much like the look of."

Bobby was walking up and down the length of the room, sending the ray of his torch into every nook and corner, seeing and finding nothing save bare walls, bare floor.

"It was there," Parkinson insisted again. "A stain of freshly-spilt blood, and now no sign of it. I saw it, touched it, it was fresh, it was damp, it was here. Now it isn't," and furtively, for he had been brought up in the Roman church, though he had long since left it, he crossed himself.

"Can't have been . . ." began Payne, but Parkinson interrupted him angrily.

"I tell you I saw it," he said. "I can swear to that. I saw it myself. I don't understand, but there it is."

"You mean, there it isn't," suggested Bobby. "Are you sure this is the same room?"

"The cotton we put in position was still there, wasn't it?" retorted Mr. Parkinson. "You saw it yourself, I showed you." He stooped to look more closely at the chalk on the floor, markings that because they no longer showed or indicated anything seemed somehow to have acquired a greater significance, gaining strangely by loss. Parkinson said: "I watched Jones make it. There, where you can see a slight irregularity, is where Jones stopped for a moment to start again." He turned towards the fireplace. "I smoked two cigarettes while we were in the room, and threw the stubs in the fireplace. There they are." He showed two cigarette stubs he had picked up. "Greek," he said, "made in Athens. Not very common. I get them from a friend. He imported them specially before the war. He still has some. No one can possibly have been in here since we left. Everything just as it was. It's . . . it's beyond me," and once again he crossed himself, and this time quite openly.

"All very odd and very interesting," Bobby commented. He was still walking up and down the room, examining ceiling, walls, flooring. He even looked up the chimney. He found nothing interesting or in any way suspicious. He noticed, peering through chinks in the boarding covering the window that there was a wide view from it over the surrounding country. Possibly, he thought, that was why it had been chosen. He said: "There'll have to be a thorough search of the whole place. Payne, do you think you could spare two or three of your chaps for the job to-morrow?"

Payne looked dismayed. He answered, when he had recovered a little from the shock:

"Well, sir, if you think it's necessary . . ." and his tone plainly implied that he did not. "You know how short-handed we are. Perhaps some of the uniform men . . .?"

Bobby smiled grimly. He knew how fierce a battle would have to be waged if any men were to be extracted from any of his superintendents. He foresaw plainly how everything that went wrong for weeks to come would always be blandly explained by the fact that these men had been withdrawn, necessary men, essential men, so that there had simply been no one to do whatever had not been done. Already every senior officer was wailing that making bricks without straw was child's play compared to carrying out duties without men to perform them. Besides, Bobby was acutely conscious that his own position was a little delicate. He was a comparatively new arrival in the Wychshire police force. He had come to it direct from Scotland Yard, an institution at which all his superintendents sniffed ostentatiously. He had been promoted over their heads, though none of them, all elderly men of the old school, all approaching or beyond the normal age of retirement, had been anxious to accept new responsibilities, or face the social activities that a Chief Constable has to be prepared to undertake. All the same, they were all much his senior in service, inclined to patronize him as a precocious though no doubt promising youngster, and could, if they chose, make things extremely difficult for their young chief. To obtain men from them would be like dragging a succulent bone from a hungry tiger.

"I would rather you tried to find them from your own lot, Payne, if you possibly can," he said pleadingly.

"Yes, sir, if you say so," said Payne formally, "only I don't quite see how. Now Jenks . . ." and he was proceeding to dilate at some length on the ease with which Jenks, the superintendent of the C division, could spare men, when Bobby interrupted.

"Oh, well, all right," he said. "We'll think about that later. Just now the thing is to have a further look round and see if we can find out why the stain Mr. Parkinson saw has vanished so completely." (Here Mr. Parkinson crossed himself once more.) "Not a sign of it left."

Bobby bent down to examine even more closely the space enclosed by the chalk line. "There's been no scrubbing or scraping, or anything like that, not been touched in any way, I'm sure of that." He stood up and said to Parkinson: "I would like a look at the gallery where the sculpture is. Can you find it? I suppose the bust that nearly did for us came from there."

"It's straight down the corridor," Parkinson answered, and, as they were all three leaving the room, he said: "Aren't you going to make the door fast?"

"Oh, I don't think so," Bobby said. "No good if it's a ghost." Here Payne made sounds indicative of annoyance and disbelief. "I suppose a locked door wouldn't keep a ghost out," Bobby continued. "And if it isn't, I don't see what anyone can do except rub out the chalk."

"Oh, well, now then," said Parkinson doubtfully, as they walked on along the corridor towards the picture gallery. On the way, he said: "According to the legend, the sooner and the more completely any such stain of blood disappears, the sooner and more certain is the death of any of the de Tallebois family who see it."

"Well, there wasn't one there, was there?" asked Payne.

"Dr. Jones is some kind of cousin, he told me," Parkinson said.

Payne sniffed again even more contemptuously than before. Bobby said:

"An unpleasant story."

Indeed it impressed him unpleasantly with some kind of dim and vague foreboding. He found himself reflecting that such tales have, at times, a way of working out their own fulfilment. He felt very certain that something, though what he had no idea, was going on in this vast deserted building where opportunities for concealment were endless. He supposed, moodily, that those of whom they had neither knowledge nor warning might well be watching, waiting. The silence, the stillness all around took on a sinister, menacing aspect, as if expectant and eager for evil things known to be at hand. Something of the same feeling the others must have had, too, for they all went warily along that dark and silent corridor, like men doubtful and on guard.

"It's through here," Parkinson said; and, though he did not know he had done so, he dropped his voice to a whisper, though a whisper that was easily heard in that all-pervading silence. Then he said: "Jones promised to wait here for me."

Bobby opened the door. Within was a long, still, silent room. As he threw the beam from his torch around, there leaped into its light, then passed into the shadows again, one after another tall, sheeted figures, like ghosts presiding over the memories of past glories or past crimes, of long forgotten festivities or of ancient mourning.

Slowly, with a kind of instinctive reluctance, Bobby moved forward.

24

Still more slowly, more reluctantly, the other two followed. Even the light of all three torches left great patches of gloom and darkness with here and there shadows yet more baffling. For the darkness was void, but the shadows seemed to contain and hide and hint at unknown menaces, only to withdraw again into nothingness when the torch rays came searching.

"Might be those things were all watching us," Payne muttered, "watching from behind those sheets of theirs."

Bobby was counting the statues, upright on their pedestals.

"Eleven in all," he observed. "You said thirteen, didn't you?" he asked Parkinson.

"Jones insisted there were only twelve. Got quite excited about it. Said twelve was the number Mr. de Tallebois mentioned, and it was twelve. But I know there were thirteen."

"There's one pedestal with nothing on it," Bobby said. "Looks as if it might have held a bust, too." He went closer and examined it. "I should think it's the one where the bust came from that didn't like us. Now, how did it manage to get from here to topple over the gallery balustrade just as we were underneath? Couldn't have walked, you know. For why? Because busts haven't legs."

"That's right," agreed Payne seriously. "No legs hasn't a bust," and he appeared to derive a certain vague encouragement from this reflection.

Mr. Parkinson was inclined to think Bobby was being frivolous, and he was quite sure this was no time for frivolity. He was still much shaken by the complete disappearance of the stain he knew so well he had seen on the floor boards where now no sign of it remained. He found himself wondering whether if he returned to the communion of his church he would be welcomed, or whether, first of all, penance and proof of repentance would be required. With a return of cynicism he told himself that probably there would be open arms at first, and then a continued pressure to keep observance and subscriptions—especially the latter—well up to the mark. This reflection was a sign that after the first shock his mind was beginning to return to its normal attitude.

Bobby had been standing staring at the vacant pedestal in deep thought for some moments. Now he turned away and began to walk the length of the room and back, pacing slowly, directing again the beam from his torch into every nook and corner of floor and wall and ceiling as he went.

The apartment answered well to the description given by Mr. Parkinson. Long, narrow, lofty, with doors at each end, windows to one side, and, between the windows, niches where stood seven of the sheeted statues. On the other side of the room were four other pieces of sculpture, equally covered with dust sheets, and two of them so much larger than the rest that Bobby supposed they must be the groups—a goddess reclining by a stag, and a river god, recumbent, with attendants, of which Parkinson had spoken. The best feature of the room, or at least the one that struck Bobby most, the ceiling decorated with a motif of birds in flight, very skilfully executed, Parkinson had apparently not noticed.

"I take it you looked behind all the coverings?" Bobby asked him.

"Oh, yes, but there was nothing, absolutely nothing," Parkinson answered.

"I think we'll have another look," Bobby said.

He began at the side where were the windows. One by one he scrutinized with care each of the pieces of statuary. All apparently represented gods or heroes of Greek mythology—Hercules resting on his club, Hermes with winged sandals, and so forth. The dust sheets had kept them all clean and fresh-looking. There was nothing to cause attention or rouse suspicion about any of them, though with each one he looked at Bobby's wonder grew—that one small gallery should hold so much so absolutely worthless stuff it would be flattery to call even second rate. When he had given a look to each of the figures on the window side of the room, he said:

"Awful stuff, all of it. Crude isn't the word. Those Italians must have thought de Tallebois a gift straight from heaven." He sniffed contemptuously, and added with a depth of scorn beyond description: "Even an art expert who was also an Honourable—what was the name? Marmaduke something or other—wouldn't need to look twice to see this lot was fit only to break up for road ballast. I don't expect the groups over the other side will be any better."

They were not. At least the first he looked at—that of the recumbent river god—moved him almost to tears.

"Could it be worse?" he demanded. "Design, proportions, workmanship. Might be kept though, perhaps, as an Awful Example. Probably turned out in a hurry for fear de Tallebois went back to England before it was ready for him. They must have sized him up pretty well, though, to expect to be able to palm off a thing like this on him. Imagine carting that atrocity all the way back to England."

He shook his head, replaced the dust sheet—or rather sheets, the size of the group had required two to cover it completely, and went on to the next, that of the goddess reclining by the side of a stag. Payne, anxious to be done with all this, had jerked off the coverings, ready for Bobby to look.

"Why, it's even worse," Bobby murmured, standing spellbound in a kind of horrible amazement. "Look at that stag—look at the goddess standing on one leg—leg—leg," he repeated, his voice trailing off into a whisper barely audible.

"What is it, sir?" Payne asked.

With a slow gesture of one lifted hand, Bobby pointed. There, in a space between the prostrate stag and posturing goddess, there showed a human leg, a twisted, motionless leg in a strained, unnatural position.

"God in Heaven," Payne muttered. "God have mercy."

"What is it?" Parkinson said, coming to join them, craning forward to look. "Why, that's Jones . . . Jones . . . is he . . . is he . . . dead?"

CHAPTER VI

MARMADUKE

An unnecessary question. There is that about death which is not easily mistaken. Bobby put out his hand to stop Parkinson, who had made as if to stoop and lift the body.

"No, don't touch anything," Bobby said. "He is past our help or any help."

"But—but—but," stammered Parkinson, and suddenly, and once more and for the last time, he crossed himself.

"That caretaker chap told us Jones had gone," Payne said.

"So he did, didn't he?" agreed Bobby absently. He had moved his position slightly, and now was bending over the body, examining it with care. "Not been dead so very long," he said. "No 'rigor mortis' yet. No visible cause of death, no wound or blood."

"Are you sure he's dead?" Parkinson asked, as if trying to confirm a certain fact that yet he found impossible, incredible. "I saw him this morning, I talked to him. Who . . . I mean, why? . . . I can't understand." In a quick, high, changed voice, he said: "Is it murder?"

"At any rate," Bobby said, "it is certain the body has been put where it is after death—to conceal it. And why should that be, unless there's foul play?"

"But Jones . . . Jones . . . why should any one? . . ." Parkinson muttered, still as if he could not bring himself to believe what he saw.

Bobby did not try to answer this, and remained silent and thoughtful.

"If that bust had been a bit more to one side," Payne commented moodily, "we might all three of us have been dumped here like this poor gentleman, all nicely out of the way."

"Oh . . . really . . . really . . .," spluttered Parkinson, in protest against a suggestion he found most disconcerting.

"Well, no," Bobby said, "hardly that. Only room for one of us here— behind that other group. No room behind the single upright figures. Necessary to think up something else for the other two of us."

27

"Oh, really . . . really," muttered Mr. Parkinson, who found this remark even more unpleasant.

Bobby, during these moments, had been examining as best he could by the light of his torch, the vicinity of the group, and the group itself, hoping to find something to give some clue to what had happened here.

"Nothing I can see," he said now. "I'm only wasting time, losing time. I wonder where's the nearest 'phone? We must get through to headquarters for help, we must have a doctor, too, though there's not much he can do. No good us three trying to search a place this size. Any one who was here when we came in is probably miles away by this time. We did immobilize the car, didn't we?"

"Yes, sir," said Payne. "Not that it makes much difference. There's ways and means."

"So there are," agreed Bobby. "If it's still there, you had better take it and find a 'phone as soon as you can. Get a doctor, and the help we need. While you're away I'll go and have a chat with the caretaker. He wasn't too anxious to let us in, and he did tell us Dr. Jones had gone. Mr. Parkinson . . ."

But Bobby got no further than the other's name. Parkinson was so bewildered, so disturbed, in such a nervous condition, that it was plainly useless to ask him, as Bobby had intended, to stay there in the picture gallery with the dead man till help arrived. He was in no condition for any such task. He was standing there in a kind of frozen horror, a picture of sheer terror and confusion. To Payne, confident that Parkinson was too lost in fear and wonder to hear or heed, Bobby said:

"Better take him with you and dump him somewhere as soon as you can. He's in no state to be any help, only a hindrance."

"Yes, sir," said Payne, lowering his voice to a whisper. "Think it could be him, sir? He was the last to see Jones, as far as we know. They had been quarrelling, he said. If you ask me, he's putting on an act, the way he is. Over-doing it."

"It's a thing to keep in mind," Bobby answered; and he remembered now that Parkinson had not waited at the Union Club as had been arranged, but had left it on some unspecified errand or another. Where had he been in the interval between leaving the club and the moment when Bobby had picked him up outside the hall where the civil defence meeting had been held? "We had better get moving now," Bobby said abruptly, telling himself these were thoughts best postponed for a time. "There's a lot to see to, and the sooner the better."

"Are we going to leave—that—alone here?" Payne asked; making his meaning plain by a glance at the body of the dead man, thrust into so strange and contorted a position between the wounded stag and the posturing goddess.

"Have to," Bobby said. "He's beyond all harm or hurt now. If the body's disturbed while we're away we shall know it, and it will tell us something, and we must have help. Not but that I would ask Parkinson to wait here if he were in a fit state. Which he isn't."

"Over-doing it," grumbled Payne agaiı.. "You don't get me to swallow any yarn about bloodstains that are there and then they aren't. Wants explaining."

Bobby was of the same opinion. An explanation was certainly required. But he made no comment except for an inarticulate grunt, and Payne went on:

"Remember all that about its being a sign someone was going to get done in. Only those prophesy who know," pronounced Payne with emphasis and conviction.

"Something in that," agreed Bobby; and, turning to the still dazed, bewildered Parkinson, told him they were leaving to get help.

Together the three of them made their way through the great, grim, silent house and out and down the short approach avenue to the entrance gates where they found their car still standing safely where they had left it. In it Payne, Parkinson with him, drove away, and Bobby turned back to knock again at the door of the small lodge. It opened more quickly this time. A woman appeared. She was fully dressed, and that, when she spoke, there was surprise and disappointment, even dismay, in her voice, was plain. She said:

"Who is it? They've gone. I heard the car. Who are you?"

"I am so sorry to trouble you again," Bobby said. "I was here before."

From above Bailey's voice called:

"Who is it, Marty? The car's gone."

"I didn't go with it," Bobby called back. "Can I have a few moments' talk with you, Mr. Bailey?"

"You had better come in," the woman said, reluctantly enough.

She drew back. Bobby followed her into a kitchen, small, tidy, well kept, still warm from the embers of a dying wood fire in the grate. The room was lighted by an oil lamp hanging from the ceiling above a plain deal table, scrubbed till it shone again. She turned up the lamp to give more light, threw some more wood—broken twigs and bits of branches—on the fire, and Bobby's impression was that these bustling activities were in part designed to gain time to hide embarrassment— or fear. She was small and slight in build, middle-aged, with a short, slightly-crooked nose that rather spoilt the effect of otherwise good features. Good looking in her youth, Bobby thought, though showing the scars of the passing years. Eyes that had once been bright were heavy now, dimmed perhaps by many tears. That she was in a highly nervous condition, controlling only with difficulty what seemed as though it threatened to become panic, was also not difficult to see. Bobby wondered why? Surely even this irruption of a stranger into her house at so late an hour was not enough to explain that pale face, those twitching lips, those sudden sideway glances. He said to her:

"You are Mrs. Bailey?"

She did not answer. She was listening to heavy footsteps descending slowly the stairs. She went out of the kitchen, shutting the door behind her, but, in her agitation, not securely, so that it swung slightly open again. The footsteps reached the foot of the stairs. They paused. Through the crack of the door Bobby heard the woman say: "Tell him it all," and in response what sounded like a surly negative.

The door was pushed open and Bailey came in, his wife close behind. He looked more sullen, more hostile, more truculent even than before. He gave the impression, with his lowering looks and hangdog expression, of one it would not be well to meet alone on some dark, solitary night. Bobby knew the type. He and Bailey exchanged quick glances, but almost as quickly Bailey looked away again. Behind him showed the white, anxious face of his wife; her dull and red-rimmed eyes full of pleading, and fearful. Bobby said:

"Your name is Bailey, isn't it? Alf Bailey? You are caretaker here, I think? My name is Owen. Here is my official card."

Bailey did not attempt to look at it. He stood there, hostile, sullen, at bay, one might have thought. He mumbled:

"I know. It was in the paper about you being deputy. So what's the odds?"

"I only want you to know," Bobby explained formally, "that I am here as an officer of police, and not out of curiosity or anything like that. I have, therefore, a right to ask for your help and assistance in every way possible. Also I have the right, as you know probably, acting as a police officer, to ask to see your identity cards. Another thing. When Mrs. Bailey left the room just now she didn't quite close the door behind her and I heard her ask you to 'tell it all'. I only want to say that that was very good advice, even necessary advice. It is not wise to keep anything back. Even small, unimportant things must be told."

"I thought cops always knew it all," Bailey muttered.

"Alf," his wife murmured; and her face was more pale even than before, and there were tears in those red-rimmed eyes of hers. "Alf," she repeated.

Bailey had turned away from Bobby, and now he was looking at her. Awkwardly he shambled across to where she stood, taking his place at her side. Half to her and half to Bobby, he said:

"All right. All right." To Bobby more directly he said: "Go ahead. Get it over, can't you?"

"When we got here," Bobby said, "you told us Dr. Jones had been here before us."

"Them ghost hunters?" Bailey asked. "They had a letter. Wasn't it O.K.?"

"Oh, yes," Bobby answered, "but you also told us that Dr. Jones had left again before we arrived?"

"Well, so he did."

"Are you sure? Did you see him yourself?"

"That's right. Knocked at the door to hand back the key and say he was done for the night."

"You recognized him then?"

"I dunno what you mean—recognized him. It was dark; and if you show a spot of light when you open the door, likely you hear about it from the O.P. up on the hill."

"What I'm trying to get at," Bobby explained, "is how you can be sure that it was really Dr. Jones?"

"Well, who else could it be? There wasn't no one else but him up there, was there? He said his name, and gave back the key, and said that was all, thank you, and half-a-crown with it, like a gentleman, and if it wasn't him, who was it?"

"That's what I want to know," Bobby explained again. "I can take it you didn't see him clearly and you couldn't swear to his voice?"

"It was a sort of gent's voice anyway," Bailey insisted. His manner had grown a good deal more confident now, and even his wife had a more relieved air. It was as though the turn of the conversation had lightened apprehensions they had felt before. "A sort of la-di-da voice," Bailey went on, "if you know what I mean, silly like, just the way you talk yourself," this last being evidently added merely in further explanation and without the least intention of offence.

"Oh, Alf," said Mrs. Bailey. "He didn't mean it that way, sir," she explained anxiously to Bobby.

"That's all right," Bobby said, smiling at her. "We can't help our voices, and we can't all be B.B.C. announcers." He hoped this small attempt at a joke would help to put the Baileys more at their ease, but it missed fire completely. They merely accepted it as a plain, if somewhat irrelevant, statement of fact. He went on: "It comes to this. Someone knocked, said he was Jones, handed back the key, said he was going. But it was dark, you didn't see him clearly, you can't be sure it was the same voice you had only heard once before. Isn't that so?"

"That's right," answered Bailey. "What's it all about?"

"Could anyone else have been in the house without you knowing?"

"I don't see how," Bailey answered. "It's all locked up, windows boarded, doors bolted, all except the side door I use when I sweep up every week, according to orders, and have a look round, and no one hasn't had the key, except Mr. Jones as brought it back—if it was him," he added doubtfully. "There hasn't been no one else except that other gent a week ago or thereabouts."

"Who was that?"

"A gent what had come to have a look at them statues. He had a letter from the agents, hadn't he, Marty?" Mrs. Bailey, thus appealed to, nodded an assent. "Very interesting they was, he said, and took long enough about it, too, so as I went up to see, in case of him having done a bunk with the key and there being only the one. But he was there all right, though I had to knock quite a time before he come along, him being so stuck on them there statues, which is more than I am, them being like ghosts you more than half expect to come walking after you."

"Do you know his name?" Bobby asked.

Bailey didn't. It was on the agent's card, but he had forgotten it. But Mrs. Bailey did remember that it was 'Marmaduke' something. She had forgotten the surname, too, but she was sure the first name was 'Marmaduke', it being 'funny like' and staying in her mind.

The soi-disant art expert again, Bobby thought with immense contempt. An art expert who had to spend time examining those deplorable specimens of sculpture when anyone who knew anything at all could see at the first glance that they were mere rubbish. But what could you expect from an art expert who was also an 'Honourable'? Or—a new idea struck him. Was it possible that this 'Marmaduke' of the unknown surname had had some other reason for so prolonged an inspection of the obvious? Was he perhaps not an incompetent 'Honourable'—and this time Bobby pronounced that unlucky word with less contempt than before—but instead a perfectly competent crook? Only what could attract any crook to pay a visit to an uninhabited, unfurnished house like Nonpareil? Something to think about there, Bobby decided. He asked a few more questions. Had 'Marmaduke' given his address? No. Had the Baileys kept the card from the agents he had shown? No. Had he said if he was remaining on in the vicinity? No. The only piece of information that came out from a fairly close examination was that when leaving he had asked if the Baileys knew a Major Hardman, and could they give him his address? But they had never heard of any Major Hardman.

"What's it all about?" Bailey asked, as Bobby fell silent, digesting this information or rather lack of it. "What's wrong?"

"If it was Dr. Jones you saw," Bobby said slowly, "he went back to the house after speaking to you, and how did he get in if he had given you the key? Unless, of course, he had left the door open. Why should he? But he is there now, or at least his dead body is, dead in the picture gallery."

CHAPTER VII

SEARCH

THIS INFORMATION DID not seem at first to be fully grasped either by Bailey or by his wife, for indeed knowledge often remains no knowledge till the emotions are as fully possessed by it as is the mind.

At any rate at first they seemed merely puzzled and surprised; and whether this apparent failure to apprehend the full meaning of what they had been told was genuine or assumed, Bobby could not decide. In any case, there was no time to spare for further explanation or for answering the questions they seemed inclined to put. He did not even stay to look at their identity cards, but told Bailey to accompany him back to the house and Mrs. Bailey to wait for and expect the arrival of a doctor and the return of Payne with help.

This was not long delayed, and soon all the accustomed routine of such an inquiry was in busy progress. With but little result, for nothing of significance emerged. All the doctor could say was that death had occurred, as Bobby had already remarked, only a comparatively brief time before the discovery of the body; and that the cause was strangulation during unconsciousness caused by a severe blow on the side of the head, delivered by the traditional blunt instrument. As soon as Bobby was satisfied that all necessary steps were being or would be taken, he sent Payne off duty, and for himself sought home and supper and bed. Both of them, he knew, would need all their faculties for what lay before them later on.

In the morning, as arranged, he and Payne met again at Nonpareil, where, after the completion of the routine work, a constable had remained on duty. Now this man was sent home. Payne had brought with him as many helpers as he could scrape together, six in all, including two secured—per impossibile—from the astonished Superintendent Jenks, so swept off his feet by the audacity of the request that he had put up but a poor resistance.

Together with Bobby and Payne to help, that made up a total of eight men available for the search of the house and grounds. Four men were assigned to the grounds and outbuildings, together with the—this morning much subdued—caretaker for additional help and guidance. Bobby and Payne chose for themselves the first and ground floors of the house; and, as is the callous way of senior officers, sent off the two remaining constables to search the cellars, an interminable labyrinth of subterranean vaults where neither air nor light penetrated, where the dust and dirt of many months had accumulated, where the cobwebs hung in thick, impenetrable sheets, where rats and mice and spiders went their ways undisturbed. The upper portions of the building were fairly free from dirt and dust, since it was the duty of the Baileys, a duty well and regularly performed, as it seemed, to keep the floors, stairs and passages of the great house properly swept. But the cellars were never visited, and when the two unfortunate constables assigned to their examination did finally emerge again into the upper world, even their seniors could not resist a pang of sympathy.

"In the force you have to take the rough with the smooth," Bobby explained to them, words received with respectful lack of appreciation; and he further resolved that if either of them put in an application for leave, it would be considered sympathetically—though probably not granted. Still, he would not at least throw it heatedly and instantly into the waste-paper basket.

"There's a locked door down there we couldn't open. Caretaker said he hadn't the key," explained one of the men as he tried to free himself from a wad of cobweb that had somehow slipped down the back of his neck. "He said it had always been locked, and spiders' webs all over it to show it hadn't been opened, so we thought it would be all right to leave it. The whole place doesn't look as if anybody had been there since the year one."

Bobby remarked that they would have to get the locked door open, but that could wait for the present, and then sent the two of them off to examine the attics. He and Payne, having completed a careful tour of the ground floor, including a vast, stone-flagged kitchen in which one felt the food must have grown cold even on the journey from oven to door, went up to the first floor, coming soon to that room in which, according to Parkinson's tale, there had been a stain of fresh blood that then had vanished quite away.

In this room they removed the boarding from the windows to gain the benefit of the daylight—elsewhere they had been content with their electric torches and the hurricane lamp they carried. They did the same in the next room they entered. Here also there seemed, at first, to reign the same placidity of entire emptiness they had found everywhere else, but as the clear light of the day flooded in there showed on the flooring, midway between the fireplace and the windows, a patch in part more fresh and clean, in part more soiled, than elsewhere. They both went to look more closely. Easy enough, then, to see what had happened. The floorboards had first been carefully and thoroughly scraped with some sharp instrument and then dust and dirt rubbed over the place in an effort to conceal what had been done.

"Parkinson was right enough then," Bobby remarked. "There was blood on the floor, though in this room, not in the other. Someone has been at a good deal of trouble to hide it. Careful and cunning. Reproduced in the next room the chalk mark, and the precautions taken to seal the door. Even the cigarette ends weren't forgotten. Quite smart work."

"Looks to me . . ." began Payne, and then paused to look at Bobby for permission to continue, in case Bobby, as the senior, wanted to expound his own views first.

"Go ahead," said Bobby, "looks to you . . .?"

"Like this," said Payne. "Jones and Parkinson were mooning round looking for ghosts, and when they saw marks of blood on the floor in here, that's what they thought. Ghosts, they thought, and they marked it off with chalk, so as to be sure where it was, and went off, meaning to come back and see if the ghosts had been up to anything else they could write a book about. Very excited they were; and, with their heads full of ghosts, never thought of letting us know, probably thinking police and ghosts don't go together. As they don't. Jones turned up first, and what he ran into wasn't any ghosts, but blokes who didn't want any nosy parkers around, and made sure that what Jones saw he wouldn't ever tell. That little job had only just been finished when we came along, so they dropped that bust thing to give us something to think about, and if it brained the lot of us, so much the better, while they themselves did a bunk fast as they knew how."

"That's rather what I was thinking, too," Bobby said. "It does look like that. Only who are 'they'? and what were they doing Jones saw and they didn't dare let him tell? and what was going on in an empty house like this?"

"How about this?" Payne said. "Washing all that out and noticing that Parkinson admits a bit of a quarrel between him and Jones. Suppose there was more to it than that. Very hot some of these literary and learned gentlemen get about things you wouldn't think mattered two hoots to anyone with any sense. Suppose words came to blows, as words do at times, and suppose Parkinson laid Jones out, not exactly meaning to, but just in the way of argument. Then he gets scared at what he has done, makes sure Jones won't ever tell and get him disgraced with all his learned friends. So he pushes the body away where we found it, and that's the way it was."

"I had something of the sort in my own mind," Bobby agreed again. "Not quite like that, but on the same lines. I don't know that it fits everywhere, though."

"Things often don't at the start," Payne said.

"True enough," Bobby agreed for the third time. "Anyhow, we'll check up on where Parkinson went while I was at the Civil Defence meeting, and why he didn't wait at the club as arranged. One more thing, though. We mustn't forget the shot Major Hardman and Reed say they heard. Shots sometimes result in bloodstains."

"But that was a good two miles from here," Payne protested. "Can't be any connection, can there?"

"There might be," Bobby answered thoughtfully. "Pistol shot heard there. Blood found here. And now a dead man. All one series? What do you think? Coincidence? I never did like coincidence."

"Coincidences happen," said Payne, a proposition none can dispute.

They continued their search, but found nothing more of interest, no indication of any sort or kind to show what had really taken place or what had caused the tragic death of Dr. Jones. The two constables had also completed their search of the attics, where they were certain none before themselves had penetrated for months, even years, so thickly lay so undisturbed the dust. For to the attics, it seemed, the caretaker and his wife had no instructions to extend their weekly sweepings.

"Time to have something to eat," Bobby announced.

They had brought some provender with them, supplied by the canteen at headquarters. By this time, too, the party dispatched to search the grounds, not very extensive for a house this size, had completed their task, and returned, reporting nothing of interest.

"Except this," one of the party said, producing a heavy walking-stick with a solid silver-mounted handle, quite a formidable weapon in its way. "It was lying in some bushes, and hadn't been there so very long, either."

Bobby asked who had found it, and was told the caretaker, Bailey, had noticed light reflected from the silver mounting.

"Some weight there," remarked Payne, who had been examining it with considerable interest. "You could give a K.O. with that all right."

Bobby, too, was thinking that here, perhaps, was the instrument that had been used to knock senseless the unfortunate psychical researcher before the final act of strangulation. Probably tests would decide whether that were so or not.

"Polished surface, sir," one of the constables said. "Take dabs all right, and we've handled it carefully."

"That was sensible of you," Bobby commended them, but without any marked enthusiasm.

"If Bailey's dabs are there," objected Payne, "what's the good if it was him found it, and perhaps knowing where to look?"

"That's another idea," Bobby remarked. "I expect Bailey's will be there all right enough—and, as you say, we're not much farther forward if they are."

"Professionals in it somewhere," Payne pronounced next. "They know their way about all right, whoever it is. Gloves, to stop leaving dabs. Knew enough to give a door a look over to see if it had been fixed. Don't you think, sir," he added directly to Bobby, "it might be as well to get Bailey's dabs, and see if he has a record?"

"Oh, I don't know," Bobby answered. "Nothing much against him yet. Except his looks. Deceptive things, though—looks. No authority to take his dabs, either."

"We could put it to him," Payne suggested, wondering vaguely why Bobby seemed so indifferent to so obvious a suggestion. "Press him a bit. If he stuck out, well, ask him why? Besides," added Payne, "there's ways and means." When Bobby still shook his head at these suggestions, Payne, a trifle annoyed, added: "Well, anyway, they're very likely on the walking-stick."

"'Very likely' not good enough," said Bobby. "No harm, though, in letting our dabs man have a go."

Their meal they had all had in common was over now, and the men had dispersed here and there on one errand or another or just for a quiet gossip away from the two senior officers. Payne, a good deal puzzled by Bobby's lack of interest in Bailey's 'dabs', went away to speak to those who had been engaged in the outdoor search and came back looking excited.

"Bailey never touched the stick," he said. "Took care not to. Called our men to show it them, and only they handled it. And now he's there in the room where he keeps his brooms and cleaning stuff. It's off the passage where we came in, and he's as busy there as you like. What do you think he's doing?"

Bobby, whose night's rest had been short, indulged in a terrific yawn.

"Most likely," he said, his yawn completed, "giving things a rub over to make sure he's left no dabs for nosy police to work upon."

"That's right, so he is," agreed Payne, disappointed that Bobby had guessed first time. "Doesn't it smell to you, sir?"

"Oh, yes," agreed Bobby. "Only what of?"

CHAPTER VIII

FOOTSTEPS

It was to The Tulips, the residence of Major Hardman, that Bobby took himself next, and thither he decided to go alone, for he did not, at this present stage of the inquiry, wish to draw attention to the Hon. Marmaduke, of the unknown surname, who had paid a doubtful visit to Nonpareil and left inquiring for Major Hardman's address. Quite possibly the illusive Marmaduke might be a perfectly innocent, if evidently incompetent, dabbler in art matters, and probably as incompetent in everything else as well, as Bobby was convinced, in his bones, all 'honourables'—ridiculous title—must necessarily be.

He knocked and the door was opened by a tall, ungainly, somewhat untidy young woman, with large, irregular features, large hands and feet, and a countenance less made up than is usual in these days when paint and powder, and lots of 'em, is regarded as beauty's secret. This young woman's tribute to fashion seemed to be confined to her hair, of a reddish-brown tint, arranged in as an elaborate a permanent wave set up as Bobby had ever seen. Her voice was deep and harsh for a woman's, and her manner was not too agreeable as she admitted Bobby and undertook to inform her uncle, Major Hardman, of his arrival.

The Tulips was not a large house, eight or nine rooms in all, perhaps. The one into which Bobby had been shown was evidently the dining-room, and was as commonplace and ordinary an apartment as Bobby had ever seen. Nothing in it to give the least clue to the tastes, the habits, or the personalities of its inhabitants. It had a well-kept appearance, though, and Bobby supposed that the young woman he had seen must be a capable housekeeper, by exception more inclined, it might seem, to give attention to her household duties than to her personal appearance. One thing at least was certain. She was not the owner of the size four shoe found on the path that led through the forest from the high road past the new bungalows to the village. This stalwart, bigly-made young person probably took a No. 7 shoe or even a No. 8, for that matter.

That meant that one small point, at least, Bobby had had in mind was settled, and now the door opened to admit Major Hardman, a bluff, smiling, red-faced man, wearing plus-fours and his Old Etonian tie, and expressing his great pleasure at meeting Bobby, of whom he had often heard since coming to reside in Wychshire. There was no trace of any family resemblance between him and his niece, for whereas she was tall and angular, he was short and round. Nor did he seem much like an invalid, for his manner was brisk and confident, he seemed in good trim physically, there was an alert look in his small, quick eyes, and indeed about his whole personality. His mouth, too, or what one could see of it beneath a moustache unusually exuberant for these clean-shaven days, seemed set in firm lines, with lips hard pressed together and showing seldom the double row of large white teeth behind.

Still expressing his pleasure at Bobby's visit, which he appeared to regard as a personal compliment, he produced cigarettes, regretted he had nothing in the shape of a drink to offer.

"Haven't," he explained, "had so much as a smell of whisky since Lord knows when. There's still a bottle of brandy left, but somehow one doesn't drink brandy in the afternoon. Not done. I don't know why. Do you?"

38

Bobby said he didn't, and he did hope Major Hardman wouldn't trouble. Anyhow he was on duty, and as constables were forbidden to smoke or drink on duty, he, as deputy chief, had to be extra careful.

Major Hardman said he quite understood. As an officer of the regular army he understood the importance of setting an example to 'other ranks'—in action, going over the top, facing the bullets, on the parade ground, everywhere in fact. But he would like to say that much as he appreciated the courtesy of this visit, he had never intended or dreamed that his small and possibly unnecessary complaint should receive the personal attention of so senior an officer as the Deputy Chief Constable. He, the Major, didn't suppose he would have ever bothered to mention it to the man on the beat—"very civil, obliging chap, name's Reed, I think, quite a pal of mine"—if his niece hadn't been nervous.

"You know what women are," said the Major benevolently. "Bombs? Yes. Mice? No. Spiders? The absolute limit. Burglars? In between mice and spiders. Ha, ha. I believe Frankie looks under the bed every night to make sure there isn't a burglar there, ha, ha."

Bobby was interested.

"I didn't know about that," he said. "Have you had a burglary here?"

"Footsteps," said the Major.

"Footsteps?" repeated Bobby.

"In the garden," the Major explained. "Frankie—that's my niece—woke me in the night. Stuck to it there was someone outside, trying to get in. I told her to go back to bed. Didn't believe it. Thought she had been dreaming. Bit cross I was, being wakened up like that. All the same I had to take it back in the morning. There were footprints all right, right under the drawing-room window, too."

"Any sign of an attempt to break in?"

"No, no. Just footprints to show someone had been there. I thought I had better just mention it. Frankie said I must or she would, and I had to give in, especially as she was right, and there really had been someone on the prowl during the night. I told Reed, and asked him to keep an eye on the place. Very civil, obliging chap, Reed. He said he would—keep an eye on the place, I mean. And you can't even give him a drink, there being nothing to drink these days—sometimes not even at the Horse and Groom."

Bobby asked if any record had been made of the footmarks. No one had thought of doing that. But the Major remembered that they were smallish and long and narrow, and probably made by a light city shoe. Definitely, said the Major, not the heavy, nailed boot an ordinary working man or farm labourer would wear. It was, indeed, partly because of that fact, that the Major had thought the incident worth mentioning. Otherwise he would have dismissed it as one of the men from the village on the prowl for cheap vegetables or for eggs.

"Eggs have their value now," he said, "and Frankie has a few hens she looks after. Very welcome, an occasional new-laid. Reed has told me of cases of gardens and allotments having been raided round here."

Bobby remarked that it was a specially mean-spirited and nasty kind of petty crime, and all too prevalent. Difficult to check, too, and some magistrates seemed to think that fining a man a shilling for stealing five shillings' worth of vegetables was enough. But he hadn't called about that, annoying as it was. He went on to tell, briefly, of the Nonpareil tragedy, and the Major was surprised, horrified, distressed. Like the Baileys, he seemed to have some difficulty in grasping the reality of what he had been told, and kept expressing bewilderment over such a thing happening in an empty and long-deserted house. He was puzzled, too, that Bobby should think there could be any connection between the shot he and Constable Reed had heard in the forest at no great distance, and the death by strangulation of this unfortunate psychical researcher at Nonpareil two miles or more away. If indeed the Major understood rightly that it was on account of the pistol shot heard by himself and Constable Reed that Bobby had honoured him with a call?

Bobby said, well, partly, and might he now broach a somewhat delicate matter? He understood complaints had been made about rowdy behaviour in the neighbourhood by a young man said to be, or claiming to be, a nephew of Major Hardman.

"Frankie's brother," admitted the Major gloomily. "That's who you mean. They're twins. He's Frank, too. She was christened Frances. He's Francis. As different in character as they are alike in looks. She's a thoroughly nice, quiet girl, and he's the black sheep of the family. Is it about that five-pound note I gave him? I heard something about its having been picked up in Wychwood."

"I suppose you can't say how it got there?"

The Major shook his head.

"I understood the boy wanted it to pay some debt or another, someone waiting for him outside, he said. Some disreputable associate or another, I expect. To keep a girl quiet perhaps. I didn't ask. No good. I don't suppose if I had I should have got the truth. I gave him the money, and told him to clear out, and that's all I know—or wanted to know."

"I see," said Bobby. "It did cross my mind that possibly he might be your last night's burglar—trying to get in touch with his sister perhaps. You know what sisters are?"

Again the Major shook his head, even more decidedly than before.

"My own idea at first," he admitted, "but it won't do. For one thing, why should he? He could easily get hold of Frankie any time he wanted. Besides, those footprints are too small for him."

"That clears that up then," Bobby said. "Thank you very much. It was just an idea."

40

"Very natural one," agreed the Major.

He hesitated, looked embarrassed, coughed, seemed about to speak and then changed his mind. Finally, Bobby waiting to hear what was coming, the Major got to his feet and went and stood in front of the fireplace and said:

"There's something I've just thought of, though I expect you'll say there's nothing in it. Only—well, there was a bloke here the other day. Called himself an art expert. Didn't strike me that way. Said he was the Honourable Something or another. Didn't strike me that way either. Might be, though. Nowadays, an 'honourable' needn't be a pukka sahib—son of some Labour lord or another perhaps." The Major laughed good-temperedly. "I'm old-fashioned, I know," he said. "I like the days when a gentleman was a gentleman. I can't say I smelt a rat exactly. I don't now for that matter. Only somehow you don't generally expect an 'honourable' to be an art expert, do you?"

"You do not," agreed Bobby emphatically, remembering how long it had apparently taken this particular 'honourable' to make up his mind about that deplorable Nonpareil sculpture.

"Only what you said," the Major went on, "made me remember that this bloke was wearing rather long, narrow, city shoes. I don't know what made me notice them, but I did."

"Did he give his name?" Bobby asked.

"It was Marmaduke something," the Major answered, frowning in an effort to remember. "I can't think of the surname. I do remember 'Marmaduke', though. Stuck in my mind somehow—silly sort of name, don't you think?"

Bobby nearly remarked that it was all you could expect of an 'honourable'. Instead he asked:

"Did he say why he called?"

"Talked round and round. I had to ask him to cut it short. Something about some valuable painting or another—an old master, I gathered, Vermeer, the Dutch artist. I'm no art expert." Here the Major paused to give a somewhat self-conscious laugh which suggested that others might hold a different opinion. "Quite the amateur. But I do know a good thing when I see it, and once or twice I haven't come out so badly when I've backed my opinion. During my time I've got together a few good things of one sort or another. Oh, not here," he added quickly as he saw Bobby give a quick glance round a room that seemed the very embodiment of the commonplace, from the 'jacobean' chairs and table to the Christmas number engravings on the walls—all snow and holly leaves and kisses. "Most of my stuff's at the bankers—for safety in these air-raid days. But I did bring one or two things up here with me. Nothing very much. A Birket Foster water-colour in the drawing-room I'm rather fond of, and some Chinese jade. Insured for two thousand guineas."

"Is the jade in the drawing-room, too?"

"Well, it was. The Birket Foster is still there, but I put the jade bowls away this morning. I didn't much like the combination of footsteps under the drawing-room window and a visit from a somewhat doubtful art expert. It's all insured, but these jade bowls mean a good deal more to me than their cash value."

"Very prudent step to take," agreed Bobby warmly. "I don't know what it all means—'too hard a knot' for me," he quoted, remembering a line that had struck his fancy in a performance of *Twelfth Night* by the old Vic company Olive had taken him to see a few nights previously. "Just as well to be careful till it's all cleared up, if it ever is. The odd thing is that this same art expert has been at Nonpareil. He had a card to view from the agents, and said he wanted to have a look at the sculpture. Also, when he left he asked the caretaker if he knew your address, which Bailey didn't."

Once more the Major hesitated, seemed embarrassed, inclined to speak and yet hesitating to do so. Again Bobby waited to hear what was coming. Finally the Major said:

"Hardly the thing, perhaps. Not playing the game, not quite cricket." He paused, still reluctant, still hesitant, shaking his head distastefully. Finally he said: "I think you ought to know. Murder—well, murder is murder, isn't it?"

Bobby agreed that it was, and waited. The Major said all in a rush, as if at last making up his mind:

"That Bailey fellow, the Nonpareil caretaker, is an old convict."

"Is he though?" Bobby said gravely. "Are you sure?"

"I knew him at once," the Major said. "I was driving by there one morning, and he was at the door, and I recognized him at once. I happened to be in court in—in 1935, was it? I was there with a barrister friend of mine, and Bailey was in the dock, charged with burglary and attempted murder, I think. I remember noticing in the paper next day that he had got three years' penal servitude. I am sure it's the same man, but I suppose you can check up."

"We can and will," Bobby said earnestly. "We always check up on everything. I can't tell you how grateful I am to you for telling me, and how useful the information will be. Of course, it doesn't prove anything. Bailey may have had nothing to do with what has been happening, but it does confirm me in following up one line of investigation at least."

CHAPTER IX

INTRUDER

LEAVING THE TULIPS in thoughtful mood, for what he had just heard seemed to him to be both significant and important, Bobby found Payne waiting for him, sitting on the running board of Bobby's parked car and looking impatient.

It seemed Payne had come, knowing that Bobby intended to interview Major Hardman and assured by the sight of the car that he was still there, to report an exciting piece of information that had just come to his knowledge.

"There's a Miss Betty Anson," he explained. "She lives with her mother in one of those bungalows they call the New Bungalows, near where the Barsley footpath starts."

"Oh, yes," said Bobby, wondering what was coming next.

"Miss Betty Anson," said Payne impressively, "is a small and slight young woman, and she is laid up with a sore foot." He paused and waited, expecting eager comment. None came. Bobby, his mind full of what he had just learned, only looked puzzled, not quite seeing what the sore foot of this hitherto unknown young lady had to do with it. Payne looked gravely disappointed. He hoped Bobby, in his new rank, was not losing touch. He had never known the deputy chief so slow in the uptake. He said, a touch of severity in his voice:

"Miss Anson works in Midwych. She has a job with Midwych Coal and Iron Consolidated. Sort of supervizing job of some kind. Working overtime recently, leaving work about nine and coming home by a 'bus the company runs for late workers. Miss Anson is the only one of the workers living about here. The 'bus drops her on the Barsley Road, and she takes the forest footpath to cut across home. Saves her going round, and brings her home half an hour earlier than if she waited for the train. So she might be coming along the footpath at ten or thereabouts. I haven't seen her myself, but Broken Reed says she might very likely take a No. 4 shoe."

"She has hurt her foot," Bobby commented, "and we found a No. 4 woman's shoe on the footpath near a cartridge case?"

"That's right, sir," said Payne. "Looks to me we've got something."

"So it does," agreed Bobby thoughtfully. "How did you get all this?"

"Well, sir, you said to try to find out if anyone else had heard the pistol shot besides Major Hardman and Broken Reed. We haven't found anyone yet, but when I tried the New Bungalows, and they are nearest, nearer even than The Tulips, Mrs. Anson said she hadn't heard anything herself. Her hearing wasn't too good, though, and she would ask her daughter, because she came home that way when she was working late, and Mrs. Anson didn't like it. It was dark and lonely, and she thought she ought to be very firm indeed and absolutely insist on Betty waiting for the train even if it did make her so much later. I said could I see Miss Betty, and Mrs. Anson said no, because she had hurt her foot and couldn't even go to work, but she would ask her. So Miss Betty didn't appear, just sent a message that she was sorry she couldn't help, she didn't know anything about it. I didn't insist. I thought I had better report first."

"Good work," Bobby said thoughtfully. "Very good work. Something to go on. Do the times quite fit, though? You might check up on that, will you? If Miss Betty leaves work at nine and there's a company 'bus waiting, surely she ought to be home before ten?"

"Yes, sir, I see that," agreed Payne. "But the 'bus may have been running late or the girl may have been hanging about or anything. How about her meeting a boy friend on the way home? You never know. Anyhow, it's a coincidence, sir. Shoe lost and injured foot. Granted it may mean nothing, but it's still a coincidence, and I never did like coincidences, and never shall."

"Quite right, too," applauded Bobby, though well aware this was a catchword of his own Payne had adopted. "Coincidences are a bit suspicious. You said the girl's mother was there, didn't you?"

"Oh, yes, sir. Mother keeps house and the girl works."

"Have they been there long?"

"Ever since the bungalows were built. Mrs. Anson isn't very strong. She was nervous about air raids long before they began, and they moved out here from Albert Park, in Midwych, soon after her husband's death."

"It's a bit late," Bobby remarked, "but if the mother's there, it will be all right for me to call." Bobby was as careful as all police officers learn to be, to have a witness at hand when interviewing a woman, since all a woman has to do is to lie down and scream to establish at once a grave *prima facie* case against any man. "I'll go and see if I can get anything more. There's a job I want you to attend to. I want all possible information about Major Hardman. His army service, his record, everything you can get. As he had a London address, get it, and ask them at the Yard if they can help. And there's that Eton tie of his. He wears it a bit more often than most Old Etonians. I would like to be quite sure about it. Anyone can buy an Old Etonian tie. I don't know how you can check up. Easy enough, to borrow a name from the Eton register. But have a good try."

"No difficulty, sir," Payne assured him. "I'll ask Burton."

"Burton?" repeated Bobby. "You don't mean Babs Burton of 'A' squad."

44

"Yes, sir, that's the man. Old Eton boy."

"Dear me," said Bobby, surprised, for though he knew he had under him many men of many trades and varied origins, he had not, till now, known there was an Old Etonian among them. Nor had he noticed any trace of an Etonian upbringing in the aforesaid Burton, except indeed that Burton had always seemed rather specially ill-informed. "Are you sure?" he asked a little doubtfully. "Burton's not just swanking, I suppose?"

"Oh, no, sir, I don't think so," Payne answered. "His father was odd job man or something of the sort at Eton—at what they call a 'house' there, really a kind of boarding establishment with guests who can't leave, and get swished if they complain. A boarding-house keeper's dream. Burton's father was an old county cricketer, too, so that helped with the boys; and Burton himself was in with them all the time, running their errands, smuggling in things they weren't supposed to have, helping them with any mischief they had on, and helping them out when they got caught. He says he gets a box of swell cigarettes every Christmas still from some cabinet minister or another he saved from being expelled probably."

"Must have been something pretty bad," Bobby commented, "to get a boy expelled from Eton."

"So it was," confirmed Payne. "A booby trap with lots of dirty water in it, and the housemaster's wife sprang it just when she was all togged up for a special do at Windsor Castle."

Bobby whistled.

"Well, well," he said. "No wonder the cabinet minister wants that kept quiet. Get hold of Burton, will you? and turn him on the job. Hardman gave me some very interesting information, and I want to be quite sure of his good faith."

"Very good, sir," said Payne, and added somewhat doubtfully: "He can't have had anything to do with the shooting on the footpath. He couldn't very well have a better alibi than being with one of our own men when the shot was fired."

"No, I suppose he couldn't," agreed Bobby, and went on to the New Bungalows.

There were four of them, side by side, all indistinguishable one from the other, but Payne had told him that that occupied by the Ansons was nearest the forest. It was growing late and nearly dark as Bobby parked his car, well away from the path he did not wish to block, and behind the tall garden hedge that bordered the Anson domain. When he knocked an elderly, frail-looking woman, white-haired and supporting herself on a stick, came to the door. Bobby explained who he was, and his errand. Mrs. Anson said her daughter was laid up with a bad foot, and couldn't see any one, and besides, another policeman had been there already.

Bobby said he knew that, and in fact that was why he had come himself, and he suggested that a bad foot did not necessarily prevent speech. Mrs. Anson still made difficulties. Bobby still insisted. Mrs. Anson yielded so far as to ask him into the sitting-room. She tried to light the lamp—there was neither electricity nor gas laid on, she explained—but found no lamp there.

"It wanted a new wick," she said. "Betty must have taken it away to get one and never brought it back. We hardly ever sit here, now it's so difficult to get oil and coal and everything."

She went away then, leaving Bobby in an obscurity rapidly increasing as the rolling up of heavy storm clouds added to the darkness of the approaching night. The door opened and a tall young man came in.

"Oh, haven't you a light?" he said, peering at Bobby, dimly visible in the gathering darkness.

"I think Mrs. Anson has gone to get a lamp," Bobby said, wondering who this young man might be, since Payne had only spoken of mother and daughter.

"Miss Anson's very sorry," the new-comer went on, "but she's not at all well, and will you please excuse her? Anyhow, she knows nothing about it."

"Nothing about what?" Bobby asked.

The young man sounded a bit disconcerted as he said:

"Well, I thought there was something about somebody shooting something somewhere. There's been another police johnny here. Wanted to know if any one here had heard anything. No one has."

"I see," said Bobby. "Might I ask to whom I am talking? A friend of the family?"

"My name's Claymore," the other answered. "Leonard Claymore. Mrs. Anson asked me to come and tell you."

"Well, Mr. Claymore," Bobby said, "We think Miss Anson may be able to give us some information. I am afraid I must ask permission to put her a few questions in person."

"Oh, that's impossible," Claymore protested. "She's not up to it. If you'll tell me anything you want to know, I'll ask her. But it won't be any good."

"I am afraid that would hardly be satisfactory," Bobby replied. "By the way, are you a relative, Mr. Claymore?"

"Miss Anson and I are engaged," Claymore answered stiffly.

"Congratulations, I'm sure," Bobby said. "Perhaps now you would be good enough to tell Miss Anson how sorry I am to trouble her, but I am afraid it is necessary for me to see her personally."

"Can't be done," said Claymore firmly. "She's not up to it, not fit."

"Is that doctor's orders?" Bobby asked. "Because, you know, this is a serious matter, and doctors' orders is about the only thing that can hold up a criminal investigation—such as this."

"You don't need a doctor," Claymore retorted, and, Bobby noticed, without showing any surprise at the expression 'criminal investigation', "to tell when a girl isn't fit to be bothered with a lot of questions about something she doesn't know a thing about."

"I should prefer a medical opinion all the same," Bobby said. "If you will give me the name of the doctor attending Miss Anson, I'll ring him up and ask."

"They haven't bothered about a doctor," Claymore admitted, "but any one can see . . ."

"Mr. Claymore," Bobby interrupted, making his voice suddenly severe where hitherto it had been quiet and suave, "is there any reason why you are trying to prevent me from speaking to Miss Anson? Please remember this is a serious matter and please understand it is necessary for me to see Miss Anson at once and in person. If more difficulty is made, I shall have to consider what further steps to take. Already I am beginning to ask myself if there is anything behind all these difficulties? And if so, what it is?"

"There isn't anything," Claymore answered sulkily. He stood there, tall and obscure in the darkness, and Bobby wished, very much, he could see his face. Difficult to form any judgment from this talk in the dark. Claymore said again: "There isn't anything except what I've said. Miss Anson isn't feeling well, and she can't tell you anything because she doesn't know anything."

"Perhaps you would be good enough to tell Miss Anson what I have said," Bobby suggested.

"Oh, well, now then," Claymore grumbled.

He still seemed to hesitate, but then went away without saying anything more, and Bobby could hear a murmur of voices from without. The three of them in consultation, he supposed. Laying plans, perhaps. The door opened and Mrs. Anson came in.

"It's past black-out time," she said. "I've got the lamp going, but I must draw the curtains first." She went to the window and began nervously to arrange blind and curtains. "We don't use this room now," she said. "We sit in the kitchen. I think it's a shame, bothering Betty like this. Mr. Claymore says he'll see a lawyer about it, and see if something can't be done."

"I am very sorry," Bobby said once more, "but surely you must understand that police work can't be held up by considerations of personal convenience. You know that Miss Anson is entitled to have her lawyer present? If you want that, I can wait till he arrives. If you give me his name I will try to get him for you on the 'phone. Or if you have his private address, I will send a car with any message you like."

Mrs. Anson seemed very startled. It did not appear that she welcomed these suggestions. Evidently they made an impression, making it all seem more serious. She went away, and again Bobby could hear the low murmur of voices in consultation. He heard another sound, too, that of heavy, cautious, careful footsteps outside in the garden. Bobby waited, listening intently. Probably merely a visitor of one sort or another, a neighbour, perhaps, and yet to his fancy there was something furtive, even faintly menacing, in that slow approach. Yet it might be merely that in the black-out one has to walk warily. The footsteps were quite near now, and yet had become even softer, more cautious, more wary. There came a fumbling at the window. It was being opened, slowly, cautiously, Bobby told himself, professionally, opened by someone who had experience in opening windows from without. It was open now. With equal slow caution the curtains were drawn aside, the blind raised. The fresh night air poured into the room. Under its influence the door Mrs. Anson had left partly open swung slowly to. Now the window was wide, the curtains were pulled aside, the blind raised. In the dark aperture that the window had become, a void opening on the greater void of the night, there showed itself a figure, a squat, heavy figure, every movement silent and careful, poised now, half in, half out, listening, waiting, sinister,

Patient, motionless, Bobby waited. If he stirred, this dark intruder would take alarm, would vanish back instantly into the shelter and concealment of the night wherefrom he had come. In a minute, two minutes, three, he would be inside the room, and then retreat, escape, would be less easy.

So Bobby waited, waited ready to leap into action the moment opportunity came. The so silent, still figure the darkness half hid and half revealed, lifted itself slightly. Bobby felt the moment had come. Another moment and whoever it was would be safe inside, instant flight no longer possible. The door opened, and Mrs. Anson stood there with the lighted lamp in her hand. Its ray shone directly on the window, showed there a man sideways, half in, half out, his head concealed by the window frame, his right leg thrown into the room across the sill, the other bent to follow it, in his hand something that looked heavy and ominous, a bludgeon, a club of some sort, a thing meant for violence, proclaiming violence in all its shape and outline.

Mrs. Anson, still clutching the lamp, screamed and turned and ran. The figure at the window vanished. Bobby leaped from his chair, hurled himself forward in one great leap, stumbled over a footstool he had not been aware of in the darkness, sent the footstool spinning, but lost himself his balance, and nearly fell, reached the window only in time to hear swift heavy footsteps dying away, dying away into the night that offered a fugitive such safe concealment.

CHAPTER X

BETTY

INTO THE ROOM, brought by Mrs. Anson's scream and flight, by the sound of Bobby's encounter with the footstool, came Claymore at a run. He seemed at first inclined to launch instant attack on Bobby, who, however, fended him off with an outstretched hand.

"Steady on," Bobby said. "Steady on."

"What is it? What's happened?" Claymore asked suspiciously. "She said there was a man at the window climbing in."

"So there was," agreed Bobby; and, as now Claymore seemed to contemplate starting in immediate pursuit, Bobby added: "He's got a good start, and it's too dark to try to follow. What about a light? Black-out must be fixed first, though. Ask Mrs. Anson for her lamp, will you?"

Claymore went off, and returned with the lighted lamp. Meanwhile Bobby had adjusted blind and curtain. To him in a tone still doubtful and suspicious, Claymore said:

"Who was it? what did he want? what's it all about?"

"I wonder," Bobby said. "Any ideas?"

Claymore made no attempt to volunteer any. He was staring moodily at the window, and looked troubled and even afraid. By the light of the lamp he had just put down on the table, Bobby could see that he was a fair-headed young man, probably about twenty-eight or thirty, good-looking, with strong, regular features. Of these the most noticeable were thick, reddish-brown eye-brows that nearly touched above a prominent aquiline nose to form one straight line, and that at the moment were drawn down in an anxious and worried frown. Into the room there next came hobbling a youngish girl, slight in build, with a small, pointed face, now extremely pale, and great brown, startled eyes that seemed the brighter for the pallor in which they were set. One foot was bandaged, and she was half hobbling, half hopping, supporting herself, too, against the wall, or by the aid of any piece of furniture in her way.

"Mother said she saw a man," she said. "Was there? who was it? what did he want?"

"It must have been a burglar," Claymore said, but not with much conviction. Then, more loudly and more firmly, he said: "The fellow saw there was someone here and he cleared off. That's all."

The girl lowered herself into the nearest chair. Claymore went to stand by her side. Bobby said nothing. He was watching the two young people closely. It was evident they were both very disturbed and alarmed. But then what had happened—an attempted burglary apparently

—was enough to disturb and excite any one. Yet was it only his imagination, Bobby wondered, that made him think it was more than ordinary excitement, more than ordinary fear, that they both showed? Somehow he was not much inclined to think that either of them believed the recent happening had been merely an attempted burglary, that and nothing more. Claymore looked a robust young man, not likely, for such a cause, to give such an impression of strain, of apprehension even. Then, too, Bobby felt there had been something more purposeful, more deadly, perhaps, behind that slow and menacing figure which had appeared for a moment framed in the night, poised on the window-sill, something ominous, too, in the dark outline of the club, the bludgeon, the heavy blunt instrument, held as if in readiness for purposed, planned intention. They were still all three silent, not one of them having spoken a word, or moved, when from the kitchen Mrs. Anson called:

"Has he gone?"

"Yes," Bobby answered. He walked out of the room, and across a short passage, or hall, to an open door that admitted to the kitchen. Mrs. Anson was huddled in a chair before the fire. She looked very scared and upset, but somehow with a terror more normal, more natural, than that the two young people showed. Bobby said: "It's all right. He's miles away by this time. No good trying to follow in the dark. We'll see what we can do in the morning. What do you think he wanted?"

"Isn't it awful?" Mrs. Anson said. She seemed a little relieved, though, by what Bobby had said. "I shall never feel easy again," she went on. "We shall have to go away."

"Have you any idea who it was, or what he wanted?" Bobby asked.

Mrs. Anson looked puzzled, and shook her head in an uncomprehending way, as if she did not quite understand the question. There came into the kitchen from the other room Claymore and the girl, who now was supporting herself on his arm. Claymore said:

"It was a burglar. It must have been. Thought he would see what he could get. Beastly lonely place. Right on top of the forest, too. Not safe for two women living alone. You'll have to get out, find some other place." A masterful young man apparently. He spoke with an air of decision and authority. "As soon as you jolly well can," he said. "Right away. Betty can get a job somewhere else. London or somewhere."

He had rather the air of rushing them both off, then and there, to catch the next train to the south. Mrs. Anson looked more terrified than ever. To her, a removal meant a crisis needing long and careful preparation. To Claymore, in his brisk, masculine way, it meant giving an order over the 'phone to the first removal contractor you thought of; that and nothing more.

"How soon can you be ready?" he demanded.

The two, mother and daughter, looked at each other rather helplessly. The girl said:

"Oh, we can't. They wouldn't let us."

The 'they' meant the Ministry of Labour, into whose hands the war has placed the destiny of all young and able-bodied women, conscripted, like their brothers, to the service of their country. Claymore was evidently about to sweep the Ministry of Labour aside—and the war with it, if necessary—when Bobby interposed to ask:

"Have you anything in the house of special value?"

"Gracious, no," said the girl, surprised.

"There's my diamond brooch," Mrs. Anson protested, "and your poor father's gold watch and chain, and the silver tea service and . . ."

She seemed inclined to continue with the full list of all her household treasures, but Claymore interposed.

"The fellow was just out for anything he could find," he declared. "Why not? why should there be anything special?"

"Well, unless there is some special reason," Bobby said, "a house like this isn't often burgled. Housebreaking is more common. Besides, burglars generally wait till people are out of the way. Watch them go or knock to make sure no one's in. Or in a large house the idea is to wait till everyone's at dinner. Somehow this doesn't strike me as if it had been an ordinary burglary. Something deliberate, purposeful about it. It gives me the idea that there was a definite object. Can't you suggest anything?"

None of them answered him, but Claymore repeated:

"You've got to get out of here, Betty. In double quick time."

Again there was, at least to Bobby's fancy, a note of urgency, of apprehension, in the young man's voice it was not easy to understand. Bobby said to him:

"Do you think it's likely to happen again?"

"Well, it's happened to-night, hasn't it?" Claymore muttered.

Bobby turned to the girl Claymore had called Betty.

"How did you hurt your foot?" he asked abruptly.

The only answer she gave was a look of extreme fear. Had it been possible for her to become more pale, so it would have been. Claymore said angrily:

"She trod on something sharp. Why? what's it matter?"

"I don't know," Bobby answered. "I am trying to find out if it does matter." To Betty he said: "Was it something sharp on the Barsley footpath?"

Betty replied this time by bursting into tears. This, of course, is a woman's trump card. It takes the trick, at any rate for the time. Claymore, with a look that showed his intense desire to slay Bobby on the spot, said loudly and angrily:

"That's enough. I won't have Miss Anson bullied any longer. Come along, Betty." He swept her out of the kitchen, through the open door, into one of the other rooms. Bobby heard him saying: "You stop there till I've got rid of this chap." He came back into the kitchen and stood glaring at Bobby. "Don't you think," he demanded, "you ought to be doing something about catching the chap instead of amusing yourself hanging round here bullying two women?"

Bobby smiled at the excited young man.

"Mr. Claymore," he said, "you are a zealous but not very wise champion of your friends. You have managed to give me a very strong impression that something is being kept back. It is, as you must know perfectly well, a very serious thing, with possibly extremely unpleasant consequences, to keep anything back in a case of—murder."

He made a slight pause before he uttered this last word. Mrs. Anson gasped audibly, but still looked more astonished and bewildered than anything else. Claymore seemed unaffected, neither surprised nor alarmed. He said slowly and carefully:

"I suppose you mean it's true something has happened at Nonpareil? We heard the caretaker there had murdered his wife, and then that the caretaker himself had been murdered. Is that it?"

"A Dr. Jones had permission to view the place. He has been found dead there," Bobby answered briefly. "That's all we know at present."

"Well, why should you think we know anything about it?" demanded Claymore with rather more confidence this time. "We don't. How could we? Why come asking us a lot of questions?"

"A lady's shoe has been found on the Barsley footpath . . ." Bobby began, and when Claymore interrupted with a sharp comment:'Well, that's not Nonpareil,' Bobby continued without taking any notice of the interruption: "Miss Anson has hurt her foot. It is easy to hurt your foot if you're walking—or running—in the dark on rough ground. A shot was heard coming from the direction of the Barsley path about the time Miss Anson was returning from work that way."

"Yes, but, well . . ." protested Mrs. Anson, looking more disturbed and distressed than ever, and then subsided into silence, as once again she received a quick warning look from Claymore. Slowly, still picking his words with caution, Claymore said:

"Miss Anson hurt her foot here, in this room. She was taking off her outdoor shoes and she trod on a broken bit of crockery as she was getting her house slippers. She knows nothing about shots or anything that may have happened on any footpath. Is that plain enough?"

"Quite plain," agreed Bobby amiably, "but I am afraid we never accept second-hand statements. I shall be obliged to see Miss Anson and question her personally. Her mother and her solicitor can be present if she wishes. But that can wait till she has a little recovered. I can understand what happened to-night has upset her. Before I go I will ask you both again: Are you quite sure you can tell me nothing?"

"No," said Claymore, giving Mrs. Anson no time to answer. "We can't. Perhaps it was one of your own lot, snooping round."

Bobby ignored this, evidently only meant to be rude. He looked at Mrs. Anson, who shook her head, muttered something indistinct, and then again subsided into silence.

"You would be wise to think it over," Bobby said.

Taking no notice of this remark, Claymore said to Mrs. Anson:

"I'll stop here to-night. I can sleep on the floor or anywhere."

"I think it will be as well," Bobby approved gravely. "I do not know who it was we saw to-night, or what he wanted or why he came. But I think he meant mischief. Why?" He paused and went on slowly: "I think Miss Anson is in danger. Serious danger. Why? Did she see something it is necessary she should not tell? I beg you both to think very seriously what you are doing, for I am certain you could tell me more if you wished." To Mrs. Anson he said: "You are the girl's mother." To Claymore he said: "You are engaged. I don't think either of you would forgive yourselves easily if harm came to Miss Anson through your silence. I should not like to be you if that happens, and I think the danger's real. I did not like the looks of that man we saw to-night."

He waited, hoping for some response. None came. Mrs. Anson continued to look helpless, bewildered, frightened, that was all. Claymore still had the same air of sullen resolution.

"I'll see no harm comes to Betty if I can help it," he said briefly.

"Then all I can do is to leave you to think it over," Bobby said. "I hope you will have changed your minds before I see you again."

He went away then, though fearing his hope was little likely to be realized, for he felt that whatever it was they knew, they had fully made up their minds not to tell.

He drove back to headquarters, and there received news of a fresh discovery, though one he had anticipated. The corpse of an unidentified man had been found in the Midwych canal, the cause of death being two bullet wounds in the back. The doctor's report had not yet been received, but photographs had been taken, and the moment they were shown to Bobby he exclaimed:

"That's Ned Doors—Lovey Doors they used to call him from a way he had of calling every woman lovey. An ugly, dangerous brute, but somehow women didn't seem able to resist him. A wheedling, coaxing sort of voice, that made them think they had the brute tamed, only they hadn't, as most of them found out in time. Last time I saw him he was in the dock at the Old Bailey. Burglary with violence, and lucky he hadn't to face a charge of murder. In the canal, was he? Well, now, how did he get there? and how does that fit in—if it does?"

CHAPTER XI

HONOURABLES

NEXT MORNING THERE was, of course, much dull desk work to be seen to, the reading and annotating of reports, the drawing up of lists of matters needing attention, the checking and comparing of results obtained, and all that mass of necessary spade work which it is so easy to dismiss impatiently as red tape, into which same red tape it is indeed only too apt to degenerate.

All this, too, had to be gone through with Inspector Payne, who had the actual charge of the investigation in detail, even though Bobby advised and directed its general course. An important point Payne brought up almost at once was that Constable Burton, formerly of Eton, had recognized Major Hardman, and had even exchanged reminiscences with him of various Etonian escapades.

"So we can take it he is O.K.," said Payne, "and then, of course, there's that alibi—he was in Broken Reed's company when they both heard the shot fired."

"There's that," Bobby agreed, "but all the same I think you might put through a call to the Yard and ask if they can scratch up any information about Hardman. After all, even an Old Etonian can turn out a wrong 'un, even if it doesn't happen very often. The only thing you can be sure of is that if he does go wrong, he goes very wrong indeed. A general rule. The better the opportunity missed, the worse the fall. Leading case. The garden of Eden. So see if the Yard can tell us anything. And I think it would be a good idea if you got Miss Hardman's birth certificate and that of her brother. For one thing it might be as well to have his name."

"Didn't Major Hardman mention it? Frank, I thought?" Payne asked, and added: "You don't think that young man can be behind all this?"

"Oh, I'm not thinking anything at all at present," Bobby declared. "A general principle, that's all. Check up on everything. First maxim of C.I.D. work."

"Oh, yes, sir, I always tell my men that," Payne agreed. "I always tell them that's the first thing to remember."

"Good idea," approved Bobby. "What about Parkinson?"

"He admitted the walking stick we found at Nonpareil was his," Payne replied. "Made no difficulty about it. He says he supposes he must have forgotten it there. He missed it, and his story is he left the Union Club, where you asked him to wait, because he thought it might be at a friend's house, where he had made a call. There was no one at home, so he got no answer. No confirmation either that that is where he really went. I pressed him about how he got on with Dr. Jones. He admitted what he called a certain divergence of view. I asked him why Dr. Jones had gone to Nonpareil by himself the second time. He said he didn't know, but he had had a feeling all the time that Dr. Jones wanted to get rid of him. So I said, if it was like that, why had Dr. Jones taken anyone with him in the first place? Why hadn't he been alone all the time? Parkinson said they were there jointly as equal representatives of the National Super-normal Research Society, and that it was through the society they got permission to visit Nonpareil. The agents would naturally have given permission to view, but not to spend the night there. Parkinson said their society always wanted at least two investigators on every job—to check up on each other, I take it. Parkinson couldn't suggest any reason why Jones should have wanted to get rid of him and be alone. It was a kind of general feeling he had that Jones was excited and wrought up and wanted to quarrel, so as to make Parkinson push off in a huff. Parkinson had clearly been huffy all right enough. The whole story sounds a bit squiffy to me, and we don't know Jones's version."

"No, that I'm afraid we shall never know," Bobby said thoughtfully. "What it comes to is that possibly all that ghost-hunting business was merely an excuse, and that Jones had some other, some secret reason for wishing to visit Nonpareil. And if Parkinson began to suspect as much, then that might have led to a quarrel, possibly with fatal results. It's a possible theory, weaker cases have been brought into court. Not yet watertight, though."

"Getting that way," Payne suggested.

"The beginnings of a case," Bobby said. "That's all. What we want to know is what was Jones's real reason—assuming there was one, and that the ghost-hunting was only an excuse. Any ideas?"

Payne shook his head.

"Not at present," he said. "We may dig it up, though." He went on: "We've got very good plaster casts of footprints in Mrs. Anson's garden. No dabs on the window frame, though—gloves, most likely. But the plaster casts aren't likely to be much help. They show a new, unworn number nine, heavy working boot. Any number of men in Midwych wearing the same sort of thing. Nothing distinctive."

"On the off chance," Bobby said, "see if you can hear of any man about there having bought a new pair of boots lately. See if anyone can remember what shoes that nephew of Major Hardman's was wearing. Though his are more likely to have been the ones of the Hardman garden incident. You might get a pointer that way. Not very likely, but everything has got to be tried. What is the connection between heavy working boots in the Anson garden and light city shoes in the Hardman garden?"

"Perhaps none," said Payne.

"Probably none," corrected Bobby, "but when you are groping in a fog you have to grope everywhere."

Payne said that was so, and went on to discuss the doctor's report. Not that it contained much of value to the investigation. Death was due to two bullet wounds in the back. Death had not been instantaneous, but had occurred before the body was placed in the canal. There had probably been a good deal of bleeding. There were various other details, but none likely to be very helpful, and to them Payne added on his own account a few more.

"Pockets empty," he said. "Nothing to help identification. If you hadn't recognized him, sir, we might have had a good deal of trouble to find out who he was."

"Oh, no, an old con.," Bobby said. "All information neatly docketed at the Yard—photos, finger-prints, all complete. Anything about the Marmaduke person—the chap who calls himself the Honourable something, claims to be an art expert, and apparently took several hours at Nonpareil to find out that the statuary there was only fit to be broken up for road making?"

"Yes, sir," Payne answered. "I got through to the agents. They say the card to view was given to the Honourable Marmaduke Clavering, a son of Lord Grandlieu. They didn't know him at all, issued the card on general principles. There is such a person, a younger son of Lord Grandlieu. I looked him up in Burke. Of course, it doesn't follow it's really the same man. Anyone can take anyone else's name. I got his address in the 'phone directory, and rang up, but couldn't get through. Quite likely this man's a fake, and if he is we shall have a job tracing him."

A knock came at the door, and a constable appeared.

"Gentleman to see you, sir," he announced. "Name of Clavering." He consulted a card he was holding. "Mr. Marmaduke Clavering," he said, and concealed a faint smile of amusement at a first name so comical.

"Good," said Bobby. "Ask him to come in, will you?"

There arrived a well-dressed—too well-dressed for war time, Bobby considered—youngish man, apparently about thirty or so, but giving an odd impression of being much younger than he looked. Plump and rosy—too plump and rosy for war time, Bobby considered—with a cherub-like face, he had wide, innocent blue eyes, that seemed to look out upon the world in perpetual surprise, and a small, pouting mouth he never quite closed. He had, indeed, a little the air of an overgrown baby, and the smile he bestowed upon Bobby was the smile of a trusting child.

"So sorry if I'm intruding," he said amiably, adjusting a monocle he seemed to have great difficulty in keeping in position. "It's really the officer in charge of the Nonpareil case the papers are full of I wanted to see, and I understand you're the Deputy Chief Constable, the Honourable Robert Owen, isn't it? A son of Lord Hirlpool, I suppose?"

Bobby gasped. He wished to speak, but for the moment his feelings were too strong—to be put down as an 'Honourable' indeed. A bit too much, he felt. And had there not been a subtle tone of underlying suggestion that as an 'Honourable' he must be, of necessity, incompetent, a mere figurehead, owing his position solely to string-pulling and influence? It was an impression confirmed when Mr. Clavering continued, still beamingly:

"You know, the bloke who does the work. No good worrying you."

Bobby, for once not quite equal to the situation, decided to ignore this. He said:

"I gather you are the Honourable"—and how bitterly he pronounced that unlucky word—"Marmaduke"—and with what cold contempt he pronounced that unhappy name—"Clavering, described as an art expert," and how clearly, and not in the least subtly, did his tone convey his belief that an 'Honourable' must owe any such reputation as he might possess solely to string-pulling and influence, being of necessity an incompetent pretender.

"When Honourable meets Honourable—" murmured Mr. Clavering, who seemed to be quick enough in the uptake to have guessed something of Bobby's feelings—"how does the quotation go?"

"There isn't one," snapped Bobby, "and I'm not an Honourable or Lord Hirlpool's son or . . ."

"My mistake," murmured Mr. Clavering as Bobby paused not quite knowing what else to deny. "I remember now. But your father only did the trick by two minutes, didn't he? Youngest of twins, and but for the grace of those two minutes, you, too . . ." He paused and beamed more than ever. "Besides," he added, "wasn't there a story that the nurse got the babies mixed, and as likely as not your father was really the eldest, and you ought by rights to be his lordship yourself?"

"A wholly unfounded tale," declared Bobby coldly, "and not a shred of evidence to support it. Mere scandal. Never mind all that. You are Mr. Marmaduke Clavering . . ."

"Generally known as 'Bill'," interposed Mr. Clavering. "Marmaduke after an uncle who added injury to insult by not leaving me a penny when he died. True, he hadn't a penny to leave."

"Occupation—art expert," Bobby went on. "You mean professionally, as a business?"

"I do," agreed Mr. Clavering. "I don't buy or sell. But I value and I advise. And I charge for my advice. Charge high, too. My fees," said Mr. Clavering putting his eyeglass up and speaking with much complacence, "have been described as outrageous. Daylight robbery. Of course, when I'm on a job for Solomon I have to be more careful. Solomon knows a thing or two, the old sinner. You know Solomon? You don't? Art dealer. King Street. W.1. Claims to be the biggest man in the racket, and I daresay he is."

Bobby waved Mr. Solomon aside. In point of fact he had heard of old Mr. Solomon, who every now and then hit the headlines by presenting the country with some specially rare and valuable work of art, and who was said to have attained his present position at the head of his profession by an unflinching and unwavering honesty which so bewildered and disconcerted all his competitors that from contests with him all of them retired utterly defeated. But all that was quite irrelevant to the present inquiry, and Bobby continued:

"I understand your object in visiting Nonpareil was to form an opinion on the value of the sculpture there?"

"One has to see before one can be sure," said Mr. Clavering. "World proverb No. 1."

"It took you some time to decide, didn't it?" Bobby asked, and could not keep a certain note of superiority out of his voice as he remembered how a single look had been enough for him.

Mr. Clavering had been screwing his cherubic face into odd grimaces as he tried to keep his eyeglass in position. Now he let it drop as he looked at Bobby with a touch of surprise in his manner. He said:

"You mean any fool could see at once they were all appalling fakes?"

"Well, you hardly need to be an expert to see that, or to take half a day about it, either," retorted Bobby.

"No, no," agreed Clavering, still evidently impressed, "only one doesn't expect police johnnies . . ."

"And one doesn't expect . . ." began Bobby hotly, and then paused. An irritating person this, with his innocent airs, his silly eyeglass he couldn't even hold in place, his even sillier name—Marmaduke, what can be expected from a Marmaduke? All the same, Bobby was beginning to feel there was more in him than his chubby, cherubic countenance showed, than appeared in his wide, innocent blue eyes, with their look of perpetual surprise. In his most official tone, he continued: "Mr. Clavering, this is a police matter and what I want to know . . ."

But again Mr. Clavering interrupted.

"Been getting in each other's hair, haven't we?" he said. "Not my fault I'm an Honourable. Not your fault you're a near Honourable. Almost worse, that if anything. Forget it, shall we? What you want to know is what I know. What I want to know is if the Dr. Jones the papers say has been found dead at Nonpareil is the Dr. Jones who is a brother-in-law of Wilkinson, Morgan and Tails, the big Mayfair Square picture dealers? Because if he is, possibly what he was after wasn't so much a ghost as a Vermeer that might run to six figures if you landed the right American millionaire."

CHAPTER XII

MOTIVE

PAYNE WAS THE first to break the silence that followed on an announcement received by Bobby with troubled consideration and uttered by Mr. Clavering with a reverence, as he spoke the name Vermeer, that one felt was not habitual with him. Payne repeated the name more briskly, and with no reverence at all.

"Vermeer? Oh, yes," he said. "Dutch artist. I remember seeing one of his things at a London exhibition years ago. Top notch. 'Delft' it was, showed the place in a sort of soft light."

Mr. Clavering—better known, according to himself, as 'Bill'—turned his innocent, surprised eyes on the speaker.

"Up-to-date blokes, the police," he murmured. "Do you have lectures on art in the force?"

"Strange as it may seem to members of the aristocracy," Bobby remarked coldly, "we are not entire ignoramuses."

"Member of the aristocracy yourself," retorted Mr. Clavering with spirit. "Sorry, all the same. I apologize, and hope same will be accepted in the spirit in which offered."

It was not a remark well received. Payne scowled. Bobby frowned. Mr. Clavering continued to beam. Bobby said:

"Perhaps you will be good enough to explain what the death of Dr. Jones has to do with an alleged painting by Vermeer, and why anyone should expect to find it in an uninhabited and empty house like Nonpareil? And I think it might be as well to remind you that this is an official investigation into an alleged murder, and that anything you have to say may be used in evidence."

If Bobby had hoped that this observation, made in his most official tones, would have any effect upon his visitor, he was doomed to disappointment. It was with a solemnity that Bobby did not at all approve that Mr. Clavering answered:

"We have some reason to believe that Dr. Jones, alleged dead, was on the trail of an alleged Vermeer. I think I had better start at the beginning—or the alleged beginning to be as prudent as one should be when making an official statement."

Bobby, suppressing a strong desire to place his visitor under arrest, in handcuffs, throw him out of the window, and a few other such strictly unofficial yearnings, snapped:

"Who is 'we'?"

"Solomon and self," answered Mr. Clavering. "I'm acting for Solomon. Expenses, a commission if the Vermeer stunt comes off, and immortal glory thrown in—entry in all future histories of art: 'This wonderful picture was restored to the world through the energy, skill, and unparalleled knowledge of the Honourable Marmaduke Clavering,' and thus the 'Honourable' restored to honourable status and e'en the 'Marmaduke' forgiven."

"I should be much obliged," said Bobby icily, "if you could tell us anything you know—if anything—without comment. We are only interested in facts."

"Sorry," Mr. Clavering apologized again. "I gather I am not making a good impression, though such is my sole aim. To start at the beginning. It is known that after Vermeer finished his 'Delft' he did another he described in a letter to a pal as a view of Rotterdam in sun and rain. The letter is lost, but is known because of another letter written by an Alderman Six of Rotterdam, in the eighteenth century, in which Vermeer's own letter is quoted. According to it, Vermeer told his correspondent it was his best work, and that in it he had been much more successful than in his 'Delft'. He goes on to describe it as so much his favourite work that he was sorry to part with it. But a travelling English 'Milord' had offered him so generous a price—forty guineas paid down in English gold—that he had felt unable to refuse. After all, Vermeer is quoted as saying, forty guineas was good provender for a twelvemonth or more, and the 'Rotterdam' took but a brief time, being painted, as it were, in a fever, in great haste, to put down a vision before it faded quite away. Sounds interesting, but you can never trust an artist. Fat-headed blokes. Throw their best work into the dustbin and call some awful daub their masterpiece. No judgment, no critical discernment," said Mr. Clavering, shaking his head sadly. "The trouble is they value a thing by what they've tried to do, instead of by what they've actually done. Possibly Vermeer may have been like that, and even if the 'Rotterdam' turns up, it may be a bad example of his work. But if it does turn up, and if it justifies Vermeer's quoted opinion—only that may have been exaggerated or even untrue or perhaps just the contemporary form of sales talk—well, it would be," and here Mr. Clavering's voice grew solemn—"the greatest art find of all time."

"Motive for a murder or two?" Payne asked; and Clavering looked at him and nodded gravely, twice over.

"I still don't see the connection between Nonpareil, Dr. Jones's death, and this more or less hypothetical Vermeer," Bobby remarked.

"Hypothetical," agreed Mr. Clavering, "is the *mot juste*. Efforts have been made to trace any mention of the picture in any catalogue or list of heirlooms. Special attention to the family of any wealthy Englishman known to have been in Holland in Vermeer's time. No result. The picture was given up. Damaged, and then destroyed as spoilt for good. Simply mislaid and finally thrown away. Burnt in some fire. That's happened often enough. There's a story of one old master found in use to stop a leak in a cowshed roof. That was on canvas, of course. Vermeer's picture is believed to have been on panel. Anyhow, hope had been abandoned, if hope there had ever been. So you can imagine the excitement when the story got about that a young man had been asking questions about it at the Wilkinson, Morgan, and Tails place. He wouldn't give his name and address, just looked mysterious and dropped hints, and went off saying that they might hear from him again if 'it came off'—which was taken as meaning if he produced the Vermeer 'Rotterdam'. But it happened that he had been recognized as a young chap named Hardman, nephew of a Major Hardman, who at one time ran an antique business off Bond Street somewhere and didn't make much of a success of it. The nephew had something to do with the business, which is how he came to be recognized. After some trouble Major Hardman was traced. He had retired, and come to live up here. But he isn't on good terms with the young man—calls him a bad egg, and says he let him down badly in some deal or another. In fact, he rather hinted the nephew wasn't always quite honest—'an unscrupulous young bounder', he called him."

"Have to try to get hold of that young man; might be as well to ask him a few questions," Payne remarked, taking out his note-book, and glancing at Bobby, who nodded agreement, though without much show of enthusiasm. "And if he is above ground we'll find him," added Payne with resolution and confidence, but Clavering looked startled.

"You don't think he may have been done in, too, do you?" he asked.

"We aren't thinking anything at present," Bobby said. "Merely trying to get together facts to think about."

"Well, one fact is that young Hardman was certainly in this neighbourhood recently, trying to get in touch with his sister, who keeps house for Major Hardman. A scallywag can always depend on a sister if he is lucky enough to have one—Claudio the exception, but that was Shakespeare's crass ignorance of human nature in sisters. Now he seems to have vanished again, unless you can trace him. Major Hardman doesn't seem to think he is likely to hear from him again for a time—gave him a fiver, he says, and told him to get out and stay out. But as soon as it was known where Hardman was living it was remembered that it was near Nonpareil, believed at one time to house a swell collection of sculpture—junk really, as you spotted yourself. But though the statues were junk, the bloke who got them together, who must have been an awful ass and badly let down, might still have hit on a good thing by accident. It could happen to anyone. The whole contents of Nonpareil was cleared out at auction, so there was a chance the Vermeer had been included in one of the job lots, and was lying about in some dealer's shop unrecognized. Another snag, though. The auctioneers who carried out the sale had their place done in in one of your local blitzes, and all records destroyed. So no way to find out who bought what or if there seemed to be any likely lot. That would have made most blokes throw up the sponge, but not the Solomon Intelligence Department—that's me," explained Mr. Clavering modestly. "Retaining fee. Grossly inadequate, by the way, though Solomon grumbles every time he draws a cheque. The next thing the S.I.D. discovered brought in Dr. Jones, brother-in-law to Tails, of the Wilkinson, Morgan and Tails concern, Tails being the junior partner, but really the boss of the show, and tough even for the picture-dealing racket, where we are all tough or in Carey Street, and generally both. Jones was trying to get permission to do a ghost hunt at Nonpareil. Well, of course, the S.I.D. at once reflected that while you are tracking down ghosts you can also, and quite conveniently, keep an open eye for a lost Vermeer. So the S.I.D. instructed me to toddle along and see what was going on. I must say this for old Solomon. He would give a fair price and be content with a fair profit. I've known him give a few odd hundreds for a Bonnington offered him for a fiver, and then he didn't do so badly on the re-sale. But Tails would pouch the whole lot—and it might be a big lot. Six figures would be a possibility."

"£100,000," said Payne, impressed. "There's your motive," he said again.

"I made up my mind I might as well have a look round first," Clavering continued. "I knew Tails was being clever—he always is, so clever it hurts him to run straight. If he has to go anywhere, he always goes round by the back streets. He wanted to stop any gossip about Dr. Jones's visit, or what he was really after, so he sent Jones on a sham ghost hunt—at least, it may have been genuine enough in itself, but it wasn't priority No. 1. That was the Vermeer, the ghost hunt was secondary. Jones is quite a well-known member of the Super-normal Research Society, so his visit was plausible enough, though I gather he didn't know, or had forgotten, that his society always insists on two investigators. One might get too scared, I suppose, and funk the ghost altogether. I don't know if he had any luck, but I drew blank though I got in first. Because I went direct to the agents and simply asked for an order to view, and got it at once, while Jones was still negotiating for his ghost hunt. Of course, when he got it he got permission, too, to spend nights there, and so had much longer time for his search, while I had only an hour or two, and even then the caretaker came to see what I was so long about. As I told you, when Nonpareil proved a washout, I tackled Major Hardman, but that was N.B.G., too."

"Thank you very much," Bobby said. "A painting worth all that money certainly provides a motive, very much of a motive. If we hear of its recovery, and it would be front page news, we shall have a few questions to ask."

"Answers will be provided," Clavering assured him. "Wholly satisfactory answers. Tails knows his onions. It'll turn up in the Argentine, perhaps, or in San Francisco, with a well-authenticated history of its discovery somewhere as far from Nonpareil as Hitler is from truth. If you want to get ahead of Tails you have to be up very early in the morning. Personally I find it better not to go to bed."

"I take it," interposed Payne, "this Mr. Tails, even if not too particular in his business methods, wouldn't be likely to mix himself up in a murder?"

"Not unless it were foolproof, and I gather murders never are," Clavering answered. "No. Tails is a perfectly respectable business man, a churchwarden and all that, with a fat bank balance, a well-established connection—and no guts. No stuff for murder there. Besides, it's his agent who's been done in. If the Vermeer comes into it at all, it looks as if some rival is concerned. That's why I thought I had better trot along here at once and come clean—that's the correct expression, I believe?"

"Quite so, but have you come clean?" asked Bobby dryly. "You've said nothing about why you were in Major Hardman's garden late at night, or what you were doing there."

CHAPTER XIII

QUESTIONS

The question went home. For once the glib, self-confident Mr. Clavering looked taken aback. He even became a little pale, and his voice seemed a little less perky than usual as he said:

"How do you know that? Did they tell you, did they see me?"

"Never mind how we know," retorted Bobby, confident now he had been right in guessing that his visitor was responsible for the footprints reported by Major Hardman as having been found in his garden, and reflecting to himself that in a good cause a good guess is of much virtue. "Enough that we do know. Well?"

"I suppose mine was a naïf question," admitted Mr. Clavering, "and if you don't know my methods, Watson, so much the better. Mystery impresses."

"Who is Watson?" interposed, suspiciously, Payne, less well acquainted than he should have been with the great classic figures of fiction.

"Modern myth, one of the greatest," explained Clavering, now once more himself, now the first shock was over. "You're quite right, of course. It's like this. In the course of my Sherlock Holmsing, I visited that perennial source of information—the local pub. By judicious pumping I learned that the lady, who, if she is like most of her tribe, obliges Miss Hardman by occasionally accepting half a crown as a reward for looking on while Miss Hardman does the work, had a story of a wonderful picture worth untold gold in the Hardman drawing-room. In the circumstances, I was interested. You might even say, excited. I didn't commit burglary. I didn't do anything you can run me in for. Hardman had already told me he knew nothing. So no good asking him again. What I did was, in the dead of night, to creep into the Hardman garden. I forced the drawing-room window. That was breaking, perhaps, but you have to add entering to breaking to make it a crime, and I didn't enter. But having got the window open and dealt with the black-out, and having provided myself with a full size torch, I made sure there was nothing like a Vermeer there. Though there was what looked like a Birket Foster—posthumous probably, in my opinion."

"Posthumous?" repeated Bobby. "He didn't paint pictures after his death, did he?"

"Not that I know of," Clavering answered, "but he got a bit queer at the end of his life. Always starting something fresh, and never finishing anything. After his death the house was full of half-finished pictures, so the dealers bought the lot, and got a rather good man who worked in Foster's own style, to finish 'em off. He made quite a good job of it, and of course put his initials on 'em all to show they were part his work, and of course the dealers took the initials out again and sold the things as pure Birket Foster. You can generally tell 'em, though. I told you what a racket it all is, didn't I?" and once more Mr. Clavering adjusted his monocle and beamed approval on his audience and on a universe where such things happened for the entertainment of the instructed.

"Isn't Birket Foster a well-known man, too?" inquired Payne.

"He is," agreed Clavering, "and in the general category both he and Vermeer rank as artists. Yet how different." Mr. Clavering paused and sighed. "How very different. But perhaps I'm prejudiced," he admitted. "The other day I had a Birket Foster to value—another posthumous, in my view. I said worth a hundred, and in twenty years not half as much. The blessed thing brought six hundred at auction the next month, and there's the name of Bill Clavering mud for ever after—

at least in that quarter. The chances and the changes of this mortal life, I suppose."

"Anyhow," said Bobby impatiently, "there was nothing like a Vermeer!"

"Nothing. The Birket Foster, which is probably the picture worth untold gold, a hundred or two soon changing into untold gold in the warm, rich atmosphere of the local; some prints; and a rather awful full length in oils slap bang over the mantelpiece so you couldn't possibly miss it—grandpa Hardman, I should judge, in full regimental rig out, Crimea period or even Waterloo. Only family affection could explain that thing, hanging there where no one could possibly escape it. Even if you shut your eyes, you saw it still in all its blaring horror. After all, even if Hardman had the Vermeer he wouldn't be likely to keep it hanging on his drawing-room wall. But after hearing that char-woman's tale I simply had to make sure."

"A most improper proceeding on your part," pronounced Bobby severely. "You owe Major Hardman an apology, at the very least."

"I owe my tailor, too," said Mr. Clavering sadly. "He still lives in hope. So will Major Hardman, probably, if you tell him."

"We shall do nothing of the sort," declared Bobby, as sternly as before, and with a glance at Payne to make sure he heard. "No offence in law except trespass. You can be sued for any damage done. Not a police matter. It all depends on your own standard of decent behaviour."

"An art expert's," Mr. Clavering told him, and added: "Need I say more?"

Bobby grunted. He asked a few more questions and Payne added a few on his own account. Mr. Clavering had, however, no more to tell. He had noticed nothing of any interest during his rapid survey of the bare, deserted Nonpareil rooms and corridors. A world's tour in minia-ture, he said. Mr. Parkinson he had never met, but he knew about him. He was the chief proprietor of a large and prosperous drapery business in a provincial town. He had come into contact with the world of art in painful circumstances. One of the wholesalers with whom Parkinson dealt had got into low water financially, and had borrowed from him a large sum, some thousands of pounds, on the security of his collection of old Italian masters. Then he had gone bankrupt, and the collection had proved to be of small value—most of the paintings were copies, and the few genuine were mostly second-rate examples of second-rate men. It had brought in on sale a thousand or two, and had left Mr. Parkinson much more than that out of pocket. An unfortunate experience, and one that seemed to have induced Mr. Parkinson to interest himself in art matters. But whether Parkinson knew or had heard anything of the Vermeer tale, Mr. Clavering had no idea. He did not think it likely, but it was possible. For his own part, Mr. Clavering explained, he intended to remain for a few days in Midwych, to watch developments, if any.

"That Vermeer, that possible, improbable Vermeer," he murmured, and seemed to lapse into a kind of mystic trance.

Then he departed, and Payne, who had been beginning to look worried, said to Bobby:

"Do you think he can be our man, sir? It wouldn't be the first time a murderer has tried to escape suspicion by coming forward with useful information."

"No, it wouldn't, would it?" agreed Bobby absently. "I wish I could make up my mind about that young man—more in him than appears, but very doubtful what."

"He knows a lot," pronounced Payne. "A lot too much, if you ask me."

"He does," Bobby agreed once more. "The dickens of a lot. I doubt if there's much he doesn't know."

"He was alone at Nonpareil for some hours," Payne went on. "Child's play to take an impression of the lock and get a key made. And there he has the run of the place."

"What about Parkinson's walking-stick?" Bobby asked.

"Fits all right," Payne said. "If Parkinson's telling the truth when he says he left it behind at Nonpareil, this bright lad could have picked it up. Suppose Jones spotted the Vermeer thing left by some accident along with all those statues and busts, but didn't want Parkinson to know, so didn't say a word, and went back on his own to get it. But our Marmaduke is on the watch and follows. He does Jones in, and off he goes with the Vermeer—a cool hundred thousand, by his own account."

"If he could dispose of it," Bobby objected. "Could he? Without giving himself away, I mean."

"He told us how," Payne reminded Bobby. "Knows all the answers, if you ask me. The Argentine. California. One of those film stars would probably give twice as much for the sake of the publicity, and trust that young man to fix up some sort of story you mightn't believe but would have to accept, because you couldn't prove anything else. Clever as a bag-full of monkeys—the S.I.D.," repeated Payne distastefully. "What do you think, sir?"

"I think it looks as if we had to find the Vermeer before we find our murderers, one or two," Bobby said, "and I think that will be the more difficult job. We've seen two dead men, but we don't even know if the Vermeer so much as exists."

"If not, why was Jones murdered?" asked Payne.

"Why was Lovey Doors murdered?" asked Bobby. "A chap like Lovey and a painting by Vermeer seem miles apart. But someone shot

Lovey. There's the other idea about Jones, too—that he and Parkinson had a row, and that led to the killing. There's still a lot that doesn't fit in. Does the Nonpareil caretaker know more than he has told us? Could he have spotted the Vermeer and brought in Lovey to help get it? I'm only thinking aloud. What about Major Hardman's young nephew who keeps popping in and out, nearly as illusive as the Vermeer itself? How did he come to know anything about the Vermeer? Where does the shot heard by the Major and Broken Reed from the direction of the Barsley footpath come in? Who fired that shot and why?"

"Isn't that when Lovey Doors was done in?" asked Payne.

"Think again," said Bobby, and Payne did so, and looked apologetic when he saw the obvious point. Bobby continued: "Then there's that bloodstain seen by Jones and Parkinson and what about it, and why did someone unknown take all that trouble to conceal it? Where does Miss Anson come in with her wounded foot and her belligerent young man? And who was that nasty customer I saw climbing in at the window, and what had he come for?"

"Oh, well, now then," muttered Payne, quite overwhelmed by this flood of questions.

"I'm uncomfortable about that," Bobby said, and looked as uneasy as he said he felt. "Murder coming in at the window was what it looked like. I don't know why, but that's how it seemed to me."

"Can the Vermeer be in their bungalow, and this man knew and meant to have it?" Payne suggested.

"Another possibility," Bobby admitted, "but no more. All that's certain is that both the young people were badly upset and frightened, and both were lying as hard as they knew how to hide something they didn't want to tell—or didn't dare to tell."

"If they are hiding something . . ." began Payne and paused.

"Oh, they are," Bobby assured him, "only what? The Vermeer? I don't think so, but it might be. Is that the connection between what happened to Jones with what happened on the Barsley footpath? Was it something the Anson girl saw, and she's been warned she mustn't tell, but now it's known we are on the job, does someone think it would be better to make sure she doesn't get the chance? Anyhow, we've got to put things together a good deal better before we can act. Two murderers to trace, a possible Vermeer to find, Miss Anson to keep an eye on or else we may find ourselves with another murder on our hands, and why? For somehow I don't think it was the Vermeer the man at the window was after—he had a deadly air."

"We'll watch out," said Payne with confidence.

"For my part," Bobby said, "I'm beginning to think Major Hardman's nephew is the crux of the whole affair."

"We'll find him, sir, and then we'll know," declared Payne once more, and with even greater confidence. "We'll find him if he's still above ground."

"If you ask me," said Bobby, adopting a pet phrase of Payne's, "he isn't."

"If he isn't, that'll make three," observed Payne, disquieted, "and if they get Miss Anson, as you think they may be trying to—well, that'll be four. A Midwych massacre," said Payne gloomily. "I don't like the look of things," he said. Then he brightened up. "We'll stop it, we'll fix them yet," he declared.

He went away then, and came back presently, looking a trifle smug, for after all, to unregenerate human nature, is there any pleasure more exquisite than that of catching out a superior officer?

"'Phone call from the Yard, sir," he reported; and added, while Bobby was still wondering what made him look so like a cat that has just emptied the cream jug: "They say the body found in the canal is not that of Ned Doors, known as Lovey Doors. The finger-prints are entirely different, and Lovey had a scar under the left eye from an injury received in prison which doesn't appear in the photo we sent them."

CHAPTER XIV

ACCUSATION

Bobby received this information in stunned silence. It had never even occurred to him that he could be wrong in his recognition of the dead man. He could almost as soon have looked in the mirror and doubted his own identity.

"But . . ." he managed to say at last, and then lapsed into silence. It even crossed his mind that perhaps for once Scotland Yard had made a mistake, or that the finger-print system was not as infallible as supposed. But recognizing that these thoughts were of the nature of *lèse-majesté*, and probably illegal as well, he hurriedly put them out of his mind. He said:

"Oh." It was all he could think of to say, so he said it again. "Oh."

"Yes, sir," said Payne, still smug, but also now a trifle alarmed by the violence of Bobby's reaction, for seldom had he seen the Deputy Chief Constable so deeply moved.

Slowly Bobby got to his feet. Payne watched him with a wary eye. Bobby went to one of his drawers and produced an old sketch-book of his. It had always been his habit, as he had considerable skill in drawing, to make sketches of people he met, and often he had found these sketches useful for identification purposes. All sketches were dated, numbered, indexed, and he soon found the one he wanted.

"Look," he said in a voice trembling with emotion, and Payne looked and made acknowledgement.

"Him all right," he said. "Spot him anywhere by that."

"Ned Doors," said Bobby gloomily. "I made that sketch directly after his arrest, and I touched it up in court during his trial when the judge wasn't looking." As he talked Bobby compared carefully his sketch with the photograph of the dead man taken after the recovery of his body from the canal. "See the ear?" he said again to Payne. "I always think the ear is as distinctive as anything. Look at the lobe."

Payne, studying sketch and photograph, was plainly puzzled.

"I suppose," he said hesitatingly, "the Yard can't have made a bloomer for once?"

"Hush," said Bobby, glancing apprehensively out of the window and relieved to see the heavens were still in place, seemed indeed quite unconcerned. "Hush," he repeated, "someone might hear. But you might ring up the Yard, tell them there is a most remarkable resemblance, and ask if there is anything known of a brother or any other relative, and if they would mind having a look through the birth registrations at Somerset House." He shook his head sadly. "A nice little bill we'll get," he said, "but cheaper than sending a man to London, even if we had a man to spare to send."

"Yes, sir," said Payne with a nostalgic sigh for the days when a trip to London was still a reasonable possibility.

So he duly rang up the Yard, and the Yard pointed out passionately that it had more work to do than provincial forces ever dreamed of. Payne replied with a hollow laugh, and the statement that he was applying for a transfer to London as his doctor had recommended a rest cure. The Yard, staggered by the sheer audacity of this, answered, bitterly, that men would at once be taken off such little jobs as guarding Buckingham Palace and set to running Wychshire errands, and was that all, or would Wychshire like the rest of the metropolitan force mobilized as well?

Therewith the receiver was banged down, and Payne went off upon his other duties, once more looking as smug as a cat who has just emptied the cream jug, for he did really feel that that 'rest cure' remark had distinctly scored.

"Got home," he told himself happily; and astonished more than one subordinate, and even aroused strange, fantastic hopes, by murmuring aloud the two words "Rest cure", at intervals during the remainder of the day, smiling seraphically the while.

It was some time later on, Payne being still out, when there was introduced into Bobby's office by an awed constable, a visitor, or rather a Presence, so impressive, so imposing, that Bobby wondered if perhaps this was no mere human visitor, but the Platonic Idea of wisdom, learning, and benevolence all here and now incarnate.

The visitor, the Presence, was tall and slim, with silvery hair and a small white moustache and beard, the latter of the imperial type. The complexion was a trifle pale, as from much thought and study; there was a slight stoop, as of one weighed down by much knowledge; the smile and manner were of one who loved his fellow men and trusted them as he hoped they trusted him; the voice was as the voice of a B.B.C. announcer, though possibly a little less aloof, a trifle more human; the long, white hands, eloquent in gesture, were all an Academy picture in themselves. As for attire—but of that, as of the last earth-shaking film out of Hollywood, it surpasses the power of human tongue to tell. Even the editor of the *Tailor and Cutter* could probably have done no more than burst into happy tears. Yet he would certainly have noted with appreciation the delicate harmony of varying shades of green whereby tie, the stripe in coat and trousers, the socks, were all brought into a subtle colour scheme.

Suppressing an inclination to ring for a constable and send him to fetch the episcopal throne from Midwych cathedral as the only suitable seat to offer such a visitor, Bobby indicated a common, ordinary chair, just as if the newcomer were a common, ordinary person, and glanced at the card in his hand.

"Oh, yes, Mr. Tails," he said, remembering the name that earlier had been mentioned by Clavering. "Mr. Tails, of Wilkinson, Morgan, and Tails, the art dealers? You are a relative of Dr. Jones?"

He added a few words of sympathy, and Mr. Tails bowed a grave and dignified acknowledgement.

"A terrible shock to us all," he said. "My sister is prostrate, confined to her bed, indeed. I am here in her place. You are aware that Dr. Jones was my brother-in-law?"

He went on to ask a few questions, and Bobby gave him further details and explanations. Bobby inquired, too, if Mr. Tails knew anything of Mr. Parkinson, but Mr. Tails seemed surprised to hear that Dr. Jones had had a companion. Of Mr. Parkinson, Mr. Tails had no knowledge whatever. After a little more talk Mr. Tails said:

"There is just one small point you may think of no importance but that I feel it might be as well to mention. In his last letter to me my unfortunate brother-in-law mentioned the name"—a faint distaste crept into Mr. Tails's beautifully modulated voice—"of a certain Mr. Clavering."

"Oh, yes," said Bobby, interested.

"A young man," continued Mr. Tails, rather as if he were referring to something not often mentioned in polite society—"of undeniably good family connections, but . . ." He paused, and Bobby reflected that never had he heard more meaning put into a simple monosyllable. "However, I need not pursue the subject." He dismissed it with an eloquent wave of his hands, a little as if drying them after they had been momentarily soiled and then well washed. "What I wish to mention is that poor Clem Jones remarked in his letter—unfortunately I attached little importance to it at the time, and destroyed it—that this Clavering young man had accosted him, had shown some curiosity as to the purport of his visit to Nonpareil, had expressed an insolent incredulity when told that it concerned psychical research. Naturally at that point my unfortunate relative cut the conversation short. He was, however, slightly disturbed on noticing that this Mr. Clavering"—odd, Bobby thought, how disparaging a simple word like 'this' can be made to sound—"appeared to be watching him, shadowing him, indeed, if I may make use of the expression appropriate I believe to your own profession. Or am I in error?"

Bobby agreed gravely that the word 'shadowing' was not unknown to him.

"I am suggesting nothing, because I know nothing," Mr. Tails continued, "but Clement, though a dear fellow, I shall miss him greatly, had a somewhat hasty temper, and was by no means likely to put up tamely with what he might have not unjustifiably considered impertinent curiosity concerning his proceedings. But my attention has since been drawn to the fact that a young man named Hardman, Frank Hardman, called recently at our establishment and made some inquiries about the possible monetary value"—here a faint intonation of contempt in the pronunciation of the word 'monetary' indicated how small was the weight Mr. Tails attached to such value—"of a painting by an old master that might, he hinted, presently be in his possession. Naturally all our representative could say was that if and when such a painting was produced and found genuine, and the title to possession considered satisfactory, the firm would be prepared either to make an offer for purchase or act as agents for sale on the customary terms. So little importance was attached to the incident that it was never mentioned to me. Quite naturally. We are continually hearing of old masters discovered in cellars and attics and similar places, and invariably they turn out to be third-rate copies, made by industrious students in the various art galleries of the world. But on the news of my unhappy relative's fate reaching us, the incident was recalled, when it was further remembered that young Hardman's uncle was now living in the district. Taken in conjunction with Mr. Clavering's behaviour, I confess to feeling uncomfortable—very uncomfortable. You will, perhaps, tell me most unnecessarily?"

"Not at all," said Bobby, "by no means. Most natural, I'm sure. Can you tell me anything about this young Hardman or his uncle?"

"Very little, practically nothing," answered Mr. Tails. "I am aware that at one time Major Hardman directed a small shop for the sale of antiques in a side street. I am not aware of the exact locality, but not far from our own establishment. He came to us once or twice on trifling matters of business. I don't think I ever saw him myself. But I did hear he had become involved in a transaction of somewhat doubtful probity through misconduct and misrepresentations on the part of his nephew. I know nothing about it, but I understood that was why Major Hardman gave up the antique business and left London. I am told young Hardman and Mr. Clavering were close associates, but I never heard that they were jointly concerned in this particular affair, whatever its nature or whatever the actual facts. But when the information reached us of my unfortunate relative's tragic end, it was suggested to me that perhaps for once there might be some truth in the familiar story of the unrecognized masterpiece brought to light by happy accident, or that, at any rate, belief in such might account for young Hardman's inquiries and for Mr. Clavering's impertinent interest in my unfortunate brother-in-law's visit to Nonpareil. At any rate, it was forcibly represented to me that the authorities should be placed in possession of such information as seemed cogent. In the circumstances I deemed it well—my sister being in a state of collapse and I being here as her representative—to call to see you in person."

Bobby expressed his appreciation of such a wise decision and his sense of deep obligation under which Mr. Tails had placed the Wychshire police force. Mr. Tails lifted a slender, gently deprecating hand. The gesture contrived to convey that Mr. Tails's actions were always wise and that he was accustomed to place those he met under a deep sense of obligation. Bobby went on:

"You were speaking of Mr. Clavering. Can you tell us anything about him?"

"As I said, of good family," Mr. Tails answered, more aloof, more gravely dignified than ever. "The 'honourable' he places before his name and of which he makes such great use he is properly entitled to. He has written, I understand, one or two what he calls monographs on art matters. I am unacquainted with their contents." A faint, almost imperceptible movement of those eloquent hands dismissed the 'monographs' for ever from human attention. "He earns his living, or so I am informed, as a runner for Solomon."

"What is a runner?" Bobby asked. "Who is Solomon?"

"Solomon?" repeated Mr. Tails, answering the last question first. "Oh, a member of my own profession. Quite well known. We ourselves have come in contact with him occasionally. I say nothing against him, I know nothing against him, but I do know there is a widespread feeling in the profession that his somewhat ostentatious professions of honesty and straightforward dealing are, to say the least, in poor taste, and quite unnecessary. I trust the standard of honesty among art dealers—no doubt we have our black sheep—is as high as in any profession or higher. Indeed it has to be. You don't get very far as an art dealer if your clients cease to feel that they can trust you absolutely—absolutely. 'Runner' is a somewhat slang term often employed to designate the go-betweens who search for and occasionally indicate possible purchasers or sellers. We do not care to employ such people permanently, though it is not infrequent to do so, as in the case of Messrs. Solomon and Mr. Clavering. I do not say it is objectionable, but it does not happen to be our way, that is all."

Bobby tactfully expressed his appreciation of, and his admiration for, such an attitude. Mr. Tails lifted a nobly deprecating hand. Bobby asked if Dr. Jones—he only just in time stopped himself from saying 'your unfortunate relative'—had any knowledge of art matters, and was likely to recognize rarity and value in a painting he happened to come across casually. Mr. Tails smiled his beautiful smile, and feared that dear Clement was hardly an expert in such matters. Possibly, though, he might have thought it worth while to mention any painting that happened to catch his attention in unusual surroundings.

"Especially," added Mr. Tails thoughtfully, "if his curiosity had been roused in any way, as certainly it had been in this case by Clavering's behaviour."

Fastidiously and unwillingly, it seemed, he appeared to contemplate unpleasant possibilities. Then he departed, and almost at once Payne came in, looking very impressed.

"There's a bloke just gone out," he began, but Bobby, slightly shocked, interrupted him.

"Not a bloke," he said, "a Presence, a Personality, an I-know-not-what."

"Not the Pope in mufti by any chance?" inquired Payne.

Bobby shook his head.

"In common parlance," he said, "Mr. Tails, the art dealer, and Dr. Jones's brother-in-law, come to tell us Clavering murdered Jones."

CHAPTER XV

SUSPECT

IT WAS LATER, in the same day, in the afternoon, that Bobby, returning from a conference at the Midwych Town Hall, came face to face with Mr. Clavering in St. Paul's Square—not altogether by accident, he suspected. For Clavering evidently wished to speak to him, and Bobby stopped, quite willing to hear anything Clavering had to say. It was a maxim of his that only when people started to make voluntary statements did you begin to get at the facts. For if they spoke the truth, that was what you wanted; and if they lied, then that was even more enlightening.

"Mr. Tails is here," Clavering began, "did you know? Has he been to see you?"

"Yes. Why?" Bobby asked.

"I just wondered," Clavering answered without specifying what it was he wondered.

"How did you know?" Bobby asked.

"I've seen him."

"Accidental meeting?" Bobby asked next, and Clavering looked at him quickly and then gave his cherubic smile.

"No," he said. "Information received. In other words, a wire from Solomon that Tails had gone off in a taxi with a suitcase. Obvious guess, Midwych. So I went round to the Midwych Central Hotel. Another obvious guess. Tails was sure to put up at the most swagger hotel in the place. His position demands it. Ask him. I saw him in the lobby. I don't think he saw me, and I didn't speak. Just withdrew. I do rather wonder why he came himself."

"In the circumstances," Bobby suggested, "it would have been odd, wouldn't it? if no relative of Dr. Jones had appeared. Mr. Tails is here instead of his sister to make necessary arrangements. We should expect one of the family to be at the inquest. Mr. Tails tells me Mrs. Jones is in a state of collapse, and unable to travel."

"Well, I suppose that may be so," agreed Clavering, "though to my certain knowledge they've been living apart for the last five years."

"Why are you interested?" Bobby asked with some suspicion. "Why did your employer send you a wire about Mr. Tails's movements?"

"My employer? who's that? Oh, you mean old Solomon. Yes, I suppose he is, isn't he? Because he thinks Tails would need some stronger motive to make him come up here than merely to represent his sister. Instructions to a lawyer are all I should have expected. What we do think is that Tails is asking himself if the Vermeer has anything to do with the murder; and, if there is a Vermeer in it, Tails means to be on the spot. Solomon thinks, too, the Vermeer may be behind it all. So do I, for that matter. Like to see the old man's wire?" Clavering produced it. He said: "You see what it says? 'Tails left Bond Street. Taxi. Suitcase. Why? Anything in Vermeer story?' Solomon doesn't believe Tails would leave London with one or two important sales coming on and plenty of rich Americans—diplomatic and military—hanging about, merely on account of the death of a brother-in-law. I don't either."

"You don't seem to have a very good opinion of Mr. Tails," remarked Bobby.

"Good lord, we're at daggers drawn, and have been for years," Clavering answered happily. "Hated rivals, ever since I sold him a faked set of Chippendale chairs for exactly a hundred and one times their value—after he had first sold them to a pal of mine for a hundred times their value. The extra one times was for expenses. If you could only have seen his face when he realized he had bought the same old faked stuff back again." A smile more than cherubic, seraphic in fact, spread over Mr. Clavering's rosy countenance. "But I gave you a close up of Tails before, and, if he has been to see you, I expect he gave you a close up of me?"

"He did," admitted Bobby briefly. "It was very illuminating. Close ups often are. Especially of those who give them."

"That's an apple in my basket, I suppose," observed Clavering cheerfully.

"Why all this excitement about the Vermeer, even if it exists?" Bobby demanded. "It won't belong to either of you even if it does turn up. If it's at Nonpareil it will belong to the de Tallebois family, won't it?"

"Are cops really as innocent as all that?" demanded Mr. Clavering, looking quite sad. "My good man, think of the publicity, think of the advertisement. You would be famous ever after. The Man Who Found the Lost Vermeer. Why, the B.B.C. would most likely let you give a special broadcast about it all to yourself—and what else is fame but a special B.B.C. broadcast? Apart from the chance of getting in a first offer or else of getting the sole sale rights as agent. Or rights of reproduction—a goldmine. And you ask me why so much excitement? My dear man," said Mr. Clavering reproachfully, polishing his monocle with vigour "be your age."

"I'll try," Bobby promised. "At any rate, you are making it plain that this merely possible Vermeer provides sufficient motive for a murder?"

"For one? for a dozen," Clavering assured him earnestly. "I wonder if Tails is really sold on the idea? Can Jones have told him anything? A wire? a letter? a phone call? There doesn't seem much time. Jones was an inoffensive sort of bloke. Why should anyone want to murder him? Someone did, though." Clavering paused. "The Vermeer's problematic. The murder—isn't. I say, did Tails drop any hints about me being the murderer? If he got you to run me in that would be one competitor safely out of the way. A real Tails touch—and he might even believe it." Clavering looked more thoughtful now, even a little scared. "Do you?" he asked abruptly.

"There's not enough for any belief yet," Bobby answered.

"You mean you're lying low and sayin' nuffen—like Brer Rabbit? The correct official attitude, I suppose."

"Could you give us a statement of your movements since you got here?" Bobby asked.

"Why, yes, I suppose so," Clavering answered, and looked more thoughtful still—and more scared. "I say, up to the neck in it, aren't I? The murder night? Let me see. It's a long time since I was in Midwych, and I spent the afternoon at your art gallery. Most of the stuff has been cleared out in case of air raids, but the miniatures are still there—they put them in a safe in the cellar if a warning comes through. Very good collection, though I'm pretty sure the Cosway Lady Hamilton is a fake. Your curator will want to murder me if I establish that. I spent all the evening in my room in the hotel writing up notes about the miniatures, and then I went to bed. I went out for a breath of fresh air before going to bed. I know the night porter saw me come back, but I don't know whether anyone saw me go out. Or if they did, if they will remember. Not much of an alibi, is it?"

"No," agreed Bobby.

"Means I'm still on the suspect list?"

"Oh, yes, but then so are several others."

"But not, I fear, Mr. Tails," said Clavering sadly. "For one thing, he was in London, and, for another, he hasn't it in him—not murder. Impressive personality, hasn't he?"

"Mr. Tails has a very distinguished appearance," admitted Bobby cautiously.

"His stock-in-trade," said Clavering. "He can strike awe into the breast of a duke, princes are proud to be seen in his company, prominent American business men have been known to say that to be done down by him is a liberal education in itself." With this parting broadside he nodded a farewell, and turned away. Bobby continued on his road, and was almost immediately caught up again by Clavering. "I say," he said. "I've just thought of something. I've just remembered the way they looked at me at the hotel this morning. I wondered why. Have you blokes been making—making inquiries? Isn't that what you call it?"

"Naturally," Bobby answered, willing to admit a fact Clavering had been shrewd enough to guess. "We didn't learn much, though. The night porter did see you go out, and did see you come in, but he has no idea of the times, so it's not much help. He seems to have trained himself to remember if guests are in or out, but never thinks of noting the time. Oh, by the way, you've been calling at a good many places in town, second-hand dealers, and so on."

"I say, though," said Clavering; and now he looked not so much thoughtful or even frightened as for once extremely grave. He even forgot to play with his monocle. "You do find out things, don't you?"

76

"What we are for," Bobby told him.

"I suppose so," agreed Clavering. "You're quite right. So I have. I've been trying to trace any purchaser of odd lots at the Nonpareil sale. The Vermeer may have been sold like that, it may just possibly be hanging up in some dealer's shop, unrecognized. One never knows. No luck, though. No trace, no sign, no hint of anything of the kind."

With a slight return to his former jaunty manner of an airy frivolity, Clavering again nodded farewell and departed; and Bobby, watching him go, told himself that for once the young man was really shaken.

"The grand manner may be the Tails way of impressing," Bobby reflected, "and is certainly deliberate. Careful preparation and long training in the Tails case. But is Clavering's frivolity put on with the same idea of getting under your guard, or is it natural—or is it both natural and cultivated?"

It was too late, and there was too much needing attention, for Bobby to undertake, that afternoon, the further task he had in mind. So it was not till the following afternoon that he could take the road to Nonpareil on the bicycle the petrol shortage compelled him to make frequent use of in place of the car of earlier and more lavish days, before all had to give way to the prime necessity of smashing the Hun and the Jap.

Arrived at Nonpareil he propped his bicycle against one of the stone pillars of the great entrance gate and knocked at the caretaker's lodge. There was no answer, and still none when he knocked again. Apparently the Baileys were out, and then he thought they might be at the back or at work in their garden. He went to the rear of the lodge, therefore, but saw no one, and there was no one in the garden. For a moment he paused to admire it. It was large, nearly half an acre in extent, and cultivated with extreme care and skill. No doubt the soil was good, washed down, probably, from the slopes around, for Nonpareil lay in a hollow, as is so often the case with the great houses built in times when the security a hill offers for defence had ceased to be required, and before light and air and a dry site had begun to be thought of as desirable. Good soil counts for little, however, without that constant loving care whereof this garden showed such plain evidence. Bobby even indulged in sentimental and perhaps not altogether sincere reflections on the enviable fate of those who work in close and innocent and fruitful contact with the good earth, as compared with the hard tasks that are the lot of a Deputy Chief Constable.

All the same, as he retrieved his bicycle and wheeled it up the avenue towards the house, he began to have a reminiscent pain in his back. A memory of a distant day when he had assured Olive, a for once unsympathetic Olive, that it was permanently broken as a result of just two bare hours spent planting out lettuce and cabbage seedlings.

Now the main building came in view; and when he turned the corner following the path that led to the side door whereby entrance was now effected, he was pleased to see the door was open.

Probably, therefore, Bailey and his wife were inside, carrying out their weekly task of maintenance and care. He wheeled his bicycle into the passage, for in these days bicycles are precious, and have a curious trick of disappearing suddenly and for ever. As he was leaning it against the wall of the passage a slight sound made him turn, and he had a glimpse, but no more than a glimpse, of a man standing there, a tall man, a young man, Bobby thought, and certainly not the short, squat, thick-set Bailey. Nor were the footsteps that he heard in swift retreat those of the heavily-shod caretaker. These were light and sure and swift, and already the sound of them was dying away. The bicycle in Bobby's hands hindered him for a second or so from starting in pursuit, and by the time he had raced up the long passage and into the central hall, the silence of the huge empty house lay once more all around like a great calm, soundless sea.

"Who's there?" he shouted, loudly and uselessly, and got no answer.

CHAPTER XVI

PURSUIT

THERE, IN THE great hall of Nonpareil, Bobby stood for a moment, motionless and listening, straining his eyes to pierce the enormous obscurity around, his electric torch ready in his hand to throw a beam of light the instant that he saw or heard anything to give him a clue to the whereabouts of the figure he had seen for that one fraction of a second.

So utter, so intense, was the silence shrouding the huge building in one vast still pall that he could almost have persuaded himself he had dreamed that momentary vision he had had of a young man watching from round the corner of the entry passage. Or that he had mistaken for a human figure what in reality had been but some chance trick of light or shade. But then there had been no light in all the long stone passage, only an all-pervading gloom, and besides he had heard footsteps.

Not much chance, he told himself resentfully, of successful pursuit in this far-stretching labyrinth of corridors and of rooms, room upon room, one opening from another, all in a gloom alleviated but little by the spare daylight that here and there struggled through chinks and cracks in the boarded windows. And then above, on the first floor, were the old reception apartments; so big, some of them, that, to one standing at the entrance, the farther end in this shuttered gloom was nothing but a great shadow, where a man might well lurk unperceived. Behind them more passages, more rooms, and behind them again still more, reaching away to the east and west wings, space enough, indeed, to hide an army.

Whoever it was of whom he had had that passing glimpse must, however, be somewhere within the building. At least unless Bailey had lied in saying that every other means of exit and entrance, save that one small side door whereby Bobby himself had just come in, had been made secure. Bobby went back to the service door beneath the stairs through which he had reached the central hall. It had neither bolt nor lock, but with the aid of his pocket knife, jammed below the lintel, he made it fast, so that any fugitive attempting to escape that way in a hurried flight would at least be delayed for a time before discovering the obstruction and removing it. As he was busy with this small task he thought, but was not sure, that someone watched him from the gallery above, and he had the impression, but again he was not sure, that a faint laugh floated down to him through the still and stagnant air, to tell him that his precaution had been noted, and that it was found amusing.

He went back slowly to the foot of the stairs, and then ran up them swiftly and lightly. At speed he raced through the great reception-rooms, sweeping the space before and around with the ray from his torch. The rooms opened one from the other, occupying the whole of the front of the building. Passing beyond, he found himself entangled in a maze of passages and other rooms, bedrooms probably, and remembered a tale of how, in former days of grandeur and hospitality, guests had been provided with bags of different-coloured wafers so that they could lay trails, red or blue or white as the case might be, to guide them to and from their rooms, much as in some of the big stores in modern cities customers are exhorted to 'follow the coloured lights' to such or such a department.

Another turn in the corridor he was following brought him, however, to the picture gallery, at the end farther from that by which he and the others had entered before. It was darker here, even, than elsewhere; but his torch showed him where still stood those silent, sheeted figures that had been the witnesses of the recent tragedy. Strange and eerie they seemed in their likeness to watchful living beings peering from under their coverings. Possible, even, that the fugitive for whom Bobby sought lurked behind their shelter. The questing ray from his torch showed nothing to support such a fancy, but he told himself it was no wonder Parkinson had been tricked by his fears into imagining that one of them had moved. Or had it been no trick of fancy, and had, that night, one sheet concealed no statue but a living man, one, who, being discovered, had been willing to use murder to make secrecy sure.

Anyhow, there was no one here now, of that Bobby made certain. And he knew now whereabouts he was. But when he left the gallery and tried to find the great central stairway again he took a wrong turning, and, as he did so, saw a shadow fall across the passage where it turned again. He ran, but when he got there he saw nothing, and he supposed that very likely it was only his fancy that made him think he felt, as it were, a movement in the air, a faint and transitory quiver, as though from some swift recent disturbance by a passing body.

The shadow had seemed to fall from the right, so he ran in that direction. He came to the head of a second stairway, the one probably in general use in former days when the reception-rooms were closed. Quite clearly he heard from somewhere below the sound of a closing door. At the risk of his neck, for on these stairs the shadows were deeper even than elsewhere, he raced down them, and found himself in a part of the house he did not think he had visited before. But again he was certain that he heard something. A cough, he thought, or was it a muffled step or perhaps a cautious signal of some kind? He hurried in the direction whence it seemed to come, his torch switched off, for he did not wish to give too clear warning of his coming. So far as he could judge he was in the west wing now, near the kitchens—he remembered there were two of them—and the other domestic offices.

He made up his mind to abandon a pursuit that had become an aimless game of hide-and-seek. Easy for any fugitive to peep and watch round corners, behind doors, through key-holes even, and so be warned in time to flee elsewhere. In this enormous and fantastic maze, where once perhaps half a hundred servants, of one sort and another, had made a bustling, active life, but which now was so silent and dark and still, it would be easy to avoid a dozen or a score of searchers. Easier still when there was but one solitary searcher.

Someone was in the house, of that Bobby was sure. Or was he sure? Had his imagination betrayed him? All old houses, no matter how silent they may seem to ears strained to listen, are in reality full of noises, echoes, rumblings, wind in the chimneys, the scuttlings of rats and mice, of this sound or of that. Even the creaking of the wainscoting can strike upon the ear and seem remote and ominous, as though in the distance men whispered secretly together.

"Getting on my nerves," Bobby told himself impatiently. "Very likely there's no one here at all."

But all the same he knew there was, he knew that he was not alone, and he thought, too, that every movement he made was watched.

He tried to think of some means by which, without leaving the house, he could summon help. Collect dry wood and make a small bonfire outside in the hope that Bailey might see the smoke and come to investigate. Not too hopeful, and even if Bailey saw and came, on whose side would he be? A point on which Bobby was not very sure. For that matter, since the side door had been open, Bailey might be already in the building somewhere, using his knowledge of its interior to help to baffle Bobby's search.

Or stand without and shout in the hope of summoning help? But he might shout all day and no one hear. Or wait till he was missed and headquarters sent to see what was happening? But that would not be till nightfall and complete darkness had come, and darkness would make search and pursuit impossible, escape easy. Even as it was, the gloom and heavy shadows in which these rooms and corridors were shrouded had proved too great a handicap for pursuit and search to succeed.

He decided again to abandon such useless efforts, and to go back to the lodge in the hope that the Baileys had returned. If so, he could send Bailey for help. He supposed, so far as he could judge his position, that straight on in the direction he was now facing should bring him back to the great entrance hall. So he followed the passage he was in, since it seemed to lead that way, and as he went the light from his torch he flashed occasionally here and there showed him to one side a door that was swinging slightly open. He looked at it cautiously. It opened on a flight of narrow stone steps leading down into utter darkness. He remembered the cellars in which two of his men had wandered for a while that other time, lost, smothered, according to their own account, in cobwebs and dirt.

But why was this door open now, swinging ever so slightly on silent hinges, and why were those hinges silent? Bobby threw the light of his torch upon them. They had been oiled recently, and so had been the bolts whereby the door was fastened.

So someone for some reason had wished to make access to the cellars silent and easy. Since the oiling had been done so recently, the explanation of the open door was not, as Bobby had thought it might be, any trifling lack of attention on the part of his two men. Since their visit someone else had descended through this door, and who and why? Or was it merely that the cellars were to be used as a refuge against search, a shelter from pursuit? Had the unknown, the unseen, whom he had followed all through the great, deserted spaces of the house with failure so complete, now sought safety there below in what seemed a labyrinth more complex, and darkness more complete, than even the labyrinth and the shadows above?

Or was it a trap?

Bobby had another look at those bolts. They looked solid. He drew them out from both top and bottom, so making sure they could not be shot against him. He had no desire to be made a prisoner in those murky regions, and he still had the feeling that he was being watched and spied upon. He pocketed the key as well; and, for additional precaution, he used one of the bolts to twist the staples out of form and place, so that the missing bolt could not be replaced by another piece of metal.

Satisfied, then, that he had taken every reasonable precaution, though none was likely to be required, he descended the flight of stone steps, and found himself in a vast subterranean region underlying the mass of Nonpareil. The darkness was intense, the walls were damp, here and there water dripped, the smell was of a noisome strength, the air was heavy and stagnant, from all around came a faint, angry rustling, as of indignant creatures disturbed in their immemorial sanctuary.

On each side of the passage along which Bobby was now making a slow and cautious progress were doors, some open, some closed, admitting to cellars. Into most of these cellars a little air, a few pale rays of light, penetrated from barred apertures. In others these apertures seemed to have become blocked by the long accumulation of the dirt of years, and in others it seemed as if such openings to light and air had never existed. All alike were empty, nothing left save the bare walls. One or two, though, had plainly been used for storing coal, since coal dust was so thick upon the floor that Bobby wondered whether, in the present shortage, it would not be worth while to remove it for the manufacture of briquettes or some similar purpose. Here and there broken shelving still remained, though generally the shelves seemed to have been removed, presumably for the sake of the wood.

He walked on, throwing around the light from his torch. Abruptly two small red lights became visible ahead, about a man's height from the ground. But when he directed his torch towards them they vanished, and he realized that it had been the eyes of a rat, gleaming in the dark, that he had seen. The creature had been perched half-way up the wall where crumbling bricks permitted climbing and some crevice had seemed to offer a safe nesting place.

Bobby made up his mind to return. He felt he had had enough of this murky and unpleasant maze. Nor did it seem likely anyone could be hiding down here. Anyhow, impossible to organize any kind of effective search without more help. He remembered that his two constables he had sent to explore these nether regions had reported one cellar with a locked door, into which, therefore, they had been unable to penetrate. He wondered if he could find it, and presently, wandering on a little farther, he came to it.

It was still locked, but now the key was there, in place. Looking thoughtful, Bobby took it out. It was quite new, and of crude manufacture, certainly not the work of a skilled man. Effective enough, though, for it turned easily and silently, so that evidently oil had recently been applied here also. The door was of heavy and substantial make, and opened outwards. Bobby pulled it back and threw within the light from his torch. There, by its strong ray, he saw the prone, still figure of a man, and around his prostrate form a circle of a dozen or more great rats, one of them already nosing at his cheek, another sniffing, nibbling at his ear.

CHAPTER XVII

CAPTIVES

Bobby's shout, the sudden flashing ray from his torch, sent that evil circle scuttling. They vanished as nightmare vanishes when a sleeper wakens. Bobby went forward and turned the prostrate man on his back. It was Clavering. Bobby looked at him thoughtfully and doubtfully, and then took out the small first-aid case he always carried, and dressed the nibbled ear. Only superficial injury, but he supposed a rat's bite might carry infection. There was a good-sized lump on the back of the head as well, and there had been bleeding from a deep scratch under the left eye. Probably it was the smell of blood that had drawn the rats from their holes, embolded them to approach so near. As Bobby attended to this scratch, too, he wondered, grimly, what would have happened if he had not seen the door, swinging slightly open, which led down to these cellars, or if he had not arrived when he did. For a rat's teeth are sharp, it can bite fast and deep, and the jugular vein might have been reached before consciousness returned.

An unpleasant thought, and grisly the picture that came into his mind of rats busy at a ghastly feast. Now he saw Clavering had opened his eyes and was looking at him. Bobby said:

"How are you feeling?"

Clavering began to struggle to get into a sitting position. Bobby helped him. Clavering rested his back against an empty packing-case and looked round him with an air of mild surprise. He felt tenderly the back of his head, and looked still more surprised. Finally he discovered his monocle, and tried and failed to put it in position. Then he said slowly:

"You, was it? I say, pretty drastic, what? You might have said something first." Then he felt his ear, and started the bleeding again, so that when he took his hand away there was a little blood on it. He said: "What did that?"

"Rats," said Bobby.

"Rats yourself," retorted Clavering indignantly. "It hurts."

"I mean," explained Bobby, "rats were starting in to make a meal with your ear as hors-d'œuvres. Who knocked you out?"

"Wasn't it you?"

"Don't be a fool," snapped Bobby impatiently. "Of course it wasn't. Didn't you see or hear anyone?"

Clavering attempted to shake his head. As a result everything started to revolve very rapidly around him, so that he felt it necessary to hold on hard to the packing-case against which he was supporting himself.

"I say, I do feel groggy," he muttered, as the cellar began to recover some degree of stability. "I say, what did you mean just now? Rats?"

"I mean rats when I say rats," retorted Bobby. "What do you suppose? Someone knocked you out and left you lying there. You hurt your face falling, and it bled. The rats smelled the blood and came along—a dozen or so. One was starting on that ear of yours when I came in. I've dressed it. That ought to stop any risk of blood poisoning."

Clavering had been slowly getting to his feet, but now he sat down abruptly on the empty packing-case. Bobby, turning the ray from his torch here and there, saw that the cellar held a collection of odds and ends of all sorts and kinds—a broken wringing machine, an old bath, some ancient and damaged gardening tools, an old iron bedstead or two, broken chairs, a good deal of crockery, all of it chipped and cracked, apparently, and so on and so on, an indescribable medley of rubbish indeed. Even in these days of salvage it hardly looked as if it would do much more than pay the cost of collection and carriage. The cellar itself seemed larger than most, and was dimly lighted by a few rays of daylight that struggled in through a small grating high up in the outside wall.

From his brief inspection Bobby turned back to Clavering, still sitting on his packing-case.

"Feeling better?" Bobby asked him.

"No," said Clavering. "Look. You—didn't mean that, did you? Kidding, weren't you? I mean to say—rats?"

"So do I," Bobby answered. "Let's have another look at that ear of yours. You've started it bleeding again, pulling at it." He wiped it with a scrap of lint from his first-aid box and put on some more dressing and then had another look at the scratch under Clavering's eye. It looked red and angry, and Bobby attended to it, too. He said: "Feel able to walk?"

"I do," Clavering answered. "My inside doesn't—it keeps trying to turn over or come up or something. Is that a rat over there? I think I've got the shivers."

Bobby threw a bit of broken crockery in the direction whence there had come a sound of rustling. It ceased. Bobby said:

"They won't bother us, they wouldn't anyone who could move. It was only because you were unconscious they dared come so close. As soon as you moved they would have vanished."

"I'll leave a legacy in my will for the endowment of rat catchers," Clavering said. He was beginning, now, to seem more normal, his voice was almost natural, his hands steadier. "I wonder if I could get some poison gas to let loose down here," he added meditatively.

"What were you doing here?" Bobby asked.

"Oh, the Vermeer, of course," Clavering answered.

"You didn't expect to find it in a place like this, did you?"

"Might—you can never tell. You spotted I was trying to trace the dealers who bought things at the Nonpareil sale. One of them told me a pal of his bought a lot of stuff—left overs that nobody wanted. He couldn't manage removal at the time, and got permission to store it in one of the cellars. But then he was killed in a blitz, and no one knew if he had left any relations or heirs of any sort to whom the stuff here belonged, or who was responsible for moving it. No one bothered. It wasn't worth anything, and it's been lying here ever since. Well, it struck me there was just a chance the Vermeer might be there—not likely, but possible. It's believed to have been on a panel, and some people seem to think a picture isn't a picture unless it's on canvas. I thought there was the off-chance it might have been put aside with odd bits of wood like bits of loose panelling. Anyhow, it seemed worth trying. I couldn't make any one hear at the lodge when I got here, so I came on to the house. The door was open, but no sign of Bailey. I thought he must be somewhere around. I couldn't find him, but I did find the door leading down to the cellars. I came across this place, and I was poking about in the rubbish— no sign of the Vermeer, of course, I didn't think there would be—when I thought I heard someone. I went to the door and called out, but there wasn't any answer. I turned to go back and have another look—and that's about all I remember. Next thing I knew you were there, and I thought it was you laid me out. But I suppose cops don't do that, they take you in instead."

Bobby listened to all this in silence. It might be true, he supposed. Or it might not. Other possible explanations crossed his mind. He said presently:

"Then you can't tell me anything to show who it was?"

Clavering again shook his head, though this time with less disastrous results. He said meditatively:

"I never did like rats."

"I thought I had a glimpse of a youngish man of middle height in a grey suit in one of the passages," Bobby said. "Did you see anyone like that?"

"I never saw anyone at all," Clavering repeated. "There was a bloke hanging about in the road outside when I got here. I remember seeing him watching me while I was trying to make them hear at the lodge. I didn't take much notice."

"What was he like?"

"I hardly know—looked like a labourer, burly sort of chap, flat nose and broken teeth, slouched along with his hands in his pockets, and looked as if he were watching you, but hoped you hadn't noticed him. I don't think I liked his looks much, but I didn't pay him any special attention."

Bobby produced a print of the photograph of the dead man whose body had been found in the canal.

"Any likeness?" he asked.

Clavering looked puzzled.

"Well, I don't know," he said doubtfully. "Might be the same bloke— I couldn't be sure. His twin brother perhaps."

"This whole case seems to be rotten with twins," Bobby grumbled, and put the photograph back in his pocket. "Had the fellow any scar on his face?"

"Not that I remember," Clavering answered. "I didn't take much notice," he repeated. "I don't suppose I should have noticed him at all but for the way I saw him watching when I was trying to make the Baileys hear." He got cautiously to his feet. "How about getting out of this hole?" he said. "I've had about enough of it, and my inside seems more restful."

Bobby said he had had enough of it, too, but he would have another look round first. He spent a few minutes turning over some of the rubbish. He brought down clattering a pile of rusty old pots and pans that had been insecurely heaped up in one corner, he used his torch to peer behind the different piles of rubbish and into the various corners. He found nothing of any interest. Clavering, watching him, said presently:

"Have you got Vermeer fever, too?"

"There's been one murder in this house already," Bobby said. "And it looks as if someone didn't much like you nosing about down here. I should like to know why."

"Isn't the Vermeer explanation enough for anything?" Clavering asked.

"Possibly," Bobby agreed, "but possibly not the complete explanation. If I were you I should give it a rest. The thing has nearly cost you your life already. Better run no more risks."

There was almost a religious fervour in Clavering's voice as he answered:

"You could risk your life for a smaller thing."

Bobby shrugged his shoulders slightly. A painting, the greatest painting, the Peruzzi frescoes by Giotto, for instance, he remembered seeing as a boy, and still remembered as vividly as though he had seen them yesterday, could not, he thought, be valued in terms of life. To do so would be to put the work of man in art above the work of God

86

in life. However, this was no time for the consideration of such questions.

"Well, come along," he said.

He went towards the door, but when he tried to open it, it resisted his efforts. Most of the time he had kept his torch switched off, to conserve the battery as long as possible, since batteries, too, are scarce. Besides, there was enough light coming through the barred aperture in the open wall to see by. But now he used the light of the torch to see what was stopping the door from opening. From behind Clavering asked:

"What's the matter? won't it open?"

Bobby was still examining the door. He said slowly:

"The key is in my pocket. There are no bolts. But someone has made the door fast while we've been talking. Wedges under the door, between it and the floor," he said. Then he added: "It opens outwards."

"Well, but . . . ." began Clavering.

"The professional touch again," Bobby said.

"What do you mean?" Clavering asked.

"I mean," Bobby answered, "that when wedges are pushed under a door the way it opens, then the more you push against that door, the stronger grows the hold of the wedge. A burglar's trick. A door fastened like that stops pursuit. The professional touch," he repeated. "You know, that's interesting."

"Wouldn't it be more interesting to know how we are going to get out?" demanded Clavering with tremendous irony.

"Oh, much, much more interesting," agreed Bobby. "Only you see I don't."

"Don't what?"

"Know how we are going to get out."

"Well, hang it all," said Clavering, more puzzled than alarmed.

CHAPTER XVIII

RESCUE

BOBBY REMAINED STANDING lost in thought. He was trying to make a coherent pattern of all these events, and not meeting with much success. Clavering gave him an impatient glance, and then started to examine the door. It was stout, well made, constructed in days when things were intended to last, before it was thought a good idea to be ready to scrap everything for anything newer. He tried to kick in its solid wood, and failed to make any impression. Then he went to rummage in the piles of rubbish for some useful tool. He found none, for what were there were either useless, like an ancient rake, or broken, or both. He came back and threw himself with all his weight against the door, again without result. Waking from his abstraction, Bobby remarked:

"You are only making those wedges hold more strongly."

"Well, do something," Clavering snapped. "We can't stop here for ever."

"Why not, if we can't get out?" Bobby asked mildly. "That door is going to be a tough job. Might be a good idea to see, first, if we can't get help."

"How?"

"We could take it in turns to stand at that grating and shout," Bobby said. "Someone might hear in time—or might not. A bit tiring, too, and we are at the back of the house, where no one ever comes. Not too hopeful. How about pushing out a sort of distress flag on any stick we can find? Same objection. No one comes to the back, and it'll be dark soon. We might start a fire outside the grating, though. That would stand a better chance of being seen. Especially during black-out."

"How?" Clavering asked again. "If we could get outside to do that, we shouldn't need to, should we?"

"There's plenty of wood down here," Bobby explained. "If we cut shavings, set them alight, push them through that grating up there and go on feeding it, we ought to get a decent sort of blaze in time. Even if no one notices it at first, as soon as it's black-out, someone is sure to spot it, and tell the A.R.P. people. You know," he added with a slightly surprised air, "I never thought to live to find any good in the black-out."

"It seems an idea," Clavering admitted.

He took out a penknife and set to work, whittling shavings. Bobby looked on. He had left his own knife in the service door above. He had matches, though, and he was gathering up the shavings into a small heap when he paused abruptly.

"What's that?" he said.

The daylight filtering through the bars of the cellar grating had been suddenly interrupted. A brick had been placed against them on the outside and now another.

"Here, I say," exclaimed Clavering. "Hi, you, what do you think you're doing?" he shouted, as yet a third brick was added to the other two. The only answer was a spadeful of earth thrown on top of the bricks. More earth followed, and the sound of blows as the loose earth was beaten down. In a very few moments every vestige of light had vanished, every vestige of air was excluded. "What's the idea?" Clavering asked, bewildered. "What's happening? Who is it?"

"Ever heard," Bobby asked, "the legend of the cavalier and his wife and family?"

Clavering looked more bewildered than ever. He went across to stand below the grating and shouted. He came back, stumbling in a darkness now intense. He said to Bobby:

"Cavalier? what cavalier? what do you mean?"

"There's an old story," Bobby explained, "of a de Tallebois who was trapped down here with his wife and family during the civil war by Cromwell's Ironsides they were hiding from. No one knew where they were, and so they starved to death down here, and the tale is that their cries and lamentations may still be heard at times, as their ghosts bewail their fate. Strikes me someone up there thinks that history should repeat itself with a policeman and an art expert taking the place of a cavalier and his family—less picturesque but equally unpleasant."

"Here, I say, stow it," muttered Clavering.

"Only making things plain," Bobby explained again.

He took a torch from his pocket. But he didn't switch it on. Batteries are soon exhausted if used continuously, and they might have desperate need of light before long. He said:

"It seems there's someone up there who doesn't mean us to get out too easily."

"Well, what are we going to do?" Clavering asked once more; and again Bobby did not answer, since he did not know.

Even yet Clavering was much more puzzled and bewildered than frightened. To him, the situation seemed to lack reality, to be too fantastic to be real. Such things as this simply didn't happen, not at least to ordinary, decent, respectable members of society like himself. True, his pursuit of art had taken him into some queer places before now; as for instance into the back slums of Marseilles, where had been reported an ancient figure of the Virgin carved on ivory, and into an Italian villa, where the owner, an Italian count of ancient lineage, had challenged him to a duel when he had denied the authenticity of a reputed Giorgione. But this present business still seemed to him more like a bad dream than anything else. He had a feeling that he might waken any moment in bed in his own small flat in central London. He began to cough, and Bobby said:

"Breathing getting a bit difficult? It was bad enough before, and it's worse now that chap outside has cut off what little air came through the grating."

"Do any of your men know you're here?" Clavering asked.

"They knew I was on my way," Bobby answered, "but I suppose there's nothing much to show I ever got here—or that I'm here now. There's my bike I left upstairs near the entrance, but—well, the professional touch shown by the wedges under the door makes it likely it'll be taken away and dumped near the canal or something like that. Obvious move. What about you? Did you tell anyone?"

"No," Clavering answered.

"How did you come?"

"Walked. Look. That idea of yours. I mean, lighting a fire outside. Couldn't we start one here and burn that door down?"

"I did think of that," Bobby answered. "But the air's got pretty foul, now the chap outside has done his stuff. It was bad enough before, it's worse now, and if we added smoke from a fire as well I'm not sure we could breathe at all. I think we'll have to keep fire as a forlorn hope. We had better have a good try, first, at breaking through."

"What's that?" Clavering asked, as a rustling sound in one corner caught his attention.

"Rats," Bobby answered. "Hope springs eternal in the rat bosom."

"That's a nice thing to say," Clavering muttered.

They set to work upon the door, using every device they could think of, availing themselves of every means of attack they could find. At the end of half an hour they had very little to show for their pains.

"A week's job at this rate," Bobby remarked.

"Can't see properly what we're doing," Clavering grumbled. He paused for a moment to mop his face. He said: "Funny how things come back to you. I remember when I was a kid an old *Pilgrim's Progress* we had. There was a picture of Christian and another bloke in the dungeon of Giant Despair, and I can remember how it frightened me because I thought it might happen to me some day, too. And now it has."

"They found out suddenly the dungeon door wasn't locked, didn't they?" Bobby asked. "I am afraid this is, though."

As he spoke, instinctively he turned the handle of the door and pushed. It opened immediately, and so unexpectedly that he almost fell into the passage without. So surprised was Clavering that for a moment or two he only stared and gaped, before, literally, coming tumbling after. Very much astonished, the two men stood and stared at each other. Out here the air, that before had seemed oppressive and heavy, almost unbreathable, now appeared to them like that of a fresh spring morning, by contrast with the foetid, suffocating atmosphere of the cellar. They both breathed deeply, and with Clavering indignation began to replace astonishment.

"The door was open all the time. You said you couldn't open it, and someone had wedged it up," he complained. "We might have stopped there long enough, all because you hadn't sense enough to turn the handle."

"But I had," Bobby protested mildly. "Just what I did."

"Only because of my happening to remember our old *Pilgrim's Progress*, and how that picture scared me," Clavering grumbled, still indignant. When Bobby, now examining the ground near by with the aid of his torch, made no reply, Clavering went on: "Of all the fool tricks . . . what made you think it was fast?"

"Because it was," Bobby answered now, having found what he had been looking for. He showed three small wedges, those by which the door had been fastened, and showed, also, the marks on ground and door where they had been inserted. "Someone came along and kicked them out," he said. "Most likely while someone else was earthing up the cellar vent, and we were too much interested in that to notice what was going on at the door. All the same, it's just as well you read *Pilgrim's Progress* when you were a kid. Everything comes in useful in time if you only wait long enough."

"Well, but . . ." began Clavering. "What's been the idea?" he demanded, and then he said abruptly: "Come on, let's get out of this. I've had enough of it down here."

"So have I," agreed Bobby.

They made their way then back to the upper regions, and once they were outside, in the open air, they stood for a time, enjoying the fresh, evening breeze, for by now it was growing late. Not much pleasure, perhaps, as a rule in the simple act of breathing, but to them both the deep breaths they drew were like renewed life. Clavering was the first to speak when he repeated his former question:

"Thank God we're out of there," he said, "but what was the idea? I mean . . . who? . . . and why?"

"Looks to me," Bobby answered slowly, "as if someone wanted rather badly to put a stopper on us and what we are doing, and someone else thought the method adopted was going a bit far. Pure benevolence, perhaps, or else fear of the consequences. So while the one was making sure by stopping up the cellar vent, the other was knocking out the wedges."

"Well, why didn't he say?" grumbled Clavering. "We might never have known."

"Didn't want to be seen, probably," Bobby suggested. "Thought he had better have a good start so as to avoid awkward questions."

Clavering looked very puzzled still.

"I can't make it out," he complained.

"Too hard a knot?" Bobby quoted once again.

"Well, I mean to say . . . who could it be?" Clavering asked.

"Three people are possibles," Bobby said thoughtfully. "Or four, rather. The Baileys. Bailey thinking he would like us out of the way, and Mrs. Bailey scared of what might happen afterwards. Or the man you saw watching you when you got here. Or the chap I had a glimpse of— youngish, I thought, in a grey suit. Only in that case, which did which? and why?"

"Anyhow, I suppose all's well that ends well," Clavering said.

Bobby, to his relief, had found his bicycle untouched where he had left it. He was preparing to mount and ride away, leaving Clavering to return, as he had come, on foot. As he started he said to Clavering:

"What makes you think it has ended, well or otherwise?"

CHAPTER XIX

SPADES

BOBBY, NEXT MORNING, found waiting for him one or two reports of interest. One was from the Yard, indicating inability to recognize Major Hardman from the description given. If finger-prints, or even a photograph, could be obtained and forwarded, a more definite answer would be given. Bobby laid this aside. Then there was information from the Lonesome sergeant to the effect that Major Hardman was absent from home on business. What business, Bobby wondered, since he understood that the Major had retired from active affairs. Again from the Yard, from another department, was word that Somerset House had no record of the birth of the Hardman twins, Frank and Frances, nor, for that matter, of Ned Doors, formerly an inmate of one of His Majesty's prisons, but not, as Bobby had at first believed, the dead man found in Midwych canal. Nothing in that, of course. People can be born elsewhere than within the Registrar-General's domain. Names can be changed. But there was also a note to the effect that a brother of Ned or 'Lovey' Doors, known as 'Shut' Doors, because of his reputed silent disposition, was said to have returned recently from the United States. But this was not certain. It was only what was said among some of Lovey's associates, none of whom were very reliable, or likely to be very anxious to provide the authorities with information. Nor was it explained how he had managed to make the journey in war time. Deck hand on a tramp, perhaps, deserting when England was reached. Bobby was interested, though. If the dead man was this brother of Lovey's, was Lovey himself in the neighbourhood? If so, was it Lovey he had seen climbing in at the Anson bungalow window? If so again, when, where and how, had the paths crossed of the professional criminal and ex-convict, Lovey Doors, and the apparently quiet, normal young woman, Betty Anson? A strange and difficult problem there, Bobby told himself. And yet another note from the sergeant at Lonesome, to say that when Frank Hardman had been ejected from the Horse and Groom he had been wearing a grey suit.

"Nothing much in that either," Bobby remarked to Payne, who had sent in these reports, and now appeared in person to ask what Bobby thought of them. "Plenty of grey suits in the world. But I think, all the same, I'll try to see Miss Frances Hardman this afternoon."

"She'll not say much," Payne prophesied.

"Did you manage to find out anything about what they think of her at the W.V.S.?" Bobby asked.

"'Fingers all thumbs,' was one description," Payne answered, smiling a little. "She's so clumsy at needlework they give her as little of that to do as they can. At the same time she's good at odd jobs, and can even drive a nail straight, which makes her one up on most women. She is said to be very willing and very regular, quite a dab at cooking, never seems tired, but, all the same, not very popular—rather sulky and won't talk, though you would think they would like that at a W.V.S. Give more of a chance to the rest of them."

"Interesting," commented Bobby.

"Do you think she comes in?" Payne asked.

"If she does, not much to show where," Bobby answered.

"A sister might be willing to do a lot for a brother and yet feel the line had to be drawn somewhere," observed Payne, and, when Bobby agreed, added: "By the way, there's a 'phone message from Lonesome. I told them to ring up if they heard of any change. A doctor called yesterday at the Anson bungalow. Miss Anson it was."

"Nervous breakdown?" Bobby asked, and Payne said he believed that was the trouble, and to himself wondered how it was the Deputy Chief Constable seemed always so lucky in his guesses. Bobby added: "I think I'll go on from Hardman's place and see Miss Anson, too, if I can. I expect I shall be told she can't be seen—doctor's orders."

"Doctor's orders," agreed Payne, "is always a trump card to play. If you ask me," he added, "those two—Miss Hardman and Miss Anson are in it together somehow."

"Yes, somehow," agreed Bobby. "Only the operative syllable is 'how'."

"I suppose, though," Payne continued, "that after what happened to you and him, we can take it that Mr. Clavering is out?"

"Why?" asked Bobby.

"Couldn't have knocked himself out," argued Payne, "and if he could, he wouldn't, not down there, not among the rats. Sort of gives you the creeps, I mean to say, being eaten alive. No one could stand for that."

"He certainly didn't knock himself out," agreed Bobby, "but he may have got an accomplice to do it for him. If so, not the first time the another victim trick has been played to suggest innocence. Makes a sore head worth while. The same accomplice may have blocked up the cellar grating just to add a further touch of realism, and then kicked

93

the wedges from under the door to let us out again. A good deal of what is going on suggests a pretty subtle mind behind it all. As for the rats, possibly they represent the unexpected, unforeseen element that's always liable to upset the best laid plans. Nothing to prove it was like that, but it might be, and nothing to prove it wasn't. It was Clavering talking about *The Pilgrim's Progress* that started me trying the door. Coincidence or design?"

"Seems," said Payne cautiously, "as if it might be either," and when Bobby signified a grave agreement with this pronouncement, Payne continued: "But if you ask me, it does seem, doesn't it? that Miss Hardman's brother is still hanging around, and, if he is, he must be above ground still. And if he is," declared Payne with undiminished confidence, "we'll lay him by the heels sooner or later."

This time Bobby shook his head.

"All I saw," he reminded Payne, "and that only for a fraction of a second, was someone who was probably young, because he was so quick in his movements, and who was wearing a grey suit. Not much for identification."

"Well, if it wasn't young Hardman, who was it?" asked Payne. "No other young man mixed up in it that we know of—except Mr. Claymore, Miss Anson's best boy. If those two girls are playing along together, he may be in it, too. He is going to the Anson bungalow every night to sleep, by the way."

Bobby said he thought that was all to the good. He still remembered with discomfort the vision he had had of that nocturnal visitor climbing in at the bungalow window. He thought it just as well the Anson mother and daughter should have all the protection possible. He shook his head again when Payne hinted that since Claymore was at the bungalow at night, it was no longer necessary to keep police watch as well.

"We haven't the man power," Payne argued; but Bobby replied, in the new war jargon, that the Anson bungalow must have 'first priority'.

"Claymore may be in danger himself, for all we know," he said. "Or it is just possible he himself is the danger. With so many cross-currents, and when we know so little about any of these people, we mustn't risk slipping up on any precaution."

Payne retired then, and Bobby applied himself to the work covering his desk and needing his attention. Of this there was so much that it was again late in the day before he arrived at The Tulips, where, as he alighted from his bicycle, he saw a waiting taxi, and inside it Mr. Parkinson, dividing his attention between a newspaper and the front door of the house towards which he kept throwing impatient glances. Nor did he look any too pleased when he saw Bobby, though he responded civilly enough to Bobby's greeting. Bobby asked him if he were waiting for Major Hardman, and Mr. Parkinson said he wasn't, he didn't know who Major Hardman was, Mr. Tails had simply said he had to see a friend and would Mr. Parkinson mind waiting a few minutes.

"Tails has been there half an hour already," Parkinson grumbled. "If it were my taxi I think I would leave him to it."

"Mr. Tails hired it, did he?" Bobby asked. "Has he been giving you a ride?"

"He asked me to go to Nonpareil with him," Parkinson explained. "He wanted me to show him exactly where it happened. He was there yesterday, but he says he couldn't get in. The caretaker was away."

"Was he, though?" said Bobby, much interested, and still more interested when he noticed a spade on the floor of the taxi. "I was there myself yesterday afternoon, having a look round, but I didn't see Mr. Tails. Was he going to do some gardening?" he added carelessly, with a glance at the spade. "Or what was that for?"

"I don't know," Parkinson answered. "I asked him, and he said something about it might come in useful."

"So it might," agreed Bobby, remembering how the day before earth had been dug to throw against the cellar grating. "I wonder if it did come in useful—to-day or yesterday. You are on your way back from Nonpareil, are you?"

"Yes," answered Parkinson. "Mr. Tails seemed very interested. I showed him everything, and told him all I could. I suppose it's only natural he should want to know. I understand he is here as family representative."

"But why the spade? Did you do any digging?"

"Oh, no. I think Tails wanted to explore the cellars, but the caretaker wouldn't let us. He said during his absence yesterday someone had got into the house and been down there, and he didn't mean it to happen again. So he had nailed up the cellar door, and he wasn't going to open it again without orders from the agents."

"Well, that's a precaution," Bobby agreed; and wondered what it was a precaution against.

"In my opinion," burst out Parkinson suddenly, "it wasn't what happened to poor Jones that Tails was really so concerned about, even if he is here on behalf of the family. He gave me the impression there was something else in his mind, something he was much more interested in . . ."

"What?" asked Bobby.

"He didn't explain. Perhaps I'm wrong, but that's what I thought. In any case, he asked me so many and such odd questions that finally I told him I hadn't come there to be cross-examined, and if he wanted to know anything more he had better wait for the inquest. When is that to be?"

"I'm afraid it will only be formal, we shall have to ask for an adjournment," Bobby answered. "Was he asking about anything special?"

"He seemed to be trying to make out that there was some cause for my slight disagreement with poor Jones I didn't want to mention. No business of his, in any case, and so I told him at last. Certainly he apologized, but had there been any other convenient means of returning I should have left him. I nearly made up my mind to walk, as it was, but it's a long way, and I've not been sleeping well these last few days."

Before Bobby could say anything more the door of the house opened and there impressively appeared the magnificence that was Mr. Tails. For a moment he stood there and looked around, a trifle as if surprised that there was no red carpet, no reception committee. Behind him the door closed, with an almost disrespectful and certainly emphatic bang, and by, Bobby thought, the fair, firm, vigorous hand of Miss Frankie Hardman herself. Mr. Tails, apparently slightly startled by so emphatic a bang, turned, and so far forgot his usual aloof dignity as to be guilty of a gesture more suitable to a small and vulgar boy than to one of his imposing personality. Probably, then, his visit had not been a great success, Bobby thought, nor, when he saw Bobby waiting for him, did he look in any way pleased. But he spoke with his usual suave dignity, as he said:

"Good afternoon, Mr. Owen. Still, I presume, continuing your researches? I am sure that if it is within the bounds of possibility, the assassin of my unhappy relative will be brought to justice. For my part," he added with that engaging frankness some of his clients sometimes had cause to remember a little ruefully, "I am continuing mine into the possible existence of the Vermeer masterpiece. I thought it possible Major Hardman might be able to give me some information concerning his nephew. You will remember he is the young man who called at our establishment to hint at knowledge of such he claimed to possess."

"Did you learn anything?" Bobby asked.

"Unfortunately, no. Major Hardman claims to have washed his hands of the young man." As he spoke, Mr. Tails was all the time edging —if that is not too disrespectful a word to apply to his almost imperceptible but always dignified progress—edging, then, his way nearer the taxi, where Mr. Parkinson sat waiting in gloomy and resentful patience. "I must not detain you longer," he explained, "and on the indulgence of my good friend, Mr. Parkinson, I have already trespassed too long."

Bobby did not attempt to keep him. He would always be available for further questioning when it seemed desirable to learn more about these visits to Nonpareil. The taxi drove off, and Bobby went towards the house where, before he could knock, the door was opened by Major Hardman himself.

"I saw you were talking to that infernal humbug," the Major said. "Any fresh developments? I've had to be away a day or two—urgent private affairs as we used to say in the army. So I haven't heard anything of what's been going on. But come in."

He led the way not this time into the front room but into the drawing-room behind, where the first thing that Bobby noticed was the strong, rank smell of tobacco, and in an ash tray on the table a dottle still warm, as if only recently knocked from a pipe. Impossible to imagine the stately Mr. Tails smoking anything so vulgar as a pipe. So apparently there had been another visitor at The Tulips, and who had that been? and had Mr. Tails been here to meet him? and had Major Hardman's cordial welcome and prompt invitation to Bobby to enter been to make sure Bobby was safely out of the way while this third and unknown visitor departed unseen?

CHAPTER XX

PORTRAIT

Major Hardman bustled about, profuse in offers of hospitality. Bobby said he hoped the Major would permit him to refuse. He was on duty. Major Hardman looked serious, and said he understood. He was a soldier, and a soldier understood discipline. He explained this at some length. Bobby, ensconced in a comfortable arm-chair, listened patiently, and as he listened, he, according to his well-established habit, looked about him, hoping that from this room he might be able to gather those hints at the characters of the inmates of the house, the dining-room here had refused to supply.

Without success. Another non-committal room, he thought, and only the most imaginative could suppose that all this careful convention hid, and was intended to hide, strange, dark secrets or purposes menacing and evil. The only object in the room in any way unusual was the small Birket Foster water-colour over the mantelpiece. Bobby thought it charming, if somewhat sentimental, and thought Mr. Clavering's condemnation too severe. The other painting Clavering had mentioned—the full-length portrait in oils of a soldier in early Victorian uniform—Bobby could not see very clearly, as it hung in a shadowy corner well out of sight. What he could distinguish of it made him, in this instance, fully agree that it was of 'family interest' only.

Major Hardman, noticing Bobby looking at it, explained that it was a portrait of his grandfather, General Sir Thomas Hardman, K.C.B.

He was evidently very proud of his forebear and told two or three anecdotes about him, all of them showing the General as having been on close and intimate terms with the great men of his day. The Major, still in chatty mood, went on to talk about his recent visit to London, and the difficulty, in this time of war, of obtaining accommodation there. He had booked his room at one hotel well in advance, and then, on his arrival, was calmly informed that it was not available. A senior officer, in possession, had unexpectedly prolonged his visit. He, Major Hardman, had 'kicked up a row', as the hotel people ought to have warned him in time, but he got no satisfaction. He supposed he was lucky to have found a room finally at another hotel. He even mentioned the restaurant where he had dined during his stay. Used to be good, he said, but now as filthy as all the rest. Oh, well, he supposed you mustn't grumble.

With this admirable sentiment Bobby concurred, without commenting on the fact that the Major had done nothing else but grumble for a good five minutes. He brought the conversation round to Mr. Tails, of whom the Major expressed an unfavourable opinion.

"His place was near mine when I was in business in the West End," he explained. "Too clever by half I thought him—a humbug, if ever there was one," and the Major bristled, and sat very upright and looked the very personification of the bluff, straightforward military man. "Tails seems to think he is on the track of a hitherto unheard of Vermeer, and I might know something about it. I don't, and, if I did, he is about the last man I should tell. Apparently that scapegrace nephew of mine has been dropping hints about some such painting. Frank never mentioned anything of the sort to me."

"It was partly about Mr. Frank Hardman that I wanted to see you," Bobby explained, taking the opportunity thus offered him, and whether by chance or design it was hard to tell. "There seems to be a story that he was seen at Nonpareil yesterday. Do you know anything about that?"

Major Hardman shook his head very decidedly.

"I haven't seen or heard of him," he said, "and I don't think I'm likely to, since I gave him that fiver and told him to get out and stay out. I hope Frankie—I told her she wasn't to have anything more to do with him. She promised, but—well, they're twins. Twins often seem closer together than ordinary brothers and sisters."

"I suppose that's often so," agreed Bobby, "especially identic twins."

Major Hardman agreed. He went to the door. Opening it, he shouted:

"Frankie. Frankie. Can you come here a minute?"

"What for? I'm busy," a voice replied from a distance.

"Mr. Owen's here, he's asking about Frank," the Major shouted back.

Sounds of movement became audible in the distance. Miss Frankie appeared, and stood, tall and sulky, in the doorway, only half visible in the shadows there, her hands still floury from some culinary operation she had been engaged upon. A hefty young person, Bobby thought, and if she wore that sullen, angry expression at the W.V.S., little wonder she was not greatly liked there. The Major asked her if she had any communication with her brother. She shook her head, and when her uncle pressed the question she repeated sulkily and emphatically that she had neither seen nor heard of him since his last visit. Major Hardman told her the police believed he had been seen at Nonpareil the day before. She said she didn't believe it. What would he be doing there? she asked. He had told her he was returning at once to London, and there was nothing to keep him in Midwych. A reference to the Vermeer only made her look contemptuous.

"Frank is always running after some mare's nest or another," she said, and went away, saying something about having the dinner to look after.

"A good girl," the Major commented as he closed the door behind her, "but a weak spot for her brother—and I think, perhaps, for her old uncle, too."

Bobby was inclined to think her looks and manner belied her if she had soft spots anywhere for anyone. But that, perhaps, was another harsh judgment. With a woman you can never tell, as Bobby sagely reflected. Then he asked if Major Hardman knew why his nephew believed he had found out something about the existence or the whereabouts of this supposed Vermeer, but the Major only shrugged his shoulders and smiled ruefully.

"You'll think I have a bad opinion of the boy," he said, "but it wouldn't surprise me a lot if he hadn't invented the whole story."

"But why?" Bobby asked.

"Well, if the story were true, it would be a big thing," Major Hardman pointed out. "A very big thing. If he managed to persuade a dealer to believe in such a possibility he might be able to get a cash advance for expenses. Or even money down to buy outright. There's a story of an art dealer who saw a very valuable Chinese vase in the window of a mall suburban villa. He didn't want to try to buy the thing by itself, in case the owner began to suspect its value. So he made a liberal offer for the whole of the contents of the house; and, once the sale was completed, walked off with the vase, making a present back to the former owner— a very astonished owner no doubt—of all the rest of the furnishings. Something like that. Frank would say he believed he knew where the Vermeer was, but he daren't inquire too closely for fear of putting others on the track. He would suggest making some sort of lump purchase,

99

including the supposed Vermeer, for a hundred or two perhaps. Quite safe, no risk of prosecution. Not his fault if it turned out the Vermeer wasn't there, or was only a worthless copy. He had always said he wasn't sure. I'm afraid I think Frank is up to all sorts of tricks. And yet," he added wistfully, "I can't help feeling Frankie is right when she says there is good in the boy still, and that presently he will settle down, once he has sown his wild oats."

"If there's really no foundation for the story and it's all just pure invention," Bobby said "is there likely to have been any reason why he should choose Vermeer rather than any other artist?"

"Well, you know," Hardman explained, "at one time Vermeer's work was often sold under other men's names—his paintings got attributed to De Hooch or anyone else they could think of. Quite likely there's still some of his stuff unrecognized, and, if unrecognized, why not unknown? I expect that's what Frank thought. Then again—well, I hardly like to mention it, but I believe Frank was at one time carrying on a rather hot flirtation with Miss Anson. The girl living at the New Bungalows, I mean. I don't know how serious it was on her side. Not at all on Frank's, I'm afraid. I imagine, from what he said, he started it chiefly because she had bought something at the Nonpareil sale he thought might be valuable, and wanted a quiet look at. Only he wasn't sure. I told Frank he was behaving like a blackguard, but he only laughed. I had told him that so often before. He always fancied himself with the girls, and I must say they seemed to like it. But I don't really know. I didn't want to know. The less you know about that young man's proceedings, the better. And it's no good saying anything to his best girl of the moment. They don't believe you. If you want to know anything more, you'll have to ask Miss Anson herself, and I don't expect she'll want to talk."

"Did you say anything about all this to Mr. Tails?" Bobby asked.

"Shouldn't I have done?" Major Hardman asked in his turn. "I wanted to get rid of him. Not a man I care much about. Not too particular in his dealings. I'm afraid I thought the easiest thing to do was to send him off to badger someone else. I hope I haven't done any harm?"

"Oh, no, no, not at all," Bobby assured him. "I wonder if you would mind telling me if there is any definite cause for your distrust of your nephew. I don't want to press you, and I certainly have no right to. I think something must have occurred while you were in the antique business yourself. If you would rather not say, I shall quite understand."

Major Hardman hesitated, looked doubtful, showed other signs of hesitation and doubt, made somewhat confused references to the stern daughter of the voice of God and how to stand and be still to the Birkenhead drill was a damn tough bullet to chew, but he was a soldier, and duty came first, and finally burst out:

"I found he was selling me things that weren't his property to sell. Things he got hold of on one pretext or another. To ask my opinion of them or just to show me, or to get a valuation. Then he sold them to me—cheap. Cheap all right till the rightful owners turned up and wanted them back. They hadn't authorized Frank to sell or, if they had, then they hadn't had the money. One or two most unpleasant incidents. I was let in for some heavy losses. Worse still, the business was getting a bad name. I shut down altogether, and came up here for a rest. The worry was affecting my health. I could have prosecuted, but naturally I wasn't willing to go as far as that, as Frank had known and calculated. I'm telling you this, Mr. Owen, hard as it is, because I feel it's my duty to keep nothing back, but I'm trusting you to keep it to yourself if you possibly can. I told Frank just what I thought of his proceedings, and that I wouldn't have anything more to do with him till he could give me proof he had turned over a new leaf. Frankie tried to stick up for him, but I told her so long as she was living with me she mustn't have anything more to do with him. I hope she won't."

Bobby expressed his thanks for such a full, frank statement, and went away, feeling convinced that now he not only knew that the Vermeer actually existed—or at least a painting believed to be by that remarkable discovery of the twentieth century—but also where it now was. That, he felt, could wait. Not primarily a matter for him, since he had no official information, and no complaint had been made, nor had he any evidence as to legal ownership. There might, for all he knew, have been a perfectly legal transfer of property rights, though he also thought that highly improbable. Besides, it was all a matter of deduction, which itself might be erroneous, from facts not yet fully confirmed. Nor did he suppose the Vermeer would disappear again just yet, not while the hunt was still in full cry, the scent still strong. So long, too, as he knew, or believed he knew if he could trust the logic of close reasoning, where the painting was, a careful watch could be maintained. That might lead to the evidence being secured that would bring home where it belonged the dreadful guilt of murder—murder twice repeated.

CHAPTER XXI

TAXI

THE NEAREST WAY from The Tulips to the New Bungalows was by a footpath across the fields. Following this, Bobby was soon there, and there he halted when he saw Mr. Tails approaching on foot. Probably, Bobby supposed, coming to visit Miss Anson as a result of what Hardman had told him. If he had also been told that story of a former flirtation with young Francis Hardman, he would be sure to think it worth following up. Only what had become of the taxi? And why the long delay? Just as well, anyhow, Bobby told himself that he had got there first. At the garden gate he waited, and on seeing him Mr. Tails came to a sudden standstill. Plainly, at first he contemplated retreat, but then changed his mind and came on. As he drew nearer Bobby thought that somehow he seemed a trifle less dignified in stately self-approval than usual, just a degree less suave in manner. Indeed, there was a tremor of a quite commonplace, even vulgar, snarl in his voice as he said:

"I have been treated abominably. A most disgraceful trick."

"Dear me," said Bobby. "What's happened?"

"An outrage," said Mr. Tails. He took out his handkerchief, of the best linen, with what one felt should be a coronet, but was really an initial, in the corner, and wiped a flushed and heated countenance. "I should be glad of your official assistance. The fellow's licence must be revoked. Parkinson . . ." He paused and glowered, sure presage, that glower, one felt, of awful consequence. "I shall inform Mr. Parkinson of my opinion of his conduct," he said, slowly and impressively.

"What's he done?" asked Bobby.

"Bunked with the taxi," said Mr. Tails, his voice bitter in the extreme. "Bunked with the taxi," he repeated, as if he could hardly believe it himself, and was certain no one else could at a first hearing. Either to provide still further confirmation of the incredible or because he felt suddenly that 'bunked' was a colloquialism little befitting his dignity, he said next: "Behind my back, Parkinson bribed the taximan to drive away."

"Did he though?" said Bobby interested. "What made him do that?"

"My call at Major Hardman's residence had naturally delayed our return to Midwych," Mr. Tails explained. "Parkinson showed temper when, after leaving Hardman's, I explained it had become desirable that I should make a further call. It happened at that moment that a man by the roadside signalled to the driver to stop. He explained that he wished to speak to me in private. I alighted, accordingly, and at his suggestion we entered a neighbouring hostelry where he intimated that liquid refreshment would be acceptable. I listened to what he had to say, and when I emerged the taxi and Parkinson had disappeared— departed. There was no trace of them. They had simply—gone," said Mr. Tails, his voice shaken by a deep emotion.

"Well, anyhow," Bobby pointed out, "Parkinson will have to pay the fare."

But this remark failed to produce any effect of consolation whatsoever.

"I gave the fellow a pound in advance," Mr. Tails said gloomily. "When I engaged him he made difficulties. He wasn't forced to go outside the city limits. He hadn't enough petrol. I imagine the fellow thought he could make more by short trips. The war gives such people many opportunities to impose upon the public. It should be stopped, but the Government remains indifferent. He only consented when I offered him payment in advance. Apparently he had been afraid of being dismissed at a considerable distance from the town and having to drive back without a fare."

"I expect so," agreed Bobby.

"Driving off in my taxi I paid for in advance," said Mr. Tails with ever increased bitterness. "It amounts to embezzlement."

"So it does, doesn't it?" said Bobby.

"It should be actionable," said Mr. Tails.

"Undoubtedly," said Bobby.

"You will see the scoundrel's licence is revoked?" said Mr. Tails.

"The least that could be done," said Bobby, still agreeing.

"I can take it then," said Mr. Tails with satisfaction, "you will see that it is attended to—immediately."

"Unfortunately," explained Bobby mildly, "that's for the city police, not the county force. I'm county, though for the sake of convenience our headquarters are in city limits."

"Red tape," said Mr. Tails indignantly. "Bureaucracy at its worst."

"Unfortunately, too," Bobby continued, "the city police people have such a perverted sense of humour I doubt if you could get them to take it seriously. In fact, I wouldn't try if I were you. They might be merely amused."

"Amused?" repeated Mr. Tails in tones of horror-struck dismay.

"Even very amused," said Bobby, even more mildly than before.

"My God," said a stricken Mr. Tails. Then he asked pathetically: "How am I to get back to my hotel?"

"Well, there's the railway," suggested Bobby.

"How far's the station?" asked Mr. Tails, and already there was apprehension in his voice.

"Three miles," said Bobby cheerfully, though well aware that he exaggerated. "Uphill," he could not help adding.

Mr. Tails groaned and surveyed—with less complacence than usual—his expensive, well cut, close fitting city shoes.

"Three miles," he said pensively.

"I suppose," said Bobby in a brisker tone, "that you were on your way to see Miss Anson? So I take it you think there may be some truth in the Vermeer story?"

"The possibility exists," Mr. Tails admitted, "though it is not to be taken too seriously. Certainly some remarks of Major Hardman's did suggest to me that it might be advisable to hear for myself anything Miss Anson might have to say. Not so much with any great hope of learning anything about the Vermeer fairy tale—I cannot help so regarding it—as because what she may have to say may throw some light on the fate of my unfortunate relative."

"May I remind you," Bobby remarked, choosing his words carefully, "that is police business, and may I also remind you that if you believe there is any chance of getting any information anywhere, you should consult us first? In an extremely delicate and complicated investigation like this, independent inquiries may do harm. They may also be dangerous. There are desperate men concerned in all this, and there have been two deaths already. There may be more to come."

Mr. Tails looked extremely uncomfortable.

"But—but——" he stammered, "but—you're there to see that doesn't happen, aren't you?"

"We can't always protect fools—or rogues—from their own folly," retorted Bobby. "And in this country," he added, perhaps somewhat regretfully, "police action can't be taken until we not merely know, but can prove we know. I suppose the liberty of the subject is more important than his safety. Who is this man you say stopped your taxi?"

"I've no idea," Mr. Tails answered. "Not the least. I never saw him before, that I know of."

"He knew you, though?"

"Many more know me than I know," explained Mr. Tails with some return of that complacent self-satisfaction which during these last moments had been less in evidence than usual. "I believe I may lay claim to a certain standing in the world, and even to the friendship of many very prominent personalities. You may consult *Who's Who* if you wish."

"I shall not fail to do so," Bobby assured him gravely. "Did this man explain what he wanted?"

"He said it was important and confidential. It seemed only sensible to hear what he had to say. I accordingly alighted, at the same time expressing to Parkinson, who I then thought did possess some vestige of gentlemanly feeling—you did say three miles, didn't you?"

"Three miles—what three miles?" asked Bobby, slightly puzzled by this change in the conversation.

"The distance to the station," explained Mr. Tails, sighing. "As I say, I asked Parkinson to do me the trifling courtesy of waiting for me. I said I hoped he wouldn't mind."

"What did he say to that?" asked Bobby.

Mr. Tails shrugged his shoulders, a delicate but perceptible gesture.

"He said he did mind very much. I imagined that he spoke in jest. I remember smiling as I reminded him that it was my taxi. That he could possibly descend to the discourteous, ungentlemanly trick he did, in fact, play upon me, never even entered my mind. I am not used . . ."

"No, indeed," agreed Bobby, cutting these lamentations short. "What was it this man had to say?"

"Nothing," declared Mr. Tails, "nothing except vague hints about a picture of great monetary value. I asked a few questions. He fenced, prevaricated, insisted he knew a lot, but it was a long story and talking was dry work. We entered a public-house near by. I paid for beer for him. It is not a beverage to which I myself am partial. I soon came to the conclusion that he was merely trying to extract a few shillings from me by repeating gossip he had picked up somewhere. I brought the interview to an end, and, as you can imagine, I could scarcely believe my eyes when I perceived that my taxi was no longer there."

"No, indeed," said Bobby. "It must have been a surprise. What was this fellow like? Can you describe him?"

"I paid him so little attention. A member of the lower orders beyond doubt. Short, broad, middle-aged. Flat nose, wide mouth with black, broken teeth. Small, light grey, bloodshot eyes. A hang-dog expression. A slouching, slinking walk, as if he wished to avoid notice. Not the sort of character one would care to meet in a lonely spot after dark, and I was little inclined to remain longer than necessary in his company."

"A very good description," said Bobby approvingly. "I suppose an art dealer is used to noticing details when he has to distinguish between a copy and the genuine thing. Your man sounds like an illusive customer we are very anxious to get in touch with. We have been thinking of broadcasting a description, but then he would probably take the alarm and disappear altogether. Easy enough just now with the whole place full of evacuees and mobile labour, and the bombed out and refugees, and all the rest of it. Especially as we are short-handed everywhere with only about half the staff to do twice the work. If you don't mind walking as far as the nearest 'phone booth with me, I'll ring up our people and tell them the chap has been seen, and will they get after him. Not much chance, though. He's a wary bird, and has probably gone underground already."

Mr. Tails said if Bobby didn't mind he would like to carry out his original intention of calling on Miss Anson, and Bobby said he wished to see Miss Anson himself, and if Mr. Tails didn't mind, he would like to be the first to hear her story—if any. Also there were one or two other small points he would like to raise. At this Mr. Tails showed surprise, and even some resentment. But Bobby made it plain he intended to have his own way, and Mr. Tails somewhat sulkily, and not without vague references to the highly-placed and important persons of his acquaintance on whose friendship and influence he could rely, both for himself and for others, expressed, finally, a perfect willingness to answer any question Bobby wished to ask. He explained that his visit to Nonpareil was simply to secure any further details obtainable of the fate of his unfortunate brother-in-law. A most pathetic letter from his sister, still prostrate from so terrible a blow, had expressed a desire for even the smallest further item of information. Of course, Mr. Tails admitted, with that engaging air of candour which his clients often found so captivating, he had it also in his mind that he might learn something either to confirm or to disprove the Vermeer fairy tale. On the occasion of his first visit he had not been able to find the caretaker or gain admittance to the house. To-day, he and the ungentlemanly Parkinson had been more fortunate. He had suggested to Parkinson to accompany him because he had wished to observe Parkinson's reactions both to the questions he intended to put to the caretaker, and to their visit to the scene of the distressing tragedy of which his unhappy relative had been the victim.

"I do not know," he said, "if it has occurred to you that this Parkinson person was the last known to be in my brother-in-law's company? If by any chance they did come across some hint to the present where-abouts of the Vermeer—not that that is likely, but it is a possibility—then with a man of Parkinson's violent temper, of which I myself have had such proof, I think there are possibilities worth your attention."

"Oh, yes," agreed Bobby. "Didn't it occur to you, though, that if Parkinson were the murderer, you were running some risk in letting him see you suspected him?"

Mr. Tails turned pale.

"No, no," he said uncomfortably, "one does not suppose—one does not suspect. I trust I may feel confident that police protection . . .?"

"We can't, as I said before," Bobby replied, "always protect people from the consequences of their own actions. I strongly advise you, though, not to try to make any more inquiries yourself. Why did you take a spade to Nonpareil with you?"

Mr. Tails, though still a trifle pale, managed to produce a hearty laugh.

"You noticed that," he said. "Foolish, no doubt. But I can't help a lingering feeling that there may be some grain of truth in the Vermeer story. Wishful thinking, I know. An art dealer's dream, but there is the undoubted fact that young Frank Hardman did talk about knowing where the supposed Vermeer might have been buried."

"Why buried?" Bobby asked.

"I have no idea. Concealment, I suppose. A spade seemed indicated. Wishful thinking again, no doubt. You smiled, probably?"

"Spades," said Bobby with some feeling, "produce in me just now no inclination whatever to smile. Someone—I would very much like to know who it was—tried to use one recently to bring off another kind of burial—and not of a picture either."

Mr. Tails showed no sign of understanding this reference, but then a picture-dealer soon learns to conceal his thoughts. Bobby continued:

"When I saw you before, you seemed to think it might be Mr. Clavering who was guilty."

Mr. Tails looked at Bobby gravely.

"It has occurred to me," he said slowly, "that they may be accomplices. I confess I should be easier in my mind if I knew they were both under suitable restraint."

CHAPTER XXII

OBSTRUCTION

THEY HAD REACHED the 'phone box now, and Bobby expressed his gratitude to Mr. Tails for having been so helpful, and said he didn't think he need impose any longer upon his kindness and goodwill. Mr. Tails said, somewhat sourly, that he was glad to have been of service, and which was the nearest way to the railway station? When he learned that this nearest way took him back past the New Bungalows, the way they had come, and that thus nearly a mile had been added to the long, weary tramp before him, he gazed at Bobby with a sad and deep reproach; too sad, too deep, for words that ought to have wrung Bobby's heart, but somehow failed to do so. He asked, however, if Bobby knew when the next train left for Midwych, and Bobby said in fifty minutes, so Mr. Tails would have ample time to catch it if he kept up a good brisk pace of about five miles an hour.

Mr. Tails repeated, a little wildly, this suggestion of a four mile walk in fifty minutes, and asked when was the next train, and Bobby said he believed it was round about half-past ten. Nor did he think there was any great hope of obtaining any sort of vehicle in the neighbourhood. One could always try. As for getting anything to eat—well, unfortunately it was early closing day. Was he, then, demanded Mr. Tails, to go without his dinner, and Bobby said earnestly that he hoped not. Then he entered the 'phone box; and as he waited for his call to be put through he watched Mr. Tails turn away to begin that long, sad pilgrimage of which he still occasionally speaks—and even dreams.

In the 'phone box, Bobby put through fresh instructions to the local sergeant. He indicated, too, some discontent that the look out he had asked should be kept for anyone answering the description he had previously given, now confirmed by Mr. Tails, had not been successful. So would the sergeant please get down to it, since here was proof the fellow in question had actually been in the neighbourhood less than an hour previously. Oh, yes, he agreed, and knew well, that no one could be everywhere at once, and probably they had to do with a wary and experienced bird, but all possible or even impossible energy must be shown. Nor must the young man in a grey suit, bearing the close resemblance of a twin to Miss Frankie Hardman, be forgotten. If seen, he was to be detained. Was that clear? It was most important that these illusive personalities should be rounded up with the least possible delay.

With that, having received assurances only one degree less satisfactory than actual achievement, Bobby returned to the New Bungalows, passing, on the way, Mr. Tails, to whom he cruelly recommended an increase of speed, if the train were to be caught that alone held out any hope of dinner. In return for this well-meant advice Bobby received a baleful glare but no spoken word from a heart too full for speech. At the garden gate of the Anson bungalow, they parted; Bobby turning in by it and Mr. Tails continuing on his way by a road that seemed to him to grow longer, instead of shorter, with each step he took.

Bobby had to knock twice before he got an answer, and then the door was opened by a young man whom he had some difficulty in recognizing.

"Hullo!" he said; and young Mr. Claymore, for young Mr. Claymore it was, though even his own mother might have been excused for failing to recognize him, said nothing, and from his one serviceable eye came a gleam of but small welcome.

"Hullo!" said Bobby again, and then with solicitude: "How's the other fellow?"

"What other fellow?" demanded Mr. Claymore as well as a much swollen and damaged mouth—the lower lip split and two teeth missing—permitted utterance.

"Well, I thought it looked," explained Bobby, "as if there had been an argument, and I was rather wondering if your arguments had been as striking as the other chap's seem to have been?"

"Think you're funny, don't you?" growled Claymore; and looked as if he would have banged the door, had not Bobby so obviously taken precautions against any such happening.

"To fallen human nature," explained Bobby, "there is always something slightly funny about the misfortunes of others. That's Rochefoucauld, isn't it? Cynical, no doubt. Can I see Miss Anson?"

"No."

"Sorry," said Bobby, "but I'm afraid I must, unless you can produce a doctor's certificate, and even then I should probably want another opinion. And even then," he added, playing a card he knew was generally effective, "I shall have to place a man on duty at the front and another at the rear, just in case Miss Anson went away for reasons of health and forgot to leave her address."

"You've no right," began Claymore furiously, but Bobby interrupted.

"Mr. Claymore," he said, speaking now with emphasis and with authority, "two men have been killed—one not far from this spot, the other at Nonpareil, which is also not very far away. There is my right to ask Miss Anson further questions—questions which I think may help to bring out the truth. Why do you wish to stop me?"

"She isn't in a fit state to answer any questions," Claymore muttered. "She wasn't able to go to work to-day."

"It must be either now or later," Bobby said: "If not now, then I must do what I said, and I must ask the police surgeon to give an independent opinion."

"Oh, very well," Claymore muttered.

"Meanwhile," Bobby added, as he followed Claymore into the small entrance hall, "what about yourself? I think you had better tell me what happened. Has the man I saw climbing in at the window here paid you another visit?"

"No," said Claymore.

"I can't force you to speak if you don't want to," Bobby admitted. "I think it would be wiser of you, though, if you did. You know, I put a man to keep a watch on this house because I felt, after that window incident, it might be better if help were not too far away. For the same reason, I was glad to know you were sleeping here. Now it looks to me as if something rather violent had happened. Will you tell me what it was?"

"It wasn't anything much," Claymore answered. "Of course, we knew all right you had put a cop to spy. He was always hanging about."

"Not to spy," Bobby said gently. "Spies don't wear uniform. As a precaution, in the interest of the safety of two women. His instructions were to keep as much out of the way as he could, consistent with being on hand if there was trouble. And it seems there has been trouble, though apparently he didn't notice it. I may be merely fussing unnecessarily, but the fellow I saw at the window had all the air of meaning mischief."

Claymore did not speak, but he gave the impression of being very much of the same opinion. Bobby continued:

"You see, I can't help feeling that you must have some idea what he wanted." Claymore shook his head this time, but still did not speak. Bobby said: "I suppose what it comes to is that some day I shall have to tell you. Because I feel pretty sure I could guess."

"Policeman's bluff," muttered Claymore, but all the same looked both alarmed and uncomfortable, so far, at least, as his battered and discoloured visage allowed any expression to appear. Then he said: "If you want to know—well, I had a fall."

"Had you?" said Bobby. "Interesting—but the truth would be more so."

"It happens to be the truth," Claymore grumbled. "It was yesterday. I came here straight from work. I had just got in. Mrs. Anson said there was a man at the back, she had seen him before. I went into the garden. There was a fellow looking over the hedge. I called out to ask who he was, and what he wanted. He moved off. I went after him. He started to run, and so did I."

"What was he like?" Bobby asked. "Short, broad, working man class?"

"No," said Claymore. "Rather small and slight, in a grey lounge suit. Youngish. He ran like a good 'un, but I was catching him up. I knew I had to before he got among the trees. I yelled to him to stop, and he yelled back over his shoulder to keep off or he would fire. He had what looked like a pistol in his hand. I put on steam. I didn't suppose he meant it, and anyhow I would wait till he did—fire, I mean. Besides, he might miss. We were chasing across the field behind here. He got to the hedge first and he went over like a bird. I put on another spurt, and I caught my foot on a beastly wire. I expect he knew it was there and that's why he picked that particular spot. Perhaps he put it there. Anyway, I came the most awful cropper, flat against the stump of a tree. When I began to sit up and take notice, there wasn't a sign of the bloke I had been chasing. A mile or two away by then. I felt too jolly sick to do anything about it. I came back here, and I had to tell them at the works I couldn't show up to-day."

"That's two of them," said Bobby disgustedly, "that we want to see and can't, and others meet them at every turn."

"What do you mean? every turn?"

"That's only being picturesque," Bobby explained, "but it's pretty foul. I want the worst possible way to have a chat with that young man— or at least with a young man in a grey suit. If you see him again, grab him and hold him and let us know. We'll be along—and we won't keep you waiting either. The same with Mr. Tails—a short, thick-set, middle-aged working man I want to meet, and I can't, but Tails can."

"Is that the man who tried to get in by the window here?"

"Suspicion only," Bobby said, "but he may be, and anyhow I would like to ask him. But if you would tell me what you know, then instead of suspecting only, I might be sure. But have it your own way. If you won't, you won't."

"I don't know anything about him," Claymore insisted. "None of us do. We've no idea what he wanted either."

"Well, think it over," Bobby said, "and now, if you don't mind, I would like a word or two with Miss Anson."

"I'll go and tell her," Claymore said, but still very unwillingly.

"It has got to be," Bobby said, and his voice had taken on an edge. "Now or later, but sometime and soon. Better get it over."

All this had taken place at the open door of the bungalow, at the entrance to the tiny hall. Now Claymore took Bobby into the sitting-room and left him there. Bobby could hear a murmur of voices coming from the kitchen. He waited patiently. Claymore reappeared. He said:

"Miss Anson isn't fit to see anyone, but she says she supposes she's got to, if you insist. Come along."

He led the way into the kitchen. Betty was sitting up in a long-chair in which she had been reclining. She looked ill and frightened, with a face like death and eyes full of terror, staring at Bobby, and yet as if they saw not him but something else whereof the vision was to them always present. Bobby felt a quick sensation of pity. Someone ought to pick her up and comfort her, like a tired and frightened child. None the less, duty had to be done and questions asked. The truth must be established, whatever it might be. An altar on which sacrifice was sometimes necessary, for justice must be done, no matter at what cost. Mrs. Anson was crying quietly by the window, a helpless, bewildered weeping, as of one who wept without knowledge, without understanding, aware only that her child suffered. Claymore went to Betty and knelt by her side, so that their eyes were on a level. They looked at each other, and it was as though the whole room was illumined by the passion and the fire of the glance that passed between them. For that one moment it seemed that their two beings merged and were one, that for each there was nothing else that mattered or that was, nothing save each to the other. Bobby turned to Mrs. Anson. He said:

"I've forgotten my bike. I'll get it and bring it up nearer the house if you don't mind. Bikes have a way of disappearing just now. I won't be a minute."

Though he did not look at them, he knew, somehow, that his voice had called back the two lovers from their moment, their brief moment, that yet, he knew, would be a living memory to them all through their lives, back again to the exigencies of the moment. Mrs. Anson made no answer, but Betty whispered something Bobby could not hear, and Claymore said:

"If they do, I'll follow you the same day, the same way, the same hour, so as to be with you again."

When Bobby returned, having placed in safety his bicycle whose security he had made an excuse for giving Claymore and Betty a chance to recover themselves, Mrs. Anson was standing in the little hall, looking more frightened, more bewildered than ever. He said to her:

"What did young Claymore mean by what he said just now?"

"He's all wrought up, I don't know," she muttered, her voice dying into a whisper as she spoke as though the sound of it made her still more afraid.

Bobby thought to himself that perhaps she did know, or at least that she guessed. He did not press her. He went on into the kitchen. Claymore looked up. He said:

"You have come back."

"I have come back," Bobby said, "for there are questions I have to ask that must be answered."

"Yes, I know," Betty said, and repeated: "Yes, I know."

She tried to sit up, and then suddenly fell back in her chair, and Bobby saw that she had fainted dead away.

CHAPTER XXIII

CONSULTATION

"Which, of course, put the lid on it," Bobby somewhat disconsolately explained to Olive that evening. "If a woman starts to cry, you're finished. But you can at least wait till she's finished, too. If she starts fainting, though, well, there you are, aren't you?"

"Girls don't nowadays," Olive observed uneasily. "If they do, it means something."

"Yes, but what?" Bobby asked. "And what did young Claymore mean when he said that about following her the same day the same way so as to be with her still?"

"I don't know," Olive said, and looked more uneasy still. She added presently: "Mr. Claymore's very young, isn't he? When you are very young you do say silly things sometimes, and then sometimes you do them, too." Then she said: "You don't really think a girl like Miss Anson . . ."

She left the sentence unfinished, and Bobby's voice was grave as he replied:

"Facts matter, not thinking. It's a fact a man was shot that night when Major Hardman and our own man, Reed, heard a pistol shot. And another fact is that his body was found in the canal. That looks like panic. A body thrown into a canal is sure to be found sooner or later, and probably sooner—as this was. And at the place where we believe the shot was fired we found a woman's shoe that may very well be Betty Anson's, though we can't prove it. If she says she hurt her foot in the house, we can't prove she didn't. Then there's the five-pound note Hardman says he gave his nephew, and how did that get where we found it, in the same place? All the same, though we know a shot was fired we don't know for certain that it took effect, or, if it did, on whom. Nor is there any evidence to show if anyone else was present, unless the Hardman five-pound note is evidence. It's all consistent with Miss Anson being the person who fired, with her having panicked when she saw what she had done, and with her having asked Claymore to help. And if so, he might well have dumped the body in the canal, not knowing what else to do with it. Not so easy to dispose of a dead body; and a bullet kills whether it is fired by a man or a woman, or by a child for that matter. When I went to the Anson bungalow I more than half intended to detain Miss Anson unless she made a much more satisfactory statement than she has produced so far. I'm asking our police doctor to see her. As soon as he says she is fit for it I shall have to question her again, and at headquarters. If she faints there, she'll have to go to the cells till she recovers. Sooner or later she's got to answer—or be charged."

"Yes, but, why should she?" Olive asked. "I mean, why should she shoot anyone? What for?"

"Didn't someone say once: 'What I would not, that I do?' Perhaps it was like that with Betty Anson. Anyhow, the Vermeer picture—existent or not—appears to be the key to the whole business, and I take it to be motive enough for a dozen murders. Old Masters aren't often stolen, because when you've got them you can't do anything with them. The 'Mona Lisa' thieves, for instance, when that was stolen, never got a penny for it. No one dared have it. Labour lost. But if this Vermeer turned up in a few months with some more or less plausible story of how it had been discovered somewhere or another, you mightn't believe it, but you couldn't prove anything. It could be sold in the market at top price, and that would be in six figures, according to Tails—Clavering too. I've got to remember Miss Anson has been mixed up in it from the beginning. Apparently it was what she said about having seen something of the sort at the Nonpareil sale that started it all. According to Major Hardman she and this nephew of his were on very intimate terms. And now, according to Claymore, Frank Hardman has turned up at the bungalow, so are they still intimate?"

"But Betty Anson and Mr. Claymore are engaged," Olive protested.

"A girl can be engaged to one man and go pretty far flirting, or more than flirting, with another," Bobby told her; and Olive looked as if she wanted very much to deny this, but didn't quite see her way to do so.

"No really nice girl would," she said finally; and then hurriedly continued, to prevent Bobby from pointing out that really nice girls never, or hardly ever, shot people: "If you really think you know where the Vermeer is, why don't you go and get it?"

"No authority. No proof of ownership, for that matter," Bobby explained. "No one to identify it as having come from Nonpareil, except perhaps Betty herself, and if she could, would she? Besides, what good would it do? My job is to bring a murderer to justice— two murderers, perhaps, or else a double murderer, for there are two deaths to be accounted for. I'm no picture-hunter. A great picture may mean a lot, but to me, anyhow, a human life means more. At least I think so, even if the highbrows don't. Besides, when I say I'm sure, I only mean that's how I've reasoned it out from what I've seen and heard, and it's easy to be both sure and wrong. I think the Vermeer had better stay where it is for the present. It won't vanish while all this is going on. Too big a risk to move it now."

"Possession is nine-tenths of the law," Olive said. "That's what you really mean."

"Well, yes," admitted Bobby.

"If I knew where there was a picture worth ever such a lot of money," declared Olive, "I should go and get it."

"Not if you wanted to go on being a Deputy Chief Constable, you wouldn't," retorted Bobby.

"Well, anyhow," Olive said, "what is Major Hardman doing? He may have an absolutely perfect alibi with a policeman to back it up, but he must be mixed up in it somehow."

"Oh, yes," agreed Bobby promptly. "He is playing his own game. So are they all, and it may be a perfectly innocent game, with nothing like murder coming in at all—or it may not. On the face of it, perfectly right and proper, and even praiseworthy, trying to trace a lost picture of such value. On the whole, I'm rather glad to be able to leave Miss Anson alone for the time. She may be more willing to speak when she's had a little time to think things over. A voluntary statement is always best. You get much more than you do under pressure. The old story— one volunteer worth three pressed men. Meanwhile, there are others. Mr. Parkinson, for instance."

"I thought you thought he was much too much the respectable provincial draper type to be a murderer?"

"Well, I did," Bobby admitted. "Middle-aged, middle-class, suburban respectability doesn't often run to murder. But it does sometimes. Consider the evidence. He's the last person known to have been in Dr. Jones's company. His walking-stick is the murder weapon. Here's a theory. Poking about Nonpareil on their ghost hunt, which was half merely an excuse as far as Jones was concerned, they find the Vermeer. Jones tries to pooh pooh it. But Parkinson recognizes its value. Both get excited. Both claim it. Possibly Parkinson was the one to spot it first. They come to blows. All that's quite possible, and it's got to be followed up. After the way Parkinson made off with Tails's taxi and left Tails to get home the best way he could, you can't help seeing he has a capacity for sudden, explosive action. To make off with someone else's taxi, ditching the rightful occupant, is almost as far from suburban standards as murder itself."

"That would mean Mr. Parkinson has the Vermeer?"

"Not necessarily. He may have panicked and made off, leaving it behind. Panicked in the way that possibly Betty Anson panicked. Murderers are apt to lose their heads. Or if it wasn't like that, he may have hidden the thing again somewhere at Nonpareil. Waiting opportunity to collect later. Buried perhaps. That might explain the sudden spate of spades. Apparently the Vermeer was painted on a wooden panel. A canvas can be cut out of the frame and rolled. A wooden panel is more difficult. If Parkinson went back to his hotel with a wooden panel under his arm, it would probably have been noticed and remembered. Or he would have been afraid it might be. Not like a rolled up canvas that might go in an ordinary suit case no one would look at twice."

"But there's the bloodstain he and Dr. Jones saw at Nonpareil?" Olive objected. "Does that fit?"

"No. Jones was knocked out and then strangled. No blood. But there's no proof there ever was any bloodstain. No evidence but that of Parkinson himself. No one else saw it, and no trace of it, only a spot on the flooring where some of the wood has been planed away and nothing to show why. The whole story may have been an invention of Parkinson's to divert suspicion. That happens. Sometimes the real criminal comes forward with a yarn meant to absolve himself and throw suspicion somewhere else."

"I would rather think it was Mr. Parkinson than poor Miss Anson," Olive said.

"Possibly it was both," retorted Bobby, grimly enough. "Two have been killed, remember. But it's early days yet. There's a lot I don't understand, a lot still to be explained. So far I don't see my way at all clearly. I can't so much as catch a glimpse of any coherent pattern beginning to emerge. Then there's the question of scientific theory and the Hardman twins. But can you trust scientific theory?"

"Gracious, no," said Olive, surprised. "Why, a scientist thinks nothing of telling you he works on one theory three days a week and on a totally different theory the other three days. My goodness," said Olive with something that almost approached a snort, "I would like to see anyone run a house like that."

"Anyhow," agreed Bobby, "you can't put a scientific theory, however scientific, in the witness-box, and Frank Hardman has got to be found —if he exists. The only evidence that there is such a person is that he was thrown out of the Horse and Groom. Since then he has disappeared. Why? How? No one has seen him since to be sure. All I saw at Nonpareil was a man in a grey suit. Claymore, by his own story, never got near enough for recognition; and there's always the possibility he invented the whole story to account for his damaged face. It may be the bloke I saw climbing in at the window has paid them another visit, and that's the reason for Claymore's injuries."

"If Mr. Frank Hardman can't be found," began Olive uneasily, "you don't think that may mean . . ."

". . . another killing," Bobby completed the sentence when Olive paused. "We haven't really got to the thinking stage yet. Just collecting facts so far. I do think, though, that young Claymore would do anything—and I mean anything—to help Betty Anson. And anything might include helping her to hang on to the Vermeer, if she's got it, or getting it for her, if she hasn't. She may have persuaded him it is hers rightfully. So it may be, for that matter. She may have bought it at the Nonpareil sale in some job lot or another. No telling."

"That would mean the man you saw at the window knew, and was breaking in to steal it."

"It might be that way," Bobby agreed. "But there again—let's keep to the facts and see where they lead us, if anywhere. What we know is that an unknown man we can't trace tried to break in there, and looked like mischief. Go on to Mr. Tails."

"But he was in London?"

"Well, was he? There are still fast trains between Midwych and London, and there are still cars and petrol and motor-cycles to be got hold of if you know how. Another theory. Jones did find the Vermeer, but Parkinson didn't know. That's why Jones wanted to get rid of him, and why he went back to Nonpareil alone. But he had told Tails—'phone or wire. Tails may have tried to double-cross Jones, and get away with the Vermeer on his own, or Jones may have made too big claims for himself—or he may even have wanted to be honest and tell about their find. Plenty of cause there for disputes and more. Men have been killed for the price of a pint. A sum in six figures might tempt anyone. The temptation would be even stronger to a dealer like Tails, who would understand its full value, and know how to make the most of it. And that goes for Clavering, too."

"But," Olive objected, "someone attacked Mr. Clavering. If you hadn't got there in time . . ." and she paused, shuddering with fresh horror at the thought of what might so easily have been.

"An old trick," Bobby told her, "to try to pass yourself off as the victim when really you are the assailant. The rats may never have been thought of—quite unexpected. Someone came along to release us. Who and why? A pal, put up to it by Clavering? And what about the bloke who was hammering down earth over the grid? Was that intended and purposeful? Or just meant for effect? It didn't strike me like that at the time. The way that spade was used to beat down the earth sounded vicious to me.

'Stay there till you starve and rot,' it seemed to be saying. Made me remember the story of the cavalier of the civil war who is said to have been trapped down there with his wife and children till they all starved to death. As we might have done had those wedges not been knocked out. Does that mean there were two of them? One who meant to do us in as against the one who let us out? If so, again who and why?"

"Oh, Bobby," exclaimed Olive, who had grown pale at the thought of the fate that might have been intended, that had indeed been so narrowly escaped. "Oh, Bobby, I do wish you were in a bank or somewhere and always came home by the five-fifteen. I think it means just everything—always to come home by the five-fifteen."

"Jolly good," agreed Bobby yearningly. "Only—a bit boring."

"I like being bored," declared Olive with passionate conviction.

"Not always," retorted Bobby, for Olive, too, in former days, had not been always in the five-fifteen class. "Anyhow, the job I've got on hand at present is to put a murderer—or two of them—out of business, and so make the world a safer place for the rest of us. There you have them, then. There are the facts and the possibilities, and out of all of it we ought to see the truth emerge. First, Parkinson and his unexpected capacity to explode into action. Then Clavering and who knocked him out, and why? And Miss Anson and her faints. Claymore and his damaged face. Major Hardman and what he told me about the Nonpareil caretakers. The Hardman nephew and niece, and does scientific theory stand up? The unidentified man of the bungalow with whom we can't get in touch, but who gets in touch himself with Tails. Again, Tails himself, and when Clavering tells us Tails is not the murder type, does he want us to believe the opposite? Oh, and the Nonpareil caretakers, who are never at home when I want to see them, but they've got to be. As pretty a jungle of contradictions," Bobby commented, "as anyone could want from which to hack out the truth. With a Vermeer that perhaps isn't there for a somewhat doubtful starting point."

The 'phone bell rang. Bobby went to answer it. He came back and said:

"That was Payne. I asked him to check up on every hairdresser in the district to get to know which of them is responsible for that coiffure of Miss Hardman's—her one concession, it seems, to fashion and vanity. Well, the final report has come in, and every hairdresser has been interviewed. Not one of them knows Miss Hardman as a client."

"That's decisive, isn't it?" Olive said thoughtfully.

"Yes," agreed Bobby. "Decisive. Only decisive of what?"

CHAPTER XXIV

TEA

WHEN, LATE ON the following afternoon, Bobby started off on his ride to Nonpareil, he had made up his mind that, if necessary, he would leave a message summoning Bailey to headquarters. The message would also inform Bailey quite plainly that unless it were instantly obeyed, steps would be taken to enforce attendance. For many reasons this was not a procedure Bobby was anxious to follow; but Bailey was evidently doing his best to avoid questioning, and that, of course, made questioning still more necessary. When suspicion of guilt was strong, it was often better that such questioning should be done in official surroundings. These had their effect on those who knew they had cause to fear official inquiry. In other cases, questioning, Bobby thought, was often more effective and apt to produce better results when carried out in the suspected person's own home, in familiar surroundings likely to put him or her more at ease, and to bring more willing co-operation. But these were only Bobby's own theories. Other and equally experienced police officers held opposing views.

Now that he was Deputy Chief Constable, he often found himself obliged, as on this occasion, to use his cycle because all available petrol had been taken by his subordinates, to whom he had not dared refuse it lest they should make that refusal an excuse for failure in their mission. But the bicycle as a means of transport has at least the advantage of silence, and as Bobby came in sight of Nonpareil he saw that the lodge door was open. He wondered if the sound of an approaching motor might not have resulted in a swift closure. Even so, he had to knock twice before he heard a movement within, and saw Mrs. Bailey peeping at him from behind the kitchen door.

"Oh, good afternoon," he called. "May I come in? Safe to leave my bike out here, do you think?"

Without waiting for a reply to either question, he propped up his machine against the lodge wall, and went on down the small entrance passage to the kitchen. A bright, clean, cheerful room as he remembered it, with the afternoon sunshine streaming in through the polished window panes. A small fire of dry twigs was burning in the grate, and the kettle was just beginning to boil. Everything in the room was scrubbed, polished, burnished to a degree that was almost awe-inspiring. Yet not quite that either, for there were many little homely feminine touches; a brightness and harmony of colour, a vase or two of flowers, cushions, slippers ready and waiting, that took away from the room any suggestion of its being too bright and good for human nature's daily use. Rather had

Bobby the impression that a spill on that gleaming table top or even tobacco ash or a mud stain upon that spotless floor would be regarded as merely another opportunity for a display of the loving care and kind attention of which the whole place seemed so spontaneous an expression.

Between the table and another door, leading, or so Bobby supposed, to the scullery, Mrs. Bailey stood, very pale, very still, with such sheer terror in her red and bloodshot eyes as Bobby did not like to s e. He felt awkward and embarrassed; he had the impression that of late she had wept much, and in secret. Trying to be friendly, trying to soothe that fear, as of a trapped animal, she seemed to be enduring with his presence, he said to her:

"Jolly little place you have here."

She did not answer. With a sense of shock he saw—or thought he saw —that the terror in her eyes had changed to hate. If she had been pale and still before, now her pallor had become corpse-like, and now she was not so much still as rigid, strangely rigid. It seemed as if, for some reason, Bobby's remark, meant to be placating, had been more than she could bear; had pushed her over the narrow edge of endurance. In a hoarse, strained, unnatural voice, she said, the words coming, as it were, in jerks:

"I'll make—you—a cup—of tea."

"Now that's very kind of you," Bobby said. "Very kind indeed. It's really Mr. Bailey I've come to see."

"He won't be long," she said, in the same jerky voice. "He isn't far. He'll be in soon. Just one little cup of tea while you're waiting."

He said again that it was very kind, but he mustn't trouble her; and she gave him a strange and tortured smile, a smile in which her eyes had no part. She took a teapot from the dresser shelf and went out with it into the scullery behind. Bobby sat down near the table. He saw her looking at him round the door from her red and inflamed eyes. When she saw that he had noticed her, she drew back quickly. He heard her moving about, and he felt that she was still watching him, peeping, this time, through the crack of the scullery door. He spread out his hands to the warmth of the fire of crackling twigs, and the singing of the kettle made a cheerful sound in the still and silent room. Mrs. Bailey came back into the room, but stood in the doorway. Bobby glanced up at her and said again:

"Jolly little place you have here."

"Yes," she said. "Yes," she repeated, and then: "Isn't it?"

She went to the dresser and took down cups and saucers. She placed them on a tray and then took a linen table cloth—clean, one of her best, Bobby guessed—from a dresser drawer. She arranged the tray, the cloth on the table. Her motions were stiff and awkward, and sometimes she fumbled the things she was holding as though she did not see them very clearly. Bobby watched her. He looked grave and puzzled. He saw she had put only two cups on the tray. He said:

"Won't Mr. Bailey have a cup, too?"

"We shall have finished before he's here," she said.

She went back into the scullery, and again he knew she was watching him through the crack of the door. He took no notice, apparently concentrating his attention on the fire and the column of steam now pouring from the kettle spout. Mrs. Bailey came back into the room with the teapot in her hand. This time she did not look at him. She went quickly to the dresser. There she opened a canister and took out tea she put in the pot. Still not looking at him, she poured on the boiling water. She put the teapot on the tray and sat down at the table, but she made no effort to pour out. Bobby said:

"Waiting a little gives it time to draw, doesn't it?" Then he said: "I like my tea strong."

She did not speak, and she still did not look at him. She put out her hand to the teapot and drew it back.

"I'll pour out for myself, shall I?" Bobby asked.

"Me, too," she said, staring at him now.

"Oh, no," he answered pleasantly. "Your house. You're hostess. You must pour out your own."

"Well, I will," she repeated, but still watching him and making no movement.

Bobby filled his cup. He added milk. He told her he didn't take sugar. "War-time economy," he chattered on smilingly. "Not that I mind much. Too much sugar and you can't taste the tea. Too little, and you can't taste the sugar, so what's the odds?"

As he chattered he lifted the cup to his lips, and she leaned across and struck it from his hand. With the same motion she seized the teapot and hurled it violently into the fire. It broke into fragments. The fire, nearly extinguished, spluttered furiously, filling the kitchen with steam and ash. She covered her head with her apron and sat, rocking herself slowly backwards and forwards. She uttered no sound. Bobby said gently:

"Rat poison, wasn't it?"

"How did you know?" she asked. Abruptly she sat upright. She threw off her apron and sat staring at him. She said: "I meant to do it, but I couldn't." Presently she said: "It was the only teapot we had, and you can't hardly ever get them now, but it doesn't matter."

"It was a pity to smash it," Bobby agreed. "I'll ask my wife if she has one she can spare. I think there's one, but I'm not sure."

"What are you going to do?" she asked.

"Well, I told you," Bobby answered. "I want a bit of a chat with Mr. Bailey, and I'll wait till he comes. You said he wouldn't be long.

Meanwhile, what about clearing up this mess? I'm not much of a hand at housework, but we must get your nice kitchen straight again."

He got up and went into the scullery. He found a cloth there and a pail. He returned to the kitchen and began to collect the fragments of the shattered teapot, and to mop up the mess in the fireplace. He was not very expert. Mrs. Bailey said:

"I'll do that."

She took the pail and cloth from him and set to work. She said: "This is the teacloth you've got. I'll get another."

She went into the scullery and came back with fresh water and new cloths. She began to work again. Over her shoulder she said once more:

"You knew all the time. How did you know?"

"It wasn't difficult to guess," he answered, smiling at her. "Teapot, cups, tea, all were here, so why did you keep dodging into the scullery? You looked it, too." Rebukingly, and in a severe voice, he said: "You oughtn't to do things like that, you know."

She went on working with busy skill, and all the time her silent tears were falling fast, so that it seemed the floor she dried was damp again at once.

"What are you going to do?" she repeated.

"I told you. Wait for Mr. Bailey, to have a chat with him."

"Now you'll have to take us both," she told him.

"There you go again," Bobby complained. "Jumping to conclusions. Just like a woman. Intuition, they call it, and generally all wrong. Give me reason every time and you can keep your intuition."

"What did you come for?" she asked.

"Because I think Mr. Bailey can tell me things to help me to find a murderer. That is, if he will." Abruptly he asked: "You have been happy here?"

"When you've been in hell for years and years, and then you aren't, and you've got everything even the Queen of England her own self could want, why shouldn't you be happy?"

Bobby looked slowly round that poor kitchen, bright and clean, but within it little beyond what many would have called the bare necessities of life, though for her containing everything the heart of man could desire. Perhaps it did, he told himself. Warmth and shelter and food, and contentment, that is rarest of all.

"Well, stop crying," he ordered. "There's no sense crying. Crying never does any good."

She began dabbing at her eyes, in an effort to obey. Not with much success. She stood up and faced him, twisting nervously between her hands the floor cloth she had been using.

"You might be a dead corpse by now," she said. "Don't you mind?"

"Well, you see," he explained, "I never had the least intention of becoming a dead corpse. Not my line at all. All the same, I think you behaved very foolishly, and I think you ought to be thoroughly ashamed of yourself. I never," Bobby explained severely, "make excuses for people. I always tell them just what I think, and that's what I think about you."

"It came over me all sudden like," she said slowly. "I knew I didn't ought, but I couldn't think of anything but you coming to take Bailey away again, and us so happy here and comfortable and all. You don't know what it's like, being on the streets. My mother was, and so I had to be, because if I got a job she turned up drunk and took me off of it, and she made me go with men while I was still just a kid like, because, you see, men pay more then. It's not their fault, it's the way they are, but it's hard on you when you're a kid and you get thrashed if you don't want. Only it's all somehow different when there's a man what wants you—I mean, you, your own self, and it gets so you're like one together, and what's for one's for both. He had just come out when me and him met. I hadn't anywhere to go because of being turned out, and he hadn't either. But I knew a doorway where there was a sort of turning inside it, so the cops weren't so likely to spot you, but he was there first. I said to him to get out, because I knew it before he did, and he told me to get out, and get out quick, or he'd bash me proper. So I said wasn't there room for two, and he said that was all right if I was down on my luck, and after that somehow we stuck it out together. He hadn't had his ticket long, and at first he reported regular, but there was a smash and grab, and the cops thought it was him as had tipped them off and so it was, and he got a pound note for it. Proper scared he was after the cops had been at him; and proper scared I was, along of thinking of being all on my own again, if he got sent back. I made him promise he wouldn't ever again, and I burned the pound note and I took a shilling we had left of our proper own, and I bought a Bible, and we promised on our bended knees, kissing the book on it, that we never would again, either of us, and we never have." She went to one of the dresser drawers and took out an old illustrated Bible. "I like the pictures," she said abruptly, "it makes you feel it's real." She went on: "It's brought us luck, and every night he reads a bit whether we can understand it or not." She put the book back in its place and shut the drawer. "It's brought us luck," she repeated. "There was a gentleman crossing the road, and a taxi came and near knocked him down, but Bailey pulled him back just in time. So the gentleman said he was much obliged, and he said did Bailey want a job, only not in London, and Bailey said as he wasn't so set on London as all that, and the gentleman said come and see him, and he went, and I told him not to let on as he had been inside. So he didn't, and the gentleman gave him this job, and we came here, and I said if he went to the cops with his ticket, same as he ought, then everyone would know, and we should lose the job. So he never did, and it's a good wage and no rent, and all we can grow in the garden like, so there's nothing we want for, and we wouldn't change places with the king and queen in their golden crowns, we wouldn't. But then you came, and Bailey knew you soon as he saw you, but he thought you didn't him, because you didn't say nothing, only he said he would keep out of your way in case it came to you. So when I saw you come to-day I knew it had; and it was more than I could bear, especial when you said that about its being jolly here, and you come to take it from me. And I thought, too, if me and you were both corpses, nobody wouldn't bother so much about Bailey, and he might have time to get away and not have to go back inside. But I'm sorry now," she said humbly.

"So you ought to be," said Bobby, still severe. "Jolly good job there's no harm done and we can forget all about it. And for God's sake," he added irritably, "don't start howling again."

There was a sound of heavy footsteps approaching. Bailey came into the room. He stood, looking at Bobby for a moment or two. Then he said:

"I thought it must be you. I knew you would be sure to come back."

"Well, if you have been expecting me," Bobby retorted, "I hope you've been a bit sensible about it, and not been working yourself into a state of excitement like your wife. Why, she was so nervous that when she started out to make me some tea, she dropped the teapot in the fire. That's the worst of women," Bobby complained. "They will fuss so."

CHAPTER XXV

LADYLIKE

BAILEY STILL LOOKED suspiciously from his wife to Bobby and back, and then round the kitchen, not yet fully restored to its pristine, cheerful brightness. A dull red glow began to glimmer in his small, close-set eyes, his open hands lifted into closed, menacing fists. He said slowly:

"Been bullying her, eh, and me not here."

"Shut your trap, you great goom, or I'll shut it for you," said Mrs. Bailey, quite without heat, but very much as if she meant it.

"I asked for it, and I done it, and I'm ready," Bailey went on, taking no notice of this, "but you leave her out. See? She ain't nothing to do with it."

"I wonder," Bobby asked pathetically, "if I shall ever get a chance to put in a word edgeways to tell you what I do want?"

"There's no cause to tell, seeing as we know," Bailey answered, "seeing as it's what I've been waiting for ever since that first time you was here and I knew you knew me again."

"Oh, very likely you knew I knew you," Bobby agreed, "but all the same you knew wrong. Quite common. Plenty of people are always knowing they know, but don't know they know wrong. All I knew then was that you knew me, and, of course, I could make a guess why. So now, if it's quite the same to you and your wife, perhaps the two of you will be so good as to let me explain why I am here, and what I do want, instead of your telling me. A change," said Bobby with deep sarcasm, "if you'll listen for once instead of doing all the talking. I haven't said a word to anyone about what I guessed about you, even though I got a hint afterwards that made me fairly sure my guess was a good one. I didn't say anything to Mrs. Bailey even. I wasn't sure if she knew you had done time, and if she didn't know—well, that was between you and her and no affair of mine. She has told me she did know, and she has told me how it is you happen to be here. Now I want to hear your side of it. I want you to tell me everything that has happened recently."

But Bailey had no power of narrative. He seemed willing enough, but to begin at the beginning, to keep to one point, to preserve a consecutive order of events, to make sure that each clause was clearly related to each, each pronoun in correct reference to its principal, all that was a task far beyond his power. Bobby, not without experience and skill in unravelling the tangled tales of those little practised in expression, would in time, no doubt, have gathered a fair idea of recent events as known at Nonpareil lodge. But it would have taken time. He was relieved when Mrs. Bailey interposed, for she had given proof that she could tell a plain, straightforward story.

"You're getting all tangled up," she exclaimed impatiently, as Bailey struggled haltingly to find words. "Let me."

Bailey looked relieved. Bobby looked acquiescent. She continued:

"I mind it well, for I had only been thinking that very morning as it was too good to last, and it couldn't ever go on like it was, not in this world, me and him together and nothing left to want. Two weeks ago it was, as he come in for his tea and I saw he was worried like, and I said what was it, and he said a bloke he didn't know had come by and stood to watch him working in the garden, and then had called him by the name he had when he was—there. Bailey, he didn't know him, and he didn't let on or answer, but he said as how he was afeared it must be some bloke as had been—there. Been in at the same time and remembered. So then I knew the good times were over, and one of them as Bailey knew before was come to fetch him back again. Bailey said he never would, and he read a piece from the Bible, but it was one of them awful hard bits, and no comfort in it, and we weren't none the better for it, not till we went down on our bended knees, same as before, and swore like we did that other time and kissed the book after, him first and then me. When it was dark the chap came knocking, and he called Bailey by his name and number what they gave him—there—and said as would Bailey join in a first-class, slap-up, easy job they had on, money for jam it was. So Bailey said to go to hell, and the chap said had Bailey turned pious, and Bailey went for him, and you can't wonder, no man as was a man being liable to take such as that lying down. I got the slop pail, and emptied it on 'em both equal like, and that parted 'em, and then I grabbed the pan what the 'taters for our supper was boiling in, and I swore to God I would let the first as lifted hand again have it full. That stopped 'em, for they knew I meant it, and a pan of boiling 'taters isn't what anyone would go asking for, not in a manner of speaking no one wouldn't. The chap cursed a bit, but I rubbed him down where the slops had gone, and I gave him our last beer, and he sort of admitted I had only acted ladylike same as any lady what was a lady did ought and couldn't help. He said there wasn't nothing neither for pals to fall out over. All he asked was to be let sleep in Nonpareil now and then, same being empty, and so no harm to none, and him having business up here, but not wanting the cops to rumble it he was around. He said if we couldn't do a little thing like that for an old pal, it was doing the dirty, and he would do the dirty on us as well, and tell the cops about us, him having rumbled to it some way Bailey hadn't reported same as he did ought, or else just guessed that was the way of it. I told him as I would put his light out if he did, but he only grinned, and said as he would know enough to keep out of my way, and if we kept mum about him, so he would about us. But Bailey said he would do what he was paid to do, and that was to look after the house and keep it proper, so the chap went away then, looking proper ugly. We never saw him no more, nor didn't want."

"Do you think he did use Nonpareil for sleeping in at any time?" Bobby asked.

"I never saw nothing to show as he did," Bailey answered, taking up the story. With an obvious effort, he added: "But I didn't go nosing round. I did my usual, and if I saw anything, then I saw it, and then I reckoned to let on to do same as I was paid for to do. But I didn't see no call to nose around; and if I didn't see nothing, then I didn't, and nothing what I need do about it. Sleeping dogs are best left lie, and I knew if it got to the cops we was done and finished. It's hard and all," he said slowly, "when you're up a bit, to be pulled down again, worse

125

than before, and I knew all right if we was, we wouldn't ever get up again. It was the rat poison we've got was in my mind and her mind, too, if the cops got on to us to send me back. What's up now?" he asked, puzzled and suspicious, for his wife had cried out at the words 'rat poison', and Bobby had looked startled.

"Nothing," Bobby answered, quickly recovering, "except that I had a look round the Nonpareil cellars the other day and saw rats, so I asked Mrs. Bailey if you never put poison down for them, and I suppose it upset her. That's all."

"It's all lies all of it, what he's saying," Mrs. Bailey said, "but I'll tell you afterwards, and you can hit me a lick or two, if you like, but it was only all along of me going funny in my head, thinking of you going back and me all on my own again, and another lady here where it had all been mine, and the only place I ever had."

"The way we thought of was the better way," Bailey said, "but what's it to do with him?" He stared at Bobby. "Better than going back," he said, "and better than being all on your own again."

"Why the Good God," Bobby exclaimed with extreme exasperation, "ever made two such outsize fools as the pair of you, no doubt He knows, but I don't. I suppose the common-sense department was closed when it came to your turn, and so you got none issued, either of you. Not that it's only you. There are plenty of others who have got it into their thick heads where there ought to be brains but aren't, that in the police we are so fond of worry and work we go chasing round looking for trouble, looking for excuses to run people in, looking for a chance to spend our time—extra time, unpaid time—hanging about stuffy police courts for hours, waiting to be bullied by magistrates always on the look-out to bite if we've gone half an inch too far. Good Lord," said Bobby, flushed with indignation, "I remember a story or broadcast or something—jolly good and exciting, too, in itself—where the author seemed to believe that when a first offender—a first offender, mark you—is released, we detail a man to tag round and watch him or her day and night. Has the perpetrator of that nonsense any idea of what size staff we should want—or what size the police rate would be jolly soon? Not to mention that it couldn't be done. Anyone can vanish in London or any big town if they want to, and big odds against us ever finding them again, even working full out. Think of our going to all that trouble for every short term discharge! Fatheadedness could no farther go."

"I don't know about that," Bailey said, blinking both eyes as if slightly dazzled by the lightning of Bobby's indignation, and indeed not having fully grasped his meaning, "but it's along of me not having reported, same as it says, and so I'm liable to be sent back."

"I know, I know," Bobby repeated, still impatient. "You've committed an offence, and more fool you, and now you're scared, and serve you right. But the object of a ticket-of-leave report is to make sure you're living a respectable life, doing honest work. Well, so you are, and that's the main thing. You're probably down as wanted, though I haven't bothered to look. The Yard is sure to have made a few inquiries among your old pals in London, and most likely that's why the chap who called here knew you had failed to report. But so long as you continue to do an honest job honestly, I shan't think it necessary to take any action, provided you report regularly in future. But you can do it by letter if you like, and no one need know a thing about it. All we shall do is to make sure you're still on the job, and haven't got a pal to post the letter for you. So now that I hope we've cleared the ground a bit, how about getting down to business? I believe you and your wife have told the truth. If you haven't, in even the smallest degree, you'll get what's coming to you. That's by way of warning, though I'm pretty sure it's not needed. I take it you always drew the line at murder. I take it you would be willing to help in a case of murder. Particularly in a case of murder that happened almost on your own doorstep. I remember you both told me once you would do anything you could to help. Well, now's your chance. I want Mr. Bailey to come to my head-quarters in the afternoon for the next few days—three hours each afternoon at half a crown an hour."

"What to do?" Bailey asked, puzzled and distrustful.

"To sit there, keep your eyes open, tell me at once if you spot anything out of the way. Dull enough. If we can think of anything to give you to do, we will. Whatever it is, it won't matter much. The real job—and that will matter—will be to say if you notice anything unusual."

Bailey was still looking very puzzled.

"What sort of thing?" he asked.

"Anything at all, anything out of the way. If you saw the station sergeant standing on his head, that would be something out of the way, wouldn't it?"

Bailey considered this. Then he said:

"No station sergeant never wouldn't."

"Well, what I mean," Bobby explained, "is anything you would tell your wife about when you got home."

"I tell her it all," Bailey said. "She always asks. You tell me what sort of thing and I'll watch out all right, but if I don't know, how can I? It ain't noway fair," protested Bailey, "to ask a man to do what he don't know as he has to do."

Bobby looked rather helplessly at Mrs. Bailey. She said encouragingly:

"That'll be all right, sir. I'll see he gets the idea."

"She's brainy she is," Bailey said with pride. "Knows what you mean before you knows it yourself."

On that note, therefore, the conversation ended, and Bobby retired, hopeful, though not certain, that when Bailey arrived in due course at headquarters he would be fully instructed in what was required of him.

CHAPTER XXVI

EXPECTED

So THERE THE next afternoon was Bailey established at headquarters, quite smart in his Sunday best Mrs. Bailey had insisted on his donning for the occasion, and a source of considerable curiosity, since no one had the least idea why this stranger had made so sudden an appearance, or what he was supposed to be doing. Nothing much, though, as far as could be seen, and in fact literally nothing, since all he did was to sit with the day's paper on his knee, but not reading it much, and never speaking, merely looking on at all the routine of an ordinary police headquarters.

Not that many of them troubled much about it. 'Our Bobby's got something up his sleeve,' one or two of them remarked to each other, and that was about all. Even Inspector Payne himself had no idea of what was the reason for this visitor's appearance, and soon he managed to convey that he was a little hurt by such seeming lack of confidence.

"Oh, well, there's been a spot of blackmail knocking about," Bobby explained then. "I want to get to the bottom of it. As a ticket-of-leave man Bailey could be sent back to serve the rest of his term for failing to report. Someone knew it would have meant fairly complete ruin, the loss of his job and his home and his garden that had all come to mean a lot to him, not to mention his wife. I went out of my way to give them a long lecture, though they aren't the only ones who think we policemen are so fond of work and worry and got so little to do . . ."

"Did you say: 'little to do'," interposed Payne, looking quite bewildered.

"Well, you know, most people think that about other people," Bobby said, "especially about police, and they think we like to fill up our spare time keeping tabs on everyone who has ever done time. Though you would think they might know better now, considering the number of men with criminal records who have managed to get responsible Government jobs since the war. But most likely that's just put down to police negligence. And in this case I had a very special reason for rubbing it into Bailey and his wife that we are only keen on spotting old lags when they are at their old games again, and that if they aren't we are just as keen on leaving them alone."

128

Payne was beginning to open his eyes very wide.

"I suppose . . ." he said slowly. "I reckon—I mean—I think I see . . ."

"Just so," said Bobby. "Quite plain now you've thought it out. But never mind saying so. I don't want even the slightest chance of so much as a look giving Bailey a hint why he's here. If it comes at all, I want it to be entirely spontaneous."

"Yes, sir, I see, sir," said Payne, now very impressed. "Very smart and clever, sir, if I may say so."

"Very obvious, I should have thought," retorted Bobby; who always hated being told he was clever, because he knew how difficult it is to live up to any such reputation.

"Yes, sir, obvious, sir," agreed Payne, "that's what I meant"; and indeed to recognize and to use the obvious is as rare a gift as any.

"By the way," Bobby added, as Payne was retiring, "there is something you could do to help, if you would. Not an order, though, not even asking. But if you could get someone—the station sergeant by preference —to stand on his head where Bailey could see him, it might help."

"On his head—the station sergeant," repeated Payne, and looked awed, and so did Bobby then, for now they both remembered that the station sergeant then on duty was full fifty years old, with a waist-girth of fifty and one inches. But Payne rallied. Not for him to shrink when the path of duty showed. "Very good, sir," he said and retired.

"Good old Payne," Bobby murmured. "I believe he's for it himself."

And it was so, and, when Bailey reported, one item, made without comment, was: 'Inspector Payne stood on his head in the corner at a quarter to four, but saying nothing.'

At which Bobby gave a satisfied nod, satisfied now that his wife had made Bailey understand.

It was the next afternoon when Mr. Parkinson appeared in response to a message he had received. He had been grumbling about the request made that he should remain for the time either in Midwych itself, or at some address where he could be found at short notice, if it became necessary, as Bobby put it with all possible politeness, 'to ask for his further assistance'. He had hoped this summons to the county police headquarters meant that his release from any such obligation had been decided upon, and he was disappointed to find that apparently all Bobby wanted was to say how sorry he was that in view of the incomplete nature and so far unsatisfactory result of the inquiry release was not yet possible.

"By the way," Bobby added, "Mr. Tails is complaining about some dispute you and he seem to have had over a taxi fare. Not a police matter. If he really wants to take action, he'll have to go to the county court. Silly waste of time if he does."

"Perhaps I was a trifle high-handed," Mr. Parkinson agreed, and he looked quite pleased with himself. "I was so annoyed I felt—well, I really felt as if . . ." He paused. "It's happened before. It's not that I lose control of myself, it's as if something not myself took control. Not my ordinary self, I mean. A deeper self, I suppose. An experience of the sort was what first interested me in psychical research. Still, I'm sorry about Tails. I heard he had some difficulty in getting back— and more difficulty in getting something to eat when he did." Parkinson paused and smiled, gently at first and then more broadly and more broadly still. "But I made up my mind I ought to call at his hotel, offer to pay my full share of the fare, and tell him I was sorry it had turned out quite as it did. I thought that ought to make everything all right."

"Did it?" inquired Bobby.

"Oh, I think so. Yes, I think so. Tails seemed in a highly excited mood. He would hardly listen. He bustled me out in such a hurry I left my walking-stick behind again—a new one I had just bought in place of the one you've got. And when I rang up to ask him about it he was quite short. Said he knew nothing about it. But I'm sure I left it there."

"Bit unlucky over your walking-sticks, aren't you?" Bobby asked with a touch of suspicion in his voice, for was this simply an attempt to make seem more probable that earlier tale of another forgotten walking-stick.

"Umbrellas and walking-sticks," agreed Mr. Parkinson. "Umbrellas necessary in this climate, but walking-sticks very old-fashioned, I suppose. Only old fogies like myself carry them nowadays. I'm sure I left mine with Tails. By the way, I saw the man who stopped our taxi that afternoon hanging about near the hotel as I went away. I wondered if he was waiting for a chance to see Tails again."

"Oh, indeed," Bobby said, more interested than he chose to show; and then a message came that Claymore, who also had been asked to call at headquarters, had now arrived.

So Parkinson was allowed to depart, and Claymore appeared, very much on the defensive, pale, sullen, and anxious-looking, his countenance not yet fully restored to normal. To Bobby's inquiry as to how Miss Betty seemed, he answered that a doctor, sent, he understood, by the police, had been to see her, and had agreed that she was still in a very nervous condition.

"Yes, I have his report," Bobby agreed. "But doctors are cautious, and I'm wondering if, with a little effort and goodwill, she couldn't manage to answer a few questions without any very serious risk?"

"What's the good of sending a doctor if you don't believe him?" Claymore demanded aggressively.

"I have to believe him," Bobby answered, "but a very little goodwill can make a very great deal of difference. It's got to happen, you know. The questioning, I mean. I can't go against doctor's orders, but it's holding up things badly. In any case, I would like you to know yourself, and to tell Miss Anson as soon as you can, that I've got to know what really happened that night on the Barsley footpath. I think I could make a good guess, but I would much rather she told me—she and you, for I think you know?"

He paused, giving Claymore a quick, sharp glance. Claymore stiffened, drawing in his breath with a sharp hissing sound, but did not speak, either to confirm or deny. Bobby continued:

"I want to know, also, what she can tell me about a painting, possibly a hitherto unknown Vermeer. It seems there is some reason to believe it was sold at the Nonpareil sale as part of a job lot. Unrecognized of course. Or possibly not sold at all. Miss Anson went to the sale, I believe. Did she buy anything?"

"I don't know. I don't think so. I shouldn't know a Vermeer if I saw it," Claymore said. "I know he was an old Dutch painter. That's all."

"I wasn't saying you did know," Bobby answered. "But perhaps Miss Anson does. You might tell her, also, that I think I know what became of it, and where it is now."

"Is that true or a try on?" demanded Claymore sharply.

"That suggests you do know something about it," commented Bobby dryly. "Well, never mind. Thirdly, there's a possibility that the young man you told me about and tried to catch, is a Mr. Frank Hardman, a nephew of Major Hardman's, though I gather disowned by his uncle. He seems to have been present at the Nonpareil sale. Do you think Miss Anson can suggest why he seems to be hanging about the bungalow?"

"It's no good asking me," Claymore repeated. "I don't know anything about any Vermeer or any Frank Hardman either."

"At any rate you can tell Miss Anson, or ask Mrs. Anson to tell her, what it is I want to know. It's got to be cleared up, and I think she could help me if she would. Only I would very much prefer a spontaneous statement made freely by her to having to drag it all out by close questioning. I don't at all want to detain Miss Anson for inquiries, as we say. But I may have to. Well, think it over, and talk it over. I've an idea Miss Anson may feel up to seeing you, even if she won't me."

With that Claymore was allowed to depart, and Bobby went to find Payne.

"The fellow we want," he told Payne, "the man who may be Lovey Doors and the dead man's brother—or may not—and anyhow is probably the same I saw at the Anson bungalow window, and the same who stopped Tails's taxi, has been visiting Tails again, at his hotel. And wasn't spotted."

"Which, I suppose," said Payne indignantly, "is what those city fellows call efficient help. A fat lot of good asking them to pick up any one."

"Well, don't rub that in when you see them," Bobby said. "No good crying over spilt milk, and they're as short-handed as we are. Put it to them as a rumour we've heard, and do they think it's true? and of course they'll say it's impossible, and you'll have to say, of course, you know, only that's our information and could they warn their chaps to keep their eyes even more open than usual? Wrap it up well in the best Danish butter, pre-war butter. And ask them if they would mind if we put on one of our men to tail Tails. That," explained Bobby, "is a joke, and nothing like a joke to smooth things down when the other fellow's a bit on his dignity."

"Joke indeed," grumbled Payne. "I would a deal rather tell them what I think of them—letting our man slip through their fingers like that. Don't you think, sir, it would be better to have a description broadcast?"

But Bobby shook his head.

"If we do that," he said, "he'll vanish into hiding. At present we know he is knocking about the neighbourhood, and we hope he doesn't know we're looking for him—or even know of his existence. Gives us a chance."

A little later on Major Hardman appeared, for he, too, had received a note asking him to call at his earliest convenience. He seemed more than a little surprised to know that Bobby was still seeking an interview with his nephew, Frank, and declared that to the best of his knowledge and belief the young man had returned to London some days previously. He believed his niece, Frankie, had had a letter from him.

"Probably asking her for money, and probably she sent it," he grumbled. "No good my saying anything."

So Bobby thanked him, and was sorry he had troubled him, and Major Hardman was very amiable about it, and departed in his turn. Later on Bobby received Bailey's report, as dictated by him to the station sergeant, since Bailey was not much accustomed to the pen. Bobby read it with interest, reminded the station sergeant that for the present it was confidential, and then showed it to Payne.

"What we both expected, you see, from what we knew," he said gravely, "and how much farther forward does it take us?"

CHAPTER XXVII

EX-CONVICT

At the midwych Central Hotel, however, when, following the instructions Bobby had so promptly given, there arrived there a plain-clothes man, no trace was to be found of Mr. Tails. All that was to be learned was that Mr. Tails had gone out. He had not said where he was going, or when he was likely to return. He had not been seen to take a taxi. Anyhow, most likely there wouldn't have been a taxi to take. Nothing, in fact, was known as to where he had gone, or why, nor was it any business of the hotel—this last said with a touch of resentment—to be informed concerning the comings and goings of guests. But as to the 'why' Bobby thought he could make a good guess. On the track of the possible, and indeed, now, almost probable Vermeer, he supposed.

"What do we do now?" Payne asked when the plain-clothes man brought back this information, or rather lack of it. "Wait till Tails turns up again and then put him through it?"

"Easier said than done," commented Bobby gloomily, not seeing much hope in the suggestion. "Tails is as smart as—well, as smart as an art dealer, and can you say more? Knows all the ropes, and then some. It's as certain as can be that the Vermeer is the key piece, and that all these people in turn are circling round it. So am I for that matter. All we really know is that Dr. Jones was killed at Nonpareil while keeping an open eye on the chance of the picture being there, and that about the same time another man was killed and his body thrown into the Midwych canal. We can show no positive link between the two murders, though I think Miss Betty Anson could help us there. As soon as the doctors allow it we'll have to make her talk."

"Makes me wonder if it's a lost picture we're looking for or a murderer, and at that we don't even know if there is a picture at all, and very likely there isn't," lamented Payne, and then he cheered up considerably as he added: "Anyhow, Vermeer or not, we've got a couple of corpses, and that's something to be thankful for."

"So it is," agreed Bobby gravely, "and I rather think we had better take a hand in the Vermeer hunt ourselves, or the thing may vanish for good. It looks to me as if Tails were negotiating, and if it's like that we had better get hold of it first. Take it into protective custody. If it gets into Tails's hands, we'll have a job getting it out again."

"You feel sure that if there is such a thing at all, it's where you said?" Payne asked, somewhat doubtfully.

"Oh, yes," Bobby answered. "Deduction from observed facts, of course, I admit that, and so subject to error. 'E. and O. E.', as they used to say on a bill when they knew they had overcharged. But I'm not saying there's necessarily a first-class, long-lost Vermeer. It may be anything. All the same, I feel the time has come to act."

"Well, anyhow," Payne remarked, "there's one thing now we do know for certain about Major Hardman. That ought to help."

"Yes, so it ought," agreed Bobby, though not with any great assurance. "Another snag is that so far as I can see there's nothing to show who is the legal owner. I suppose we can ask for proof of rightful possession. But suppose it turns out to be a fake. Not a Vermeer at all, or spoilt by rough handling, or only a copy. It may be worth all these people seem to think, or it may be worth just nothing at all."

"I take it they think the gamble's worth while," Payne answered. "Two dead men to show, anyhow. If you ask me, sir, I'm not all that happy about the caretaker—Bailey, I mean. He may be playing a double game."

"Oh, yes," agreed Bobby, "though I don't think so. Apart from everything else, I don't believe Mrs. Bailey would let him do anything to risk the little home she's built up. Now she's got a home and a man of her own, she jolly well means to keep 'em. But I'm not easy about Tails. He may be running a bigger risk than he knows. The game he knows and is good at is a smooth game, played within the rules. He's taking a hand now in a rougher game, played without any rules at all, an all-in game."

"Only hope," grumbled Payne, "he doesn't mean to get himself knocked on the head. Two murders are quite enough to handle at one time."

"Two too many," Bobby said. "I think you had better wait here and I'll push on to Hardman's by myself. Just as well for me to tackle him alone. It's a bit irregular. There's not much to go on, and even if he has the Vermeer he may be able to claim rightful possession. I'm not too happy about it."

"It's that alibi of his sticks in my throat," Payne sighed. "If it hadn't been for that I should have said long ago—pull him in. But how can you, with one of our own men he can call as a witness?"

"Better be sure than sorry," Bobby told him. "A waiting game—waiting for the suspect to make a false move. They generally do sooner or later. Anyhow, I'll go and see him. I may find Tails there, and I rather hope I do. Alibi or none, I think the time has come to ask Hardman a few questions."

Accordingly Bobby, lucky enough this time to find a car none of his juniors was using, drove off to The Tulips. Arrived, he was admitted by Miss Frances, whom he found in the garden, hanging out some of the family washing she had apparently been doing herself.

"The laundries are getting so difficult," she explained. "The one we go to is talking about rationing customers."

Bobby agreed that the laundry question was indeed getting very difficult. Every woman her own laundry-maid apparently. Total war even—or very much—in the laundry now. And was Major Hardman at home?

Miss Frances said no, he wasn't. Nor did she know when he would be back, and, as she said this, there issued from within, from behind the partially open drawing-room door, a loud, reverberating sneeze. So Bobby said he thought perhaps Major Hardman must have returned without Miss Hardman's knowledge, and Miss Hardman, without turning a hair—not that it would have been easy for any one hair to turn in that hairdresser's masterpiece, her coiffure—agreed that it seemed like it.

"Uncle, is that you?" she called; and forthwith Major Hardman appeared, bland and smiling, radiating welcome, more than delighted to see the Deputy Chief Constable again, and perhaps this time they could have a drink together, and what were the prospects of bringing to justice those guilty of the two atrocious murders that had so shocked and alarmed the neighbourhood?

"Well, the position," Bobby explained, "is that we have got together a mass of evidence, but there are still links needed before we can take action. By the way, have you seen anything of Mr. Tails?"

"Tails, the art dealer?" Hardman asked. "He called the other day, and I heard that his taxi drove off and left him behind. Some dispute with another man sharing the taxi, I understand. He wanted me to put him in touch with Frank. I had to explain I knew nothing about Frank's movements. You don't think Tails has anything to do with these murders, do you?"

"I hope not," Bobby answered. "He seems to be prolonging his stay in Midwych rather longer than one would have expected, and he has been seen talking to a man we are anxious to interview. We have no very good description of him—no one appears to have had more than a passing glimpse. But he does seem to bear a close resemblance to the dead man found in the canal. Might be brothers—twins even. Odd how often twins turn up in this affair. A minor complication, but interesting, all the same."

"Like my nephew and niece, Frank and Frankie," Major Hardman remarked. "But if this man and the dead man are brothers, you don't suspect him of being the murderer, do you? Or could it be that they were both mixed up in the murder of Dr. Jones, and one of them got killed doing it? That would mean that actually there's been only one murder."

"A very ingenious theory," agreed Bobby, regarding the Major admiringly. "It must be considered. Even a peaceable, respectable, elderly citizen like Dr. Jones will defend himself if attacked; and, as he was visiting a deserted old house at night, he might have taken it into his head to go armed. Certainly if anyone else was put on trial, it's a theory the defence would raise. And argue that it was, perhaps, Dr. Jones himself who began it. I suppose you can't tell me anything about him—the man Tails has been seen talking to, I mean?"

"I know nothing about anyone of the sort. I only hope it's not somebody Frank has got himself mixed up with. More likely some pal of that caretaker chap at Nonpareil, the ex-convict I told you about. I expect you meet a queer lot of customers in gaol?"

"Well, yes, I expect that was your own experience, wasn't it?" Bobby asked casually.

Major Hardman, hitherto sitting easily in his arm-chair, comfortably chatting, one leg carelessly crossed over the other, jerked upright. His manner, hitherto that of friendly co-operation in a business not very directly concerning himself, changed in a flash into one of mingled rage and panic, that most dangerous of all combinations. Bobby watched him warily. Not that Bobby did not feel himself a match for half a dozen Hardmans, elderly, gross with self-indulgence. As well to be on the look-out though. Hardman made an effort to recover himself. He said with all the dignity he could muster:

"Deputy Chief Constable, if you mean that for a joke I consider it in the worst possible taste."

"No joke at all," Bobby assured him. "You as good as told me yourself. If you hadn't, I should never have thought of it. Why should I? One doesn't expect an old public school man, from the swellest school in England, a retired army major, to turn out to be an old lag. But when you said you recognized Bailey from having seen him only once in court, and then seeing him again years later in quite different circumstances, I did rather wonder. It struck me that possibly you had seen him rather oftener, and rather more closely. When you came to H.Q. you didn't see Bailey, but he was there, in a room you passed through, in a corner, reading a paper. He knew you again."

"The fellow's lying," Hardman broke out. "Of course he recognized me. After you had given him a full description and told him who to look out for."

"We told him nothing," Bobby answered, "not even what he was there for. I even got one of my chaps to stand on his head, so that Bailey shouldn't even be sure he was wanted to identify anyone. He says you were at Parkhurst together. You were serving a seven-year sentence—finishing it. Easy to confirm, of course. If you deny it, I mean. I have checked up on your record. A gap of some years you spent travelling abroad, I believe you told your friends later on. I think your identity was never disclosed, was it?"

CHAPTER XXVIII

DISAPPOINTMENT

MAJOR HARDMAN HAD become first very red, then very pale, and now against the pallor of his countenance his small and angry eyes burned like pin-points of fire. Physically he seemed to have shrunk, to have coiled in upon himself as it were, so that to Bobby he seemed to have acquired an odd resemblance to a snake about to strike. A warning to be wary, Bobby told himself, even though he had small fear of Hardman as an open-adversary. Not a man to let slip behind you, but not so very formidable face to face. Hardman was speaking now, snarling angry oaths.

"A dirty trick," he declared. "Mud raking. Just like police. Anything to throw dirt. What has it to do with you? It's over, isn't it? Done with. I made a mistake. I know I did, and I paid. It's no business of yours, nothing to do with you. Get out of it," he roared. "Get out of my house."

"If I do," Bobby said quietly, "I take you with me. Do you want that?"

Hardman glared in answer, hesitated, tried again to control himself, and said more quietly:

"All that's behind me, done with. You've no business to rake it up. Naturally I didn't want you to know. Suppose it's true. You can't do anything. I know cops, ferreting things out . . ."

He paused, breathing heavily, and Bobby said:

"Sometimes it is necessary for us to ferret things out. At present it is my duty to try to ferret out what happened at Nonpareil on the night Dr. Jones met his death there, and also what happened to the man, still unidentified, whose body was found in the canal."

"I know nothing about all that," Hardman declared sulkily. "How could I? You know yourself I was talking to one of your own men when the fellow was shot. Or do you think he and I did the murder together?"

"I'm quite sure you didn't," Bobby answered. "I only wish I were one half as sure of many other things."

"I don't mind telling you now you've nosed it out," Hardman said bitterly, "that Frank knows about me, and where I was when I was supposed to be abroad. That's how he gets money out of me, that's why I gave him that five-pound note you found."

"Do you think he may be the murderer?" Bobby asked.

"You can't expect me to say a thing like that about my own nephew."

"Do you think he is alive?"

"Alive? What do you mean?" Hardman asked quickly, evidently both startled and puzzled, and yet a little as if the question were a relief. "Why shouldn't he be?"

"I don't know," Bobby answered. "There seems to be a medico-scientific theory against it."

"What's that mean?" Hardman asked, very puzzled and even more suspicious. "What are you getting at?"

"Never mind," Bobby answered. "A sort of side issue. That's all. At this stage it doesn't matter. Major Hardman, I want to give you a very serious warning. It is your last chance. If you wish to make a full statement I am prepared to listen to it. You see, I feel sure you know a great deal you have not told me, though I think I know enough now to be sure of being able to put it all together in time. But I'm not sure yet who is at the head of the queue, not quite sure what the queue was lining up for. If you choose to make a statement you can do so, either to me now, or at headquarters, in the presence of a lawyer if you like. You would understand, of course, that anything you said would be made use of as and when required."

"I don't know what you think all that means," retorted Hardman. "Typical police bluff. I know your ways. Bluff you into thinking everything's known so as to make you talk, and then twist what you say. That won't work with me. Because there's nothing I know, and nothing I could tell you if I wanted to."

"Not even where the Vermeer picture is?"

It was a sudden thrust, and Hardman winced and looked more furious, more frightened, even than before.

"I don't know anything about any Vermeer painting," he declared sullenly. "What Vermeer painting? What are you talking about?"

"Well, there's been a lot of talk about one," Bobby explained. "Even the chairman of my watch committee has heard about it. Quite excited him. A side issue in my opinion. Murder is more important than art, even the greatest art. But this painting does seem as if it were a kind of focal point. I see all this as a kind of circling and weaving here and there, with always this picture I have never seen as the centre of it all. I was hoping you might be willing to show it me."

"I know nothing about any Vermeer," Hardman persisted sullenly. "All I know is that Frank talked about the chance of finding it. Nobody else had ever heard of it. You know all that, and it's all I know. Ask Frank, if you want to know more."

"Unluckily he is so hard to find, always supposing that he is living," Bobby answered. "In the meantime I'm asking you, and I'm going to ask how it comes to be in your possession?"

"I tell you I know nothing about it," Hardman shouted. "You're talking rot." He was on his feet now, gesticulating, shouting. His voice

138

sounded hysterical, his face was contorted, ghastly. All at once he subsided. He sat down again. "I don't believe there is such a thing," he muttered. "I don't know what you've got into your head. It's all rubbish, nonsense."

Bobby made no answer. He strolled over to the fireplace and stood looking at the water-colour hanging there.

"Birket Foster, isn't it?" he said. "All his own work, or one of those only half completed the dealers bought up after his death and got a well-known Scots artist to finish for them?"

"I don't know anything about that," Hardman growled. "It's a genuine Birket Foster all right. What's it to do with you?"

"I was only wondering," Bobby explained, "why the Birket Foster has displaced the portrait of your grandfather, isn't he? the one that used to hang over the mantelpiece where the Birket Foster is now. Poor grandfather banished to a dark corner, I see. I wonder why? May I look closer?"

He moved across towards the corner of the room where the portrait now hung. Hardman was on his feet again, dismayed, gesticulating.

"Leave it alone, leave it alone, I tell you," he shouted. "You've no right . . . don't touch it, I tell you. Leave it alone, put it down."

"Oh, I think I'll have a look," Bobby said gently. "No harm, surely, in giving grandfather the once over. Why do you object?" he added sternly, as Hardman came angrily and threateningly towards him.

For the moment Hardman looked as if he had so entirely lost all control as to be about to launch a personal attack, even though Bobby had so obviously every advantage of height and strength and youth. Bobby watched him. Hardman cried out a violent oath, and turned and rushed out of the room. Bobby had already taken down the portrait from the nail on which it hung. Now he propped it against a chair and crossed swiftly the room to stand against the wall by the door, on the side against which it did not open. He heard Hardman racing wildly down the stairs, hurling himself across the entrance passage. He heard someone crying out, in surprise and terror. The niece, he guessed, running from her kitchen to know what was meant by this wild running and shouting. Hardman dashed against the door, threw it back with the violence of his rush, dashed into the room, a revolver ready in his hand. Bobby thrust out a leg. Hardman tripped over it, and went sprawling, headlong on his face. Bobby stooped over him, picked up the revolver, pocketed it, left Hardman lying there, shaken and dazed, and proceeded with his examination of the portrait he had taken down.

A glance was enough to show him there was not, as he had so fully expected, another picture secured at the back of this one. But nails had recently been driven into the frame, and from these nails bits and pieces of string were still hanging. Something had been attached there, held in position by a network of string stretching from one nail to another. But nothing to show what that something had been, or why it had been so secured, or, more important, what had now become of it. Bobby sat frowning and baffled, very disappointed. At the door appeared the pale, frightened face of Miss Hardman. Hardman, badly shaken by his heavy fall, still badly dazed, was struggling to his feet. Bobby took no notice of either of them. Hardman cried out suddenly and violently.

"Put it down. Where is it?" he shouted. "You've no right . . . it's mine . . . I . . . where is it?"

"Where is what?" Bobby asked.

Miss Hardman came from the doorway farther into the room.

"What's the matter? What's happening?" she asked. "Uncle, what's he doing with grandfather's portrait?" More directly to Bobby, she said: "What's it mean?"

"Don't you know?" Bobby asked.

Hardman was beginning to recover himself slightly. But he was still dazed, shaken, bewildered. He muttered:

"Isn't it there? What's happened? Who's got it?"

"What isn't there?" Bobby asked. "Well," he said again, when Hardman did not answer, but stared and blinked and gasped, "what isn't?"

"I wish someone would tell me what's been going on," Miss Hardman interposed, and Bobby swung round on her, and she looked back at him calmly and quietly. There had even come a faint hint of mockery in her voice as she said: "What are you doing with grandfather's portrait? Uncle, do you know what it's all about? First, you take it away from the mantelpiece because you said the light was too strong, and it was fading, and now Mr. Owen's got it down again. What for?" she asked innocently, even too innocently. She came forward and took the portrait from where Bobby had placed it, leaning against a chair. She started to replace it in its former position. "I wish you would tell me what's been happening," she said over her shoulder.

"Oh, you both know," Bobby told her moodily, "only I'm a bit too late."

"I'm sure I don't know," Miss Hardman said. "Unless you've both been drinking," she added brightly. "You both look like it," she concluded, stepping back to regard critically the rehung portrait, and then giving it a touch to straighten it a little.

Hardman was seated now. He was still looking very dazed, not yet fully recovered from the violence of his fall. He was muttering something to himself, and Bobby thought he caught the name 'Tails'. Miss Hardman went to him, began to brush his clothes. She went out of the room, and came back quickly with a glass of brandy and water, Bobby thought.

"Drink that," she said, giving it to her uncle; and then, stooping over him, and adjusting his collar and tie, she said something to him in a low voice, but Bobby could not hear what.

Major Hardman drank off the contents of the glass, gave it back to her, began to look more composed. His voice was still unsteady, though, as he mumbled:

"I don't understand all this . . . I think we are entitled to an explanation."

"So am I," retorted Bobby. "What did you mean to do with that revolver you ran upstairs for in such a hurry?" He took it from his pocket into which he had hurriedly thrust it. "Fully loaded," he said. "Safety catch off. I'll put it on again. Better like that. Well, what was it you wanted it for in such a hurry?"

"Oh, that," said Major Hardman slowly. He was more himself now. He spoke slowly and carefully. "It's like this. I've had it on my mind long enough. I've had it ever since the last war. Just in case of burglars. Or because an old soldier likes to feel he isn't quite defenceless. I never bothered about getting permission, a licence, all that sort of red tape. But what's been going on recently made me think perhaps I had better. I told you I was going upstairs to get it."

"Told me?" repeated Bobby, considerably taken aback.

"Well, didn't I?" retorted the Major, telling this bare-faced lie with the utmost composure. "I said: 'Wait a moment and I'll get you my old nineteen-fourteen pistol, and then you can go through all the motions, and put me right with your blessed regulations.' That's what I said to you, isn't it?"

"No," said Bobby, beginning almost to be amused at the audacity of this invention. "Not a word of it. Never mind. Go on."

"When I got back here," Hardman continued, "and saw you had taken down grandfather's portrait, and had it there for all the world as if you were going to run off with it, I was so surprised that I sort of jumped forward. I thought the house was on fire or something. And I suppose I tripped over the carpet or something. Anyhow, I went over flat on my face. Shook me up a bit. I hardly knew where I was or what I was saying for a time."

He paused and cocked a confident eye at Bobby, as much as to say: "That's my story, and it's as good as yours any day."

"You ought to be more careful," said his niece solicitously. "You might have hurt yourself badly. I'm glad you've got rid of that thing at last. It's months since you promised you would, months since you started saying you would give it to Mr. Owen or someone."

"Kept putting it off, forgetting it, one thing and another," said the Major. "You know how it is," and again he looked at Bobby, this time with the faintest possible grin of triumph, plainly saying that here was confirmation of his story, and now it was two stories to one.

"Or is it," Bobby asked, "that you got it in such a hurry because you had it in your mind to shoot me before I had time to find what both you and I believed to be hidden there?"

"What hidden where?" asked Hardman. "I don't follow." Then he added: "I ran upstairs, I believe. I often do. But hurry? No. Did I?" He appealed to his niece.

"Oh, no," she answered, "not a bit."

"Was it because he wasn't hurrying that you cried out so loudly?" Bobby asked her.

"Oh, I didn't," she answered. "Did I?" she appealed to her uncle.

"Oh, no," he answered, "not at all."

Bobby had to laugh, though somewhat wryly. They were both, he thought, showing a readiness of wit, a gift for improvisation, really remarkable in its way, slightly disconcerting indeed. He sat down at the table and took out his note-book and looked at the revolver again.

"I'm going to keep this for the time," he said, "but I'll give you a receipt. And if you care to make an application now for its return, that'll perhaps save time later on, and trouble."

Major Hardman, though slightly surprised at finding Bobby so mildly accommodating, said he thought that was a very good idea, and very kind of the Deputy Chief Constable. A wink he gave his niece plainly intimated that in his opinion Bobby was now singing very small indeed, a proof of his complete defeat and overthrow now that he had been obliged to accept an explanation entirely plausible and simple, even though they all three knew it to be also entirely untrue. But one story's as good as another, isn't it? so a second wink bestowed upon Miss Frankie seemed to say. Then the Major wrote out and signed the application Bobby had suggested, and Bobby put it away with care in his pocket-book.

After that, Bobby took a polite and regretful leave, and both the Major and his niece expressed the most friendly hopes that he would come and see them again. Bobby promised he would do his best to pay them another call, and he said this with an edge to his voice that chilled just a little the warm glow of their triumph. For disappointed and puzzled, though Bobby was by the disappearance of the Vermeer he had so confidently counted upon finding, still he felt convinced that now at last he had secured the evidence he had so long sought, the conclusive, decisive evidence that leaves no doubt. Though of course, he reminded himself, it had to be checked and confirmed before it could be really accepted. And indeed there was in a corner of his mind a tiny murmur of a suggestion that perhaps it was not going to be quite so simple as all that.

CHAPTER XXIX

CONFESSION

INSPECTOR PAYNE, MUCH more interested in catching murderers than in the whereabouts of any painting whatsoever, however great a masterpiece it might be, was inclined to consider Bobby's visit to The Tulips as a much greater success than did Bobby himself.

"That evidence you got is just what we wanted," he declared, though adding more thoughtfully: "Of course, that is, if Wakefield confirms."

Bobby agreed. Wakefield has won a reputation for scientific police work that gives its verdicts authority; and until Wakefield pronounced, Wychshire county police must wait. Then Bobby asked if any message had been received from the Midwych Central Hotel, of which the management had been asked to ring up the moment Tails returned. They had not done so, and Bobby looked uneasy.

"It may be all right, of course," he said, "but I don't feel too comfortable. A big fortune on the loose, two deaths already, and Tails used to auction rooms, not rough houses. He does you down with a smile not with a club, and some of this present lot are more accustomed to use the club."

"Nothing we can do about it," Payne declared. "I take it, sir, you feel sure the Vermeer was tacked on behind the Hardman portrait?"

"There had clearly been something there," Bobby said, "or why all that business of nails and bits of string?"

"Yes, sir," agreed Payne, wrinkling his brow, "the fact is, sir, I don't quite see what made you suspect it was there."

"The portrait," Bobby explained, "was evidently shown as a sort of guarantee of respectability, social standing, to impress the vicar or the doctor or anyone else who happened to call—including the daily help when there was one. Grandfather a general, and there he was in full view over the mantelpiece in full uniform, and if that doesn't impress—well, it ought to. And then all at once it is moved into a dark, out of the way corner. There's a reason for everything, and I wondered what it was this time. One picture pushed out of the way in the corner. Another missing. Any connection? I thought there might be, and I thought that if the Vermeer had to be hidden in a hurry, then that was as good a place as any. No one very likely to look behind one picture to find another. The old story though. Being too clever. If Hardman had been content to leave grandpa where he was at first over the mantelpiece, I should never have given him another thought. As it was, I saw there had been a change since Clavering was there and described the room to me. So I wondered and I worried till I guessed what the answer might be."

"From observed fact to reasoned deduction," said Payne thoughtfully. "Simple enough if you know how. Perhaps Clavering worked it out that way, too?"

"There's that," agreed Bobby gravely.

"I take it," Payne went on, "Hardman's hiding the thing is clear proof he knows he can't put in any claim to rightful possession. Do you think there's any chance Hardman moved it himself somewhere else?"

"The way he lost his head," Bobby pointed out, "is pretty good proof he had no idea the picture had gone again. Shook him off his balance altogether when I began to take an interest in grandpapa, and he saw I knew where the Vermeer was, and meant to have it. Upsetting when you see a fortune you thought all snug and secure suddenly threatened. I don't know whether he actually meant murder when he rushed away for that revolver of his. I expect he couldn't think of anything except that he had got to stop me walking off with the Vermeer. And a worse shock still when the Vermeer wasn't there to walk away with. Miss Hardman kept her balance much better. Quite calm and composed, made him pull himself together. Probably she told him if the Vermeer had gone there was nothing he could do about it, and anyhow his revolver was safe in my pocket."

"Just as well it was, too," commented Payne. "Next thing—where's the Vermeer thing now?"

"Anybody's guess," Bobby told him, not too happily. "Not our job, really, even if some of our local big-wigs are beginning to hint it would be a good idea if we could nobble it for the Midwych art gallery."

"Oh, Lord," groaned Payne, "and I suppose we'll get it in the neck if we don't."

"Most likely," agreed Bobby cheerfully. "That's what police are for. But I did just drop a gentle hint that our job is spotting a murderer, not a picture. And even if we did manage to trace it, that wouldn't prove that whoever has it now is also the murderer. Possibly someone quite different. Possibly Clavering. He is quite smart enough to make the same guess I did if he knew grandpa had stepped down from the mantelpiece. But did he? Then there are the Hardman twins, and are they or aren't they? Anyhow, I don't trust Miss Frankie. Playing her own game all right. And there's Parkinson. A dark horse," he pronounced gloomily.

"Yes, sir," agreed Payne, and nearly added: 'And so are they all.' Instead he said: "And now the city blokes have rung up to say he's been talking to Mr. Clavering, and they didn't seem to be agreeing any too well, either."

"If we question them," Bobby remarked, "all they'll say is that they are trying to find the Vermeer, and why not? Tails, too, takes the same line. A public duty. But I shouldn't be a bit sorry to hear he was safe back again. It looks as if the man he's been in touch with might be Lovey Doors, the dead man's brother. I don't see how the likeness can be merely a coincidence. But we can't be sure till we can bring him in and have him properly identified. There's always the chance that Lovey wasn't in it at all, or dropped out, and that the man we want, the man who talked to Tails, I mean, is someone else altogether."

"Looks to me," declared Payne, "as if, whether it's this Lovey Doors or not, he is working in with the Nonpareil caretaker. Bailey and his wife, I mean."

"We mustn't forget them," Bobby agreed, "or young Claymore and Miss Anson either. She's got to be made to tell what she knows—or what she did."

"Did?" repeated Payne, startled by this last word.

Without replying, Bobby went on:

"Difficult to get the truth out of anyone who collapses into a faint or worse as soon as questioned. All the same, Miss Betty will have to face it—and young Claymore, too, for I'm pretty sure she's told him all about it. Anyhow, there is the one piece of evidence I got at The Tulips."

"Conclusive," agreed Payne. "Absolutely."

"Unless Wakefield turns it down," Bobby reminded him; and Payne looked rather taken aback, for this was a contingency he had not before seriously contemplated. "That's the way it goes," Bobby complained. "One point cleared up or so we hope, and two fresh ones turn up at once—who has the Vermeer and what's become of Tails?"

"Done a bunk," pronounced Payne. "Perhaps because he's managed to get hold of the Vermeer. Or perhaps because he is guilty and scared. Running away is as good as confession."

"Yes, I know," agreed Bobby, "only is it a case of running away, or is it something else?" and what that something else might be he did not specify, and Payne did not ask, because he knew.

To these two questions, the whereabouts of Mr. Tails, of the Vermeer painting, the morning of the next day brought no answer, nor was there as yet any reply from Wakefield concerning the Major Hardman revolver sent to them. Not that a quick reply was to be expected since the examination had to be careful and detailed. As for the Will-o'-the Wisp of a Vermeer—Bobby was beginning to think it a veritable Mrs. 'Arris among paintings—of that, too, there was no news, nor had Bobby expected any. But the continued absence of Mr. Tails was making him really anxious. At the hotel they still knew nothing; and indeed were beginning to cast an anxious and a doubtful eye upon an unpaid bill, though a much-comforted one upon the personal belongings left behind.

"We'll have to get cracking," declared Payne, who now he was an inspector felt it incumbent on him to keep fully up-to-date. "Get cracking," he repeated, pleased with an expression that sounded so thoroughly efficient and effective.

Before, however, the 'cracking' process could get really started, Payne, who had it in hand, came back to tell Bobby that Miss Betty and young Claymore had arrived, and were asking to see the Deputy Chief Constable.

"Come to confess, do you think, sir?" he asked, though somewhat doubtfully.

"Hope so," Bobby said. "Have them in, and we'll hear what they have to say."

Payne told a constable to bring in the two visitors. Betty looked pale but composed. She had the air of one who had at last decided to face the worst, and in doing so had found both courage and resignation. That she was still weak physically was, however, sufficiently apparent and the chair Payne put for her she accepted with both thankfulness and evident relief. Young Claymore was plainly much more agitated; had himself under much less strong control. If either of them broke down, Bobby thought, it would be the young man, not the girl. He had, indeed, a wild and desperate look, and it was he who began the talk, blurting out in a high, unsteady voice:

"It's all been me. She would have come before if I hadn't stopped her. So it's me just as much as her. If you want her, you must take me, too. I'm in it just as much."

"Hush, hush," Betty said, and put her hand on his, an odd contrast, hers small, slender, and steady, his large, strong, shaking.

"Suppose," Bobby said, "we let Miss Anson tell her own story." He added sharply, for he thought the warning needed: "If you interrupt I shall clear you out. And I think Miss Anson would rather you stayed."

"Oh, yes, yes," the girl said, with a grateful look, and Claymore said nothing, but took out his handkerchief and began dabbing at his face and wiping his wrists, which had become damp and clammy.

"Now, Miss Anson, if you'll begin and tell us all about it," Bobby said, "perhaps you may find it's not so bad as you think."

"Oh, it is," she answered, and then with a little sort of gasping rush, she said: "I killed him." When Bobby, listening gravely, made no comment, she repeated: "I shot him."

"Please begin at the beginning," Bobby said. "Who and where?"

"A man. I don't know who he was. In the wood, on the Barsley footpath. I didn't mean to, but I did, and so it's murder, isn't it."

CHAPTER XXX

RE-ASSURANCE

"ALL DEPENDS," BOBBY said. "Please go on. Tell us all about it. From the beginning, mind."

Betty's voice was steadier again, her self-control fully regained. In a quiet, narrative tone, she said:

"I get home much quicker if I come by the company's Barsley 'bus. It puts me down on the Barsley Road, and then I have to cross Wych-wood by the footpath. It's always very dark and lonely. Mother was nervous about me using it, and so was I. Mother wanted me to wait for the train but that's such a long time, and there's the long walk from the station as well. Mother was nervous, too, herself, about being alone, I mean, after it got dark, and there were the air raids. So I went on coming by the 'bus, and I used to run home along the path as fast as I could, only it was difficult to run fast in the dark. It was all right at first, but then I began to meet a man, and he tried to follow me, and he whistled. He got so close up once I slipped behind a tree and he went by, and somehow that made me awfully frightened, seeing him, I mean, because he looked so horrible."

"When I could get away in time, I tried to meet Betty," Claymore interposed, "but I couldn't always. I had an idea I knew who it was Betty had seen, but when I tackled him he swore it wasn't, and, anyhow, he's gone away now, so he can't have had anything to do with what happened. I did think once or twice it might be Frank Hardman, because I heard he had turned up again and he used to be fond of boast-ing about girls. But I don't know."

"It wasn't Mr. Hardman," Betty said. "It was someone quite different. I didn't tell mother, but I knew where she had the pistol thing that belonged to father when we lived in China when I was little. I put it in my handbag. It was the very next night." She paused a moment, struggling to retain her self-possession. "I was hurrying along as fast as I could in the dark when a man came out suddenly from some bushes, just as if he had been hiding there waiting for me. He called out something, I don't know what, and I said: 'Go away. I've got a pistol. I'll shoot you,' and I ran, and he ran after me. He kept calling, and I could hear him swearing most awfully, and he ran so fast I thought he would catch me. So I thought I would try to frighten him away, and I pointed the pistol over my shoulder up in the air, and I pulled the trigger, and it went off most awfully loudly, and I heard him cry out and fall down, and I ran and ran. I fell down twice, and I lost my shoe and I cut my foot, but he wasn't after me any more, and I knew that, because it was all quiet, only I never once thought that I had killed him. Because I meant to shoot it off right up in the air, only I suppose I didn't with running so hard, and then the letter came, and I knew what I had done. It was in the papers, too, and I knew that I had killed a man, and so I must die as well. I am quite ready now."

"For God's sake, Betty, don't talk like that," Claymore groaned. Then he said very wildly: "If they do, I'll hang myself, too."

"Oh, shut up, you young ass," Bobby said roughly. "We don't want heroics, we want common sense. Much rarer, too, and much more difficult." To Betty he said, as gently as he had spoken roughly to Claymore, whom, indeed, he judged to be nearer hysterics by a long way than was the girl: "I see. Yes. Well, what did you do with the pistol?"

"I gave it to Len," she answered, looking at Claymore. "You mustn't let him."

"Let him what?" asked Bobby. "Hang himself, do you mean? Of course not. Though it's not such a bad idea, either. A good deal to be said for it." To Claymore he said: "Where is it?"

"I threw it in the canal," Claymore answered.

"Nothing you've forgotten," Bobby observed resignedly, "to make it more difficult. I suppose you can show us where? We'll have to get hold of it, even if it means draining the canal and holding up war transport. I'm getting more and more to feel that that idea of yours about going off and hanging yourself has more and more to be said for it."

Claymore was too relieved by the turn things seemed to be taking either to look or feel either sheepish or annoyed. Betty had passed beyond the stage of feeling anything, she was just waiting. Bobby was speaking aside to Payne. Payne left the room and returned with some half-dozen pistols—automatics and revolvers from the small police armoury. Asked to select the one most like that used by Betty, both she and Claymore picked out separately a point thirty-two automatic. Pressed about this, they were both emphatic that Betty's weapon had exactly resembled this one. Satisfied, Bobby had the pistols returned where they were kept. He asked Betty:

"How was it your pistol was loaded? Did you load it yourself? Were there clips with it?"

Betty looked puzzled. She said hesitatingly that she didn't know. What did he mean by 'clips?' What sort of 'clips?' She had apparently taken it for granted that a pistol is always ready to fire, just as it has always a barrel and a stock.

"It was just as I took it from where mother kept it in one of her boxes," she explained. "I never thought about whether it was loaded."

"What about the safety catch?" Bobby asked, though slightly bewildered by this apparent tendency to regard the loading of the weapon as a mere detail. "Did you touch that at all?"

"I don't think so. What is a safety catch?" Betty countered.

Bobby looked at her sadly. Apparently a fully-loaded automatic, the safety catch off, had been lying about, probably for years, in the Anson household. Why no one had been killed he could not imagine.

"Oh, well, never mind," he answered Betty's last question. "I suppose you never heard that a licence is required for firearms?"

"Oh, yes," Betty declared, quite triumphantly this time. "I know that. If you buy one, but we didn't, we've always had it."

Bobby gave it up then, and went on to ask about the letter to which Betty had made a passing reference.

"What letter did you mean?" he asked.

"I found it in the passage next morning," Betty explained, "when I went to take in the milk. It said the man who wrote it had been there, and had seen it all, and I was a murderess—it began 'Dear little murderess.' It said I was a good shot to hit anyone when firing over my shoulder, and I must have worked it all out very carefully. And it said it was rather cold blooded of me to have shot and killed a man I had met there before when I had kissed him other times, but that wasn't true, because I never had. I expect it was someone else he used to meet, but I don't know. And the letter said the writer wouldn't tell if I kept quiet and said nothing, because then no one would know, and so I would be quite safe. But if I said anything he would tell what he had seen, and then I would be hanged, and there was a little picture of me hanging, and it was awful—I can't tell you how awful. I think it was worse than it will be when it happens. I don't think it will matter so much after seeing that."

"My good girl," interrupted Bobby irritably, "for the dear Lord's sake, don't be in such a hell of a hurry to jump to conclusions." He paused, vaguely aware there was something a trifle odd about the juxtaposition of the words he had used. Betty looked puzzled; and now a faint relief began to show, dawning behind her desperate self-control. Claymore started to say something, and then stopped when Bobby made him an abrupt gesture to keep quiet. To Betty, Bobby continued: "A very interesting and suggestive letter; and if either you or that young man of yours had as much common sense as would go on the point of a needle, you would have guessed at once that it was phoney, that its one object was to make you believe yourself guilty, and so make sure you wouldn't say anything. And then you would have brought it straight to us. Where is it? I suppose you have it still?"

But Betty shook her head.

"I put it in my drawer," she said. "When I went to look, it wasn't there any more. Someone had taken it, and left instead half a sheet of note-paper just like it, and folded just the same, only with nothing on. I think it must have been the man you saw climbing in at our sitting-room window, only I can't think how he knew where it was, or how he got into my room without our knowing."

Bobby looked at her more despairingly then ever.

"I suppose you two innocents never heard of such a thing as vanishing ink—only vanishing cream," he said at last. "And I suppose you don't know what became of that half sheet of note-paper, folded the same way but with nothing on it?"

"I showed it mother," Betty answered. "I thought perhaps she had taken the letter. She didn't know anything about it. I don't know what became of the paper. I think, perhaps, mother used it for the laundry list or something."

"I expect she did, especially something," agreed Bobby, resignedly this time. "Did you show the letter to anyone?"

"To me," interposed Claymore. "It was I who stopped her from giving it you. I told her not to. I said she mustn't. I couldn't stand thinking what it would mean—a trial and the liar who wrote the letter coming forward to make sure she was found guilty. I was nearly off my head. How could I let her? Would you?"

Bobby did not attempt to answer this question. Instead he said to Betty:

"Now I want to ask you about something else. I think you went to the sale at Nonpareil some time ago, and I want you to tell me all about it."

"About the picture I saw there?" Betty asked. "I don't know anything about it or what became of it. Mr. Frank Hardman came about it once or twice, and at first I don't think he believed me when I said I hadn't got it, and I didn't know who had, but I think he did afterwards. Anyhow, he stopped coming, at least till that time Len ran after him. I don't know if it was because of that he came back again."

"Tell me about it," Bobby repeated.

"The sale was in my holidays," Betty explained, "so I was able to go on the view day. I thought I would like to see the things, and I thought if there was anything going cheap we wanted I would buy it, but there wasn't. In one of the attics there was a picture painted on wood. I only noticed it because it was standing against the wall and my frock caught on it and it fell over. It was most awfully dirty and dusty, all cobwebs and things, and it fell on some dirty straw packing that made it worse. So I dusted it a little, and where it wasn't too dirty it looked so nice I thought perhaps I would buy it if it went cheap."

"What was it like?" Bobby asked.

"There were buildings and water and there was rain and sunshine, and it all sort of glowed—at least it did what you could see, only it was all over dirt and cobwebs and things. It made you catch your breath, somehow, what you could see, as if you had never known before what light was. Mr. Frank Hardman saw me looking at it, and he looked, too. I didn't know who he was then, only afterwards, when he came to the bungalow. He said it was nice, only spoilt by being so dirty, he didn't seem much interested. He said all the dirt and stuff ruined it and he went away. I looked in the catalogue I had and it was in a lot with all sorts of other things."

"What were they?" Bobby asked.

"There was a tin bath they had all been put in to keep them together. There were some books and a box with shells on the lid and an old ink-stand and an engraving of 'Bubbles.' Mr. Hardman said he thought it much nicer than what I had been looking at; and so it was nice, too, only a different sort of nice. Mr. Hardman said anyhow it was clean. There was a Dutch oven too, I remember, and a hand mirror. I asked the auctioneer's man if he thought I could buy the pictures separately, because I liked the 'Bubbles', too, but he said no, he said you had to buy lots as a whole, but of course what you didn't want you needn't take away. I said it was silly to buy things you didn't want to get something you did, and I didn't think I would. I went back to have another look, but it wasn't there any more. The 'Bubbles' was, but not the other picture. Mr. Hardman was just going down the stairs and I told him, and he was very surprised, and he went to look, but he couldn't find it either. We told the auctioneer's man, and he said some of the people there were trying to pinch things, and he would tell them at the door to look out, and anyhow it wouldn't be easy to go off with a wooden panel like we said without being noticed. And I remember Mr. Frank Hardman laughed, and said no one would be likely to try, and anyhow it wasn't worth bothering with. But when he came afterwards I thought he believed somehow I might have managed to get hold of it, only that was silly, and I told him so, because I couldn't, even if I had wanted to, and of course I wouldn't. It would have been stealing."

"So it would," agreed Bobby absently, a little awestruck by this description of how a painting of such extreme value had been put with other odds and ends into a tin bath for sale.

"It was lovely," Betty said again. "What you could see, I mean. It was as if light were caught in it and held, like in the sky after sunset. It made you feel the man who did it had been able, he too, to say 'Let there be light', and it was so."

Claymore broke in impatiently, nervously.

"What's it matter? What's a picture got to do with it? Now you know it all, what are you going to do?"

"I'm wondering that myself," Bobby said. "The picture Miss Betty saw is probably very valuable. But for it nothing of all this would have happened, most likely. It is why there have been two killings already, and why there may be more. It's bedevilled the whole affair, so that we never know whether what's happening is because there's someone guilty trying to make himself safe or because there's someone innocent trying to get hold of this picture. Quite legitimate in itself. But these attempts to find it provide the perfect camouflage for the actual murderers."

"But I don't know anything about it," protested Betty. "I only saw it that once."

"What's it got to do with the man who got himself shot?" Claymore asked, still impatient, still highly nervous. "It was all his own fault. He had only himself to blame if he happened to get hit when Betty fired."

"Oh, he didn't," Bobby said, and spoke with real concern. "I ought to have made that plain before. All the same, if you and Miss Anson have been through a bad time, it's been your own fault for not coming forward to tell us what really happened. Miss Anson may put her mind at rest. It's quite clear from the evidence that she killed no one. The actual killer is obviously whoever wrote the letter she got. As I said just now," Bobby went on to Betty, "the idea was to make you believe yourself guilty, and then you would hold your tongue. That's quite plain, and by itself is almost enough to clear you. Also the dead man was killed by two shots from a revolver, and it was clear that there had been only one shot fired on the Barsley footpath and that from an automatic—because there was only one cartridge case, and it is only automatics that throw out cartridges. They stay in the cylinder of a revolver. But we couldn't be sure there might not be some link somewhere. Again, you fired when a man was running after you, and so it wasn't very likely that you would shoot him twice in the back. The papers reported all that, or most of it. Don't you ever read the papers?" he asked reproachfully.

"Oh, I couldn't, not about that, it was too awful," Betty said. She asked: "Do you mean it wasn't me . . . ?"

"I do," Bobby assured her. "Your shot went high, I expect, as you meant, though most likely the fellow was badly scared, and let out a yell and dropped on his face to be safe in case you fired again. Then someone else shot him later in deadly earnest, taking advantage of what had happened before to get you to believe it was you had done it, and for goodness' sake," added Bobby in alarm, "don't go and faint again."

But Betty was not fainting, she was only crying as if she would never stop again. Nor was Claymore in much better case.

CHAPTER XXXI

SHOES

Young leonard claymore and Betty Anson had departed, chastened indeed by a further lecture given to them on the folly of attempted concealments, but at the same time so relieved that to them the world no longer seemed the same place.

"A brace of young idiots," Bobby said of them tolerantly when they had gone, "but I suppose you can't much wonder that they shirked telling a story they both believed would send the girl straight to the gallows."

"I take it we can accept Miss Anson's story as correct?" Payne asked, though still a trifle doubtfully.

"Oh, I think so," Bobby answered. "It fits. It was always clear that if Hardman and our fellow, Reed, were correct in saying they had heard one shot, then that didn't explain why there were two bullets in the dead man's back. Of course, two shots fired in quick succession might have sounded to them like one, if they weren't listening very carefully. Now we've the girl's own story, and seen it fits, we can be sure the real murderer saw the opportunity the one shot she fired at random gave him to push suspicion on to her. That was a devilishly clever letter sent her. You can't wonder it worked, and convinced her she was the killer. And if she thought so herself, why shouldn't we?"

"There does seem quite a lot straightened out," Payne agreed. "Only are we much nearer the truth? Where's our evidence? Is it certain we are on the right track? And where's the picture got to?"

"One question at a time," retorted Bobby. "We are nearer the truth because we've reduced the field of the possibles by two—Claymore and Miss Anson. They are clearly out. It's not certain we're on the right track, because nothing's ever certain till you know. Why, the Anson girl and her young man may be back in again before we know where we are. There's nothing whatever to show what has become of the picture, but for the first time we have first-hand evidence that it does exist. Or did. Till now, there was nothing to prove it wasn't merely imaginary—possibly a deliberate invention to put us off. Probably after Miss Anson found the picture, and while she was talking to the auctioneer's man, young Hardman, who had recognized its value, took it and hid it away somewhere. He wouldn't dare risk trying to walk off with it on view day. There would be a much better chance after the sale, when he could pretend to be a successful bidder taking away his purchase. He may even have hoped to get a chance to buy, though probably he was afraid of its value being recognized. But as

Fe

he clearly didn't succeed, or why the present hunt? someone else, probably one of the auctioneer's men clearing up, came across it, where it was hidden and moved it. What became of it after that is anybody's guess. But something must have become known recently, and set in motion all this activity that has meant two killings so far—and may mean more to come. As to what we do next, we go round to the Central Hotel and have a look at anything Tails may have left there. We may pick up some hint and we are justified in calling him 'missing' now."

The hotel was near by, facing St. Paul's Square in the centre of the town. The hotel management knew nothing, had heard nothing. The London office of Mr. Tails's firm had rung through to make inquiries, and seemed puzzled and anxious at his silence. No difficulty was made in allowing Bobby to see what few possessions had been left behind. But there was nothing to help. Only a little clothing, toilet articles, and so on. The management wasn't sure there would be enough to pay the bill, but was reassured when Bobby told them Mr. Tails was a well-to-do man, partner in an established and responsible firm. In one corner Bobby noticed a pair of shoes evidently meant for city wear with their thin soles and narrow toes. These were the shoes, Bobby supposed, he remembered Tails was wearing when he had started on his long tramp to the railway station after the so regrettable and unjustifiable abduction of the taxi. Bobby looked at them thoughtfully. Had Tails brought two pairs of outdoor shoes for so brief a stay? If not, what was he wearing now? A tactful question or two elicited the fact that before Tails's disappearance there had been delivered for him from a shop in Market Street a pair of stout walking shoes. Owing to the paper shortage they had been left with the hall porter unwrapped. He remembered the incident, and remembered having commented to another of the staff that they looked a good, stout pair. Bobby remarked, vaguely, that evidently Mr. Tails's recent experience had taught him the benefit of strong shoes when on a walk, and then he asked the name of the shop. A little to Payne's surprise he suggested calling there.

"If Tails was going for a walk," Bobby said, "just possibly he may have said where, or asked the best way, or something like that."

Payne didn't think that very likely, nor did Bobby, but then you never know your luck. So they interviewed the assistant who had sold the shoes, and who remembered the transaction well, because his customer had tried to evade giving coupons for the shoes by suggesting that he might be allowed to hire them for a couple of days. This had been rejected, on the grounds of doubtful legality, backed by a serene assurance that in any case a sale would not be long delayed, since at present the difficulty was not in selling goods but in getting goods to satisfy eager customers. So the coupons had been reluctantly surrendered; and, though Mr. Tails had said nothing about any destination he had in view, he had remarked that he wanted a specially good and easy fit, as he had a long walk before him, nine miles there and back—a distance and a task he had spoken of as another might have spoken of walking from one end of the country to the other.

"Very interesting," said Bobby, and thanked the assistant and departed. To Payne he said when they were in the street again: "What do you make of that? Why walk instead of taking a taxi or even a bicycle?"

"Fed up with taxis after what happened last time," Payne suggested, "and he may have never learned to use a bicycle—a bit too plebeian."

"Or else he didn't want anyone to know where he was going. How far is Nonpareil from the nearest train terminus?"

Payne considered.

"About nine miles, there and back," he said, and looked enlightened.

"And we know he's been in touch with our unknown unseen friend who may be Lovey Doors, and who seems to be more or less making Nonpareil his headquarters."

"That might mean," observed Payne, wrinkling a thoughtful brow, "that he has this blessed picture, or knows where it is—and is going to hand it over to Tails. Then it might be him took it from where Hardman had it hidden?"

"Ye-es," agreed Bobby, slowly, and still more thoughtfully. "We know that that day—the day of the taxi incident—there was another visitor at The Tulips besides Tails himself. I saw a dottle on the table still warm from the pipe it had been knocked out of. Tails is much too dignified ever to smoke a pipe in public. I've never seen Hardman with a pipe, and he certainly wasn't smoking one then. So there had been a third person present. Who? A fair assumption, I think, that the man who stopped the taxi, the pipe smoker who had been at The Tulips, and our unknown friend who haunts Nonpareil, are all one and the same. Why was he visiting Hardman? And apparently on more or less familiar terms with him, since he was smoking his pipe and knocking out his dottle on Hardman's table. Another fair assumption is that his visit had something to do with the Vermeer. Did he know Hardman had it, and where it was hidden? Or wasn't he sure, and did he suspect Hardman of wanting to do him down? If he was present while Tails and Hardman were talking, did it strike him that he could do better for himself by making a direct deal with Tails, meaning, in his turn, to do down Hardman? Rogues tend to fall out, since, of course, they can never trust each other. So he waits for Tails outside, and Tails promises him a good fat sum, cash down, for any information about the picture. Next step, this bloke—he was seen near Tails's hotel—calls there and tells Tails he has the picture, and will hand it over for the cash promised. Tails goes to keep the appointment with a good fat wad of bank-notes in his wallet. But uppose there's no picture? or suppose the bloke in question thinks he will keep the picture and have the cash as well? Quite likely that only Tails's eagerness to pay big money for it made our man realize how valuable it really was."

"All that's a lot to get out of a dottle lying on a table," Payne said, half-admiringly, half-doubtfully.

"It's a train of reasoning that may have flaws," Bobby said, "but it seems to me to hang together."

"Strikes me we had better get along to Nonpareil quick as we can," suggested Payne, now as uneasy as was Bobby himself at this prospect, or possibility, of a fresh killing. "I take it Nonpareil is most likely where Tails would go for delivery?"

"If it was, we may be in time," Bobby said. "If it was anywhere else, there's not much chance. Tails deserves to get whatever's coming to him. He's been playing crooked all along. But I suppose it is part of our job to stand between fools and scamps and their deserts."

Their way, as they talked, took them past the Central Hotel. Clavering was outside, having apparently just emerged. He nodded a recognition, but would have passed on without speaking, had not Bobby stopped to ask if he knew or had heard anything of Mr. Tails or his present whereabouts.

But Clavering shook his head and looked very gloomy and depressed.

"He's cleared out," he said. "Half-way to America by now if he could wangle a passage, or else giving a dinner at the Savoy to a bunch of millionaires and pressmen and critics—the first as possible buyers, the others for publicity. It'll put even the war news in the shade when it comes out."

"When what comes out?" Bobby asked sharply.

"Didn't you know?" Clavering asked. "I thought a Deputy Chief Constable knew everything. But I suppose you blokes are still hunting around after a mere commonplace murderer or two. Lots of murderers in the world, especially just now. You'll never run short of them. But there's only one Vermeer lost and now recovered—by Tails," added Clavering with an intensity of bitterness no words can convey.

"Are you sure?" Bobby asked.

"Oh, yes. He didn't say he had it—if he had I mightn't have believed him. He could match lies with Hitler if he wanted to, and come out evens. But he stood me a drink—if you knew Tails you would understand that meant something—and he gave me hints on where to look for it, and suggestions about our working together if I brought it off, and a lot more guff. And he talked about what it would be worth. He expects a knighthood at the least. He was just oozing triumph—rubbing it in he had trumped the trick. He even asked if I would like to give old Solomon the go-by and work for him—the dirty dog. Oh, he has it all right," and

156

these last words Clavering pronounced as if all hope had fled, all brightness from the earth for ever more.

"If it's like that," Bobby said, only half convinced, "why has he gone away without saying anything, without paying his bill, leaving his things behind?"

'As if,' said Clavering pityingly, "anyone would even think of all that when he had brought off the coup of all time—of all eternity for that matter. Can't you get it into your head—your thick head—what it means? Recovering a lost and till now unknown first-class Vermeer?"

"The search for it seems to have had consequences anyhow," Bobby said grimly. "What did you want with Tails?"

"To eat humble pie," said Clavering sadly—though sadly is but a poor, inadequate word; "to lick his boots, or anything else for a chance of a look." A faint glow of enthusiasm shone for a moment through the heavy gloom of his expression. "Next best thing to recovering it, would be a long, quiet look all to yourself. But I expect Tails will keep it back till he can produce it with a good big blaze of publicity. You know, I don't believe the Vermeer means a thing to him except in terms of cash and credit." Clavering paused, and looked slightly ashamed. "Envy," he admitted. "Envy, spite and malice. You oughtn't to say a thing like that about any man, not even about Tails."

"Did he say anything about Nonpareil while you were talking to him?" Bobby asked.

"No," Clavering answered. "Is that where he found it? How could he? Nonpareil has been gone through with a small tooth comb. I thought it was through Major Hardman. I'm pretty sure Hardman has had something to do with it only he's been let down. By Tails very likely."

"Why do you think that?" asked Bobby.

"Oh, Hardman's nearly off his head. I've seen him. Near frenzy. I couldn't get anything coherent out of him, but he cursed every one he could think of, including you—and me. Not Tails, so I take it it was Tails he meant. And his nephew, young Frank Hardman. Young Hardman is in it somewhere, somehow. They must have had hopes of nobbling the thing themselves, and Tails has got in ahead. I suppose it's nothing to do with all this business, but there is a story that young Frank sometimes dresses up as his sister. They're like as two peas, you know. I don't know if there's anything in the yarn. Very likely there isn't."

"No, I don't much think there is," Bobby said thoughtfully.

They parted then; and as Bobby and Payne continued on their way, Payne remarked, glancing over his shoulder at Clavering's melancholy, drooping, retreating figure:

"Do you think he is O.K.? He sounds to me a bit cracked about this picture of his. After all, a picture's a picture, isn't it? To hear him, you would think he was talking about something holy."

"He thinks he is," Bobby said.

Payne greeted this with an incredulous grunt, and as they reached headquarters he remarked that it was time they heard from Wakefield. Wakefield had taken their time about it. When the report did come in, however, he supposed they would be able to see their way better, perhaps even proceed to an arrest.

Bobby agreed. He went to his room, and Payne went to his, where he found waiting for him the Wakefield report, so ardently, so confidently expected. A little later he came in to Bobby, looking as woebegone, as depressed, as melancholy, as even Clavering had done when expressing his belief that the Vermeer had passed finally into the hands of triumphant Mr. Tails. Bobby was quite startled. His mind flew rapidly from one possible catastrophe to another. He said:

"What's up?"

"Wakefield," said Payne, and Bobby almost thought he was going to cry. "Wakefield reports that the murder bullets and the revolver you got from Hardman are not complementary."

"Oh," said Bobby.

"Complete wash out," said Payne.

"Com-plete," agreed Bobby.

So all that astute care by which he had secured Hardman's signature to an avowal of the ownership of the weapon had gone for nothing. Probably, Bobby reflected now, Hardman would not have given his signature so readily had his revolver been, in actual fact, the weapon used. Not that that would have proved his guilt, but it would have needed a good deal of explaining, and would certainly have justified arrest. Oh, well, detective work was like that, life itself was like that. You built up with infinite care what seemed a secure position, and then all at once everything gave way, everything crumbled, and you had to start again from the very beginning.

CHAPTER XXXII

IMPRISONED

But this set-back, if set-back it were, made still more urgent that unease and sense of instant need of which Bobby was conscious. He decided that this was an occasion for prompt action, and one when the use of petrol would be justified, even though every drop was precious, brought as it was at the risk of men's lives. He got out, therefore, his own small Bayard Seven he now often used on duty, since it was so economical in fuel consumption. In it he and Payne were soon on their way, nor did they talk much, for Payne, too, was aware of an impression that a climax was near, and that it was a climax holding dark threat of more tragedy to come. Indeed, Payne only spoke once, and that was when Bobby was slowing down as they neared their destination. With a memory stirring in his mind of a remark Bobby had made just before their start, he said abruptly:

"When a man thinks a thing is holy, he can do strange things."

Bobby gave him a startled glance, for the remark ran parallel with a latent feeling of his own.

"Yes, I know," he said. Then he repeated. "Yes, that's so."

He brought the car to a standstill and Payne said, as he was alighting:

"What about Tails? It might be he has engineered the whole thing."

"It might be," Bobby agreed, backing his car on to the grass verge by the roadside. "We shall soon know, I think. 'Too hard a knot,' I remember calling this business once, with its double thread of murder and treasure hunt. But it'll soon be unravelled now—or unravel itself."

They went through the great Nonpareil gateway. Bailey, working in his garden, had heard their approach, and was coming to meet them.

"The missis is gone to ring you up," he said. "Did you get it?"

"No," Bobby said. "What about?"

"It's young Hardman," Bailey said. "I thought I saw him first thing, soon as I was up, but I wasn't sure. It was someone dodged away among the trees, and I shouted, but soon as he saw me he did a bunk, and I didn't see him no more. And I'm not so sure there hasn't been someone inside up there, for things didn't seem the same like, and such a maze of a place half a dozen might be there and you never know."

"Anything else?" Bobby asked.

"I thought I twigged him again," Bailey answered, "and if it wasn't him, it was mighty like. But bunked off so quick I couldn't be sure, and the missis said to ring you up, so she done it, and not back yet, it being near a mile to the road box. But if anyone's been inside up there, I don't see how. I put a screw in the door now when I leave, as well as locking up careful. And all other doors and windows boarded, and none of 'em touched. So what's the odds?"

"Not difficult to get out a screw," Bobby said, "and I expect an impression of the lock was taken sometime when you were at work cleaning inside. Easy enough then to have a key made. We'll have a good look. You had better come, too. I suppose you can get to the house at the back without coming this way?"

"Easy as winking," Bailey agreed. "Nothing to stop 'em, but a fence full of gaps." Then he said, somewhat defensively: "No one couldn't expect there was a bunch wanting to get into an old house full of nothing but emptiness."

"Of course not," agreed Bobby. "No fault of yours, but it looks as if there had been more in there than any of us ever dreamed of."

They had drawn close to the house now, and as they skirted the angle of the left wing wall, so as to get to the side door Bailey used, there rang out, clear and loud, a pistol shot, as it seemed, from just above their heads, from one of the rooms there—one shot, and then another, loud, clear and ominous.

Bobby began to run. He got first to the door, with Payne close at his heels, but they had to wait for Bailey, slower and more awkward in movement, and fumbling for his keys. He got the right one at last. The screw holding the door had been removed. He opened the door and instinctively they all waited, drawing aside a little, more than half expecting to be greeted by more shots. But there was only silence, the vast and empty silence that weighed so heavily upon these huge deserted rooms, and long and twisting corridors and passages, where it seemed that only the past existed, since for them the present had neither value nor significance.

"There's no other way out, is there?" Bobby asked. "How about putting a screw inside this time? In the floor to stop the door opening. Then no one could get out in a hurry."

Bailey nodded, and said he could soon manage that. He added an inquiry as to what were the odds. He went into the room where he kept his tools and cleaning material. When he opened the door the first thing they saw was Mr. Parkinson sitting at the table, eating bread and cheese.

"Good day," he said affably.

Bobby's reply, after a moment of speechless surprise, was much less affable.

"What are you doing here?" he demanded suspiciously.

"I came to meet Tails," Parkinson replied, though stiffly, and with eyebrows lifted in protest at Bobby's harsh, abrupt tone. "He asked me to. He said if he wasn't back at his hotel last night, would I come on here, and if I couldn't find him then I was to let you know. I was thinking of doing so."

"Pity you stopped at thinking," Bobby snapped, perhaps a little unfairly, but he was growing more concerned every moment. "You've seen nothing of him?" When Parkinson shook his head, Bobby went on, his voice still full of doubt and suspicion: "Didn't you hear anything just a moment or two ago? A pistol shot?"

"A pistol shot? Certainly not. Whereabouts? When?"

Bobby did not answer. In his ear Payne whispered:

"Perhaps he didn't hear it because perhaps he fired it."

Bobby nodded. It was a possibility that had occurred to him, too. To Parkinson, he continued:

"Didn't Mr. Tails say anything more? Explain at all?"

"Well, no. I understood it was something about a highly valuable picture he hoped to recover. He thought it as well to be on his guard, so he asked me to be here this morning."

"What good did he think that was going to do?" growled Bobby, feeling more worried than ever. "A client may be a child among dealers, but a dealer is a child among gangsters."

"Or their boss," murmured Payne doubtfully.

Bobby made up his mind.

"We'll have to have a good look round," he said. To Parkinson he said: "You had better stay here, and, for your own safety, I'm locking the door." To Bailey, he said: "Is there a key? Have you it? Yes? Good." To Parkinson, he said: "It won't be for long."

"Here. You've no right," began Parkinson, getting to his feet.

"No. I know I haven't," Bobby agreed, "but I'm going to, all the same. It's for your own safety," he repeated.

He went quickly into the passage, before Parkinson fully realized what was happening. Payne and Bailey followed. Bobby banged the door to. Bailey locked it. From within came a volley of shouts, kicks, and other violent sounds.

"False imprisonment," said Payne doubtfully, two words of which he stood, as do all policemen, in great awe and dread. "For his own safety," he repeated, still more doubtfully, "or to make sure he's still there when we want him?"

For a moment they stood listening to Parkinson's very energetic protests. Under them the door was shaking. But it was old and solid and held fast.

"It'll hold," Bobby said; and added, as there reached them the sounds of a specially fierce and vigorous assault: "You know, for an elderly man, a draper by profession, he does rather run to violence. You don't expect drapers to be violent people, though I don't know why not."

He moved on down the passage as he spoke. The other two followed him. Behind them there died away the sound of those unceasing thumps, bangs, kicks. In the great hall in the centre of the house they stood listening. They heard nothing, not even now the steady drumming of Parkinson's assault on the door of his prison. Bailey was told to wait there, in the main hall, so as to cut off any attempted escape. He was to keep out of sight as much as possible. He was also handed an unloaded pistol, though this he flatly refused to accept until twice assured that it really was unloaded.

"I've got this," he had explained, holding up a certainly solid-looking fist. "That's good enough for me."

"Looks as if it ought to be, but I don't want any more scrapping than can be helped," Bobby explained.

Leaving thus Bailey on guard, Bobby and Payne made a quick circuit of the ground floor of the great building. They found nothing, heard and saw nothing of interest, though now and then, listening, they recognized the distant hammering Parkinson was still keeping up with vigour and determination.

"Doesn't give in easily," Bobby remarked, listening. "There are formidable possibilities in that man."

They ascended, next, the great stairway, to search the upper floors. Once or twice they shouted, but got no reply. They looked in the nearer rooms, and found them all empty, deserted, wrapped in their usual silence and desolation. Hard to believe that once here the full tide of life had flowed and ebbed day by day in unceasing change and bustle. They went into the great picture gallery where the sheeted figures still stood undisturbed. They left it, and came to the corridor whence opened that room where, as Parkinson had told, he and the unlucky Dr. Jones had once seen a fresh bloodstain.

"This is where it started," Bobby remarked, opening the door.

Within, once again, much where it had been before, there showed upon the bare boards of the flooring a stain of newly spilt blood.

CHAPTER XXXIII

CUPBOARD

"THAT'S THE SHOT we heard," Payne said, staring at the small red, ominous pool, remembering the sharp double crack of pistol shots that had greeted their arrival.

Bobby nodded gloomily. They were too late, he feared. He began to look round the room, hoping for further indications of what had happened. In the wall he discovered a hole, wherefrom, with care and patience, he extracted a bullet. A revolver bullet, he thought. He put it away carefully. Two shots had been heard, but there was only one bullet to be found. Where was the other? A question that might, they both felt, have a tragic answer. Bobby went to the window, that window whence so wide and far a view could be obtained. On the frame were plainly-marked finger-prints, clear on the recent dust that even in empty rooms accumulates so quickly. Payne, who had at one time made a special study of finger-prints, examined them carefully, producing a small though powerful magnifying glass for the purpose.

"Look to me like Hardman's," he said.

"If they are," Bobby said, "was he shooter or shot? and who else was in it—shooting or shot?"

"There are some more dabs here," Payne said, "but they don't look as if they will be much good—more of the same perhaps."

Bobby went back to the window to look. He could not make much of them. Through the chinks and cracks in the boarding covering the window, whereby a little daylight filtered through into the room, he peered out over the wide country-side.

"I suppose we had better have another look round the house," he said. "Not much good, though. Too late. An easy get away while we've been up here, or before we got here, for that matter, or while we were talking to Parkinson." He stiffened suddenly, as his idle glance, wandering over the country-side, caught sight of movements in a distant field. "Come here, come and look," he said to Payne.

Payne came up. He stared through another crack. He said:

"What is it? Oh, see that? Someone ran in behind those trees, half-way across the field with the three cows."

"See who it was?" Bobby asked.

"No. Too far off. He didn't want to be seen, the way he was crouching as he ran."

"I saw another man in another field," Bobby said slowly, "creeping along a hedge, farther away, and I think the first man was following the other, and I think the second man was hiding from the first."

"Could you see who they were?" Payne asked.

"No," Bobby said. "Too far."

"What do we do?" Payne asked.

"Carry on here," Bobby answered. "More urgent. Whatever's going on out there, it's too far away for us to interfere. We must clear up here first. Besides, what's out there may have nothing to do with us. Boy scouts perhaps."

But this he did not really believe, not for one moment, nor did Payne. They continued their hurrying search of this upper floor. They went swiftly, almost running at times, they looked into every room, opened every cupboard and closet. Or so they believed, for though they marked their progress with chalk, it was hard to keep any sense of direction in that bewildering maze of twisting corridors and unexpected rooms and sudden stairs, all appearing where it seemed they could not be.

"We've been down here," Bobby said when they came upon one abrupt turning. He pointed to their chalk mark on the wall. "Haven't we?" he said doubtfully. "Or did we put that mark when we came the other way?"

Payne didn't know. They had hurried so.

"Better be on the safe side," Bobby said, turning down the passage. "It ought to take us towards the main stairway, oughtn't it?"

Payne said he didn't know. He said the famous maze in the Midwych Pleasure Park was nothing to this place. He said finding your way in one of the celebrated Midwych fogs during black-out was child's play to this. Bobby was inclined to agree. It was only a short corridor, though, with a small window to one side, very effectively boarded up so that the darkness here was greater than elsewhere. Opposite the window was a cupboard, easily overlooked in that gloom. Probably it had been used at one time for keeping brooms and pails and so on. Hurrying as they were, uneasy about what might be happening elsewhere, they very nearly passed that cupboard by unnoticed. But Bobby paused, as they were rushing by, to pull at the door handle; and when it resisted his tug and would not open, he stopped and tried again.

"Locked," he said. "What for?"

Like all the doors, windows, furnishings, in this old house, built before mass-production had been heard of or conveyer belts invented, the door was strong, solid, meant to last. Bobby, having tried a kick or two, was just about to say they would have to get tools from Bailey to force it with, when Payne pointed to the floor a yard or two away.

"There's a key," he said. "It may belong."

He picked it up as he spoke, and gave it to Bobby. Bobby tried it. It seemed to fit. When he turned it the door opened and there tumbled out the inanimate body of Mr. Tails.

Bobby bent over him, tried his pulse, felt his heart.

"Alive," he said, "but not very much so."

A further hasty examination showed no injury except a bad bruise at the back of the head.

"The skin's broken," Payne remarked. "It's bled a little."

"Not enough to make the blood we saw," Bobby said. "Besides, that was quite recent. This is twelve hours old at least." He added, looking into the cupboard, now quite empty, and then feeling Tails's pockets, "No picture and no wallet either."

Between them they carried the still unconscious man down to the great hall. Bailey was sent to get water. There was, of course, none in the building, for the well by which it had been supplied was out of action, but there was a big rainwater tank outside. From this Bailey brought a pailful. As he set it down, he said:

"That bloke you've locked up is banging away good and proper. Sounds as if he had got my hammer out of my tool box, and when he heard me he started yelling blue murder through the keyhole and all, so what's the odds?"

"I don't know," said Bobby, intent on Tails, now beginning to show signs of returning consciousness under the influence of the free application of water and of Payne's industrious fanning in the most approved first-aid style.

"Best be ready for him," Bailey added. "He'll be out soon, and by the way he's cursing there'll be trouble when he is."

Tails opened his eyes. He stared hard at Bobby. He put up a hand to stop the flapping of the handkerchief Payne was using so energetically as a fan. He said:

"Was it you?"

Bobby said:

"Drink this." He had in his pocket a small flask of brandy. He put it to Tails's lips, supporting his head to let him sip a few drops. He said: "How do you feel?"

Tails considered the point, but did not seem quite sure. He said, and shuddered as he spoke:

"I thought I was buried alive."

"Not you," said Bobby, producing a loud laugh for the occasion, though a grim picture flashed into his mind of consciousness awakening to darkness, silence, boards all around, then panic, then merciful swoon again. "What's it all about? Had a fall or did someone knock you out? You're all right now, of course, but you've had a bad whack on your head. Feeling better now?"

He let Tails sip a few drops more brandy. They had a strongly reviving effect. Tails tried to sit up.

"It's you, isn't it?" he said. "It was dark."

"So it was," agreed Bobby, "but it's daylight now. Where's the Vermeer painting?"

The last two words seemed to galvanize Tails into renewed life and energy. He struggled upright, though he held himself so with some difficulty, and only by the aid of Payne's grasp upon his arm.

"Clavering," he said. "That's it. He guessed. He guessed from what I told him. The young scoundrel. He guessed, and he was here first. He laid me out, and he got the Vermeer." He began to feel in his pockets. "My wallet's gone," he said. "You're witnesses. I'll prosecute. I'll have him into every court in the land. It's criminal, theft, it's theft."

"Did you see Clavering?" Bobby asked.

"Yes, I did, of course I did, who else could it be?" Tails tried to take a step forward, but nearly collapsed in doing so. Payne said "Steady on", and held him up. But if Tails's legs were still somewhat untrustworthy, his tongue was in good working order, and he let out a stream of oaths and anger and abuse that would have much astonished some of his élite clientele. "Who else could it be? That young scoundrel would stick at nothing, murder, he tried to murder me, didn't he? He's been watching, waiting, spying, and now he's tried to kill me, and he's stolen the Vermeer painting. Why don't you arrest him? Clavering."

His voice rose to a scream. He collapsed, and Payne lowered him gently to the floor. The door at the back, giving admittance to the hall, opened, and Clavering himself appeared.

"Did I hear my name?" he inquired suavely.

CHAPTER XXXIV

GIRL—BOY

IT WAS CLAVERING himself who had to break the staring, surprised, suspicious silence that ensued upon his unexpected appearance.

"Quite a party," he said, putting up his eyeglass to survey benevolently the small assembled group. "I thought I heard . . ." He broke off abruptly. "Good Lord, it's Tails," he said. "What's up now?"

Tails had managed, somehow, to get to his feet again.

"That's him," he cried. "Where is it?" he shouted at Clavering. "You've got it, you lying, swindling, thieving . . ."

' Quiet," snapped Bobby.

"What's he mean? Got what?" Clavering asked. "Looks as though poor old Tails has had it, though. What's going on here? There's a bloke rying to kick a door in and raising Cain generally, and young Frank Hardman's been hurt and wants help. He's been shot up. Did he do that?" Clavering added, nodding at Tails. "Or was it the bloke you've got locked up?"

"What's that about Frank Hardman?" Bobby asked.

"He's out there hiding in the rhododendrons at the front," Clavering answered, "with a bullet in his arm, and looking pretty sick. He said there was someone in the house, so I came to get help. He wants a doctor, he looks bad."

"Where's the Vermeer? What have you done with it?" interrupted Tails suddenly, and then collapsed.

Payne caught him, and again lowered him gently to the ground. Bobby said to Clavering:

"What do you know about the Vermeer? Have you got it?"

"Good lord, no," Clavering answered, astonished. "If I had, I shouldn't be here. I should be half-way to London. What about the Hardman boy? He wants looking after."

Bobby gave a quick look at the now again half-swooning Tails, and decided he could be left for a few moments. To Bailey he said:

"Get along quick as you can to the nearest call box. Put a police call through. Tell them I want the ambulance, a doctor, four duty men, all most urgent. Hurry up. Get your bike."

"O.K." said Bailey. "So what's the odds?"

With this cryptic question, he departed at a clumsy trot, and to Clavering Bobby said:

"Front of the house? In the rhododendron bushes? Come along then."

They all three hurried off, Bobby leading the way, and Payne keeping a suspicious eye on Clavering, in whom he felt small confidence. They passed the door of Parkinson's prison, where, as the captive heard them coming, the violence of the assault upon it increased, accompanied by such a torrent of lurid threats as can but seldom have issued from the lips of a peaceful, respectable draper.

"Just a minute, Mr. Parkinson," Bobby shouted to him. "I'll let you out as soon as I can."

Probably what he said was not fully understood. At any rate the only results were a spate of even more remarkable language surely never learned in the drapery trade, though indeed all trades have their secrets, and an even fiercer assault on a door now clearly showing signs of surrender, just like a cornered German army. "Old Parkinson, is it?" Clavering said as they all three still hurried on. "What's he been doing?"

Bobby said to him:

"Tails says you knocked him out. Did you?"

"Me? no," Clavering answered, with apparent surprise. "What did he say that for? The old liar. What's the idea, saying it was me?"

"His story is he saw you," Bobby said. "Why should he tell me that if it isn't true?"

"Oh, just the first lie he could think of," Clavering suggested. "Or perhaps to stop you knowing who it really was. For ways that are dark and tricks that are vain, &c. He says he hasn't got the Vermeer? How do you know he hasn't? Perhaps he's got it salted down somewhere. More likely he's been double-crossed, though, with that broken head of his. Perhaps he really thinks it was me. If it had been, I shouldn't be here. I should be miles away with the loot."

"Why are you here?" Bobby asked, still with suspicion in his voice, though he admitted the force of this last remark.

"'Phone call from old man Solomon," Clavering explained. "In the picture racket we all know all about the other fellow, and what he's doing, and Solomon and every one else knew the Tails outfit was badly rattled because they hadn't heard from him, and didn't know what he was up to. But only Solomon and self knew Tails was playing around up here, and why, and as Tails was missing from his hotel it struck me something had gone wrong with the deal I told you he was boasting to me about. I tried Major Hardman's place to see if he knew anything about it, but there was no one there. You said something about

Nonpareil, so I came on here. Lots going on apparently, including the Hardman boy. There he is."

They had reached, now, the great rhododendron beds that lay in front of the house, about a hundred yards distant. In front of them half lay, half sat young Hardman, the right arm roughly bandaged, though blood was still oozing from it. Sullenly, silently young Hardman watched their approach. Bobby bent to examine the wound. He did what he could, though that was not much. He thought the bullet was still there, embedded in the bone. He said:

"Who did this? Was it your husband?"

The only answer he received was the same sullen, angry stare. Payne, surprised, for he had not anticipated the word 'husband' repeated it under his breath, and looked very bewildered, and Clavering, open-mouthed, all his surface sophistication slipping from him, gasped out "Oh, I say," and then subsided. Bobby went on:

"That arm of yours wants looking at. Dirt in it, I think. I've sent for a doctor. It was your husband, wasn't it? Were you running away from him with someone else or with the Vermeer painting, or was it both?"

"Think you know all about it, don't you?" she muttered.

"Well, I know a good deal," Bobby agreed, "and I can guess the rest. But not yet where you hid the Vermeer painting when you took it from behind the portrait in The Tulips drawing-room. Where is it now?"

She made no answer, only looked as sullen and defiant as before. Clavering burst out:

"Her brother's got it. That's it. She's given it him. That's why he's been hanging round all this time. Ask her where her brother is."

"She has no brother," Bobby said.

"Yes, of course, you know, her twin," Clavering exclaimed eagerly.

"There isn't any twin," Bobby said, but again Clavering interrupted.

"Yes, there is," he declared. "I've seen him, I've spoken to him. I had an idea sometimes he dressed up to pass off as his sister, but I never thought of her playing the same trick. It's being twins."

"There's no twin," Bobby said. "There couldn't be. I always knew that. But I didn't know what it covered. You see," he explained, speaking directly to the girl whose air of sulky and defiant reserve was now giving way to an expression of uneasy surprise, "there are two sorts of twins—ordinary twins, who come from two different eggs and are just ordinary brothers or sisters who happen to be born at the same time, and who no more resemble each other than do ordinary brothers and sisters—family likeness and no more—and identic twins who come from one egg, who were meant to be one personality, who, there-fore, always resemble each other, and who sometimes show an odd psychic link with each other. But they have to be both of the same sex, either both male or both female, because sex determination takes place before the splitting of the one egg into two. So it was certain, unless medical and scientific theory was wrong, which I didn't think likely, that the twin story was a fake, and used merely to provide a useful scapegoat, and set us police looking for someone who didn't exist, and therefore couldn't be found. Major Hardman did his best to push suspicion on the non-existent Frank. Only I couldn't be sure, at first, whether it was a boy pretending to be a girl or the other way round. What settled it was when I found out you had been working a lot with the W.V.S. A boy can pass as a girl easily enough for a time, but I wasn't going to believe that any young man could associate regularly with a lot of women as you did at the W.V.S. centre without their spotting him. That swell coiffure of yours rather gave the game away, too. Not quite your general style. So why were you wearing it? Because, you know, there's a reason for everything. And it was certainly a wig, or why did no hairdresser round here—and we asked them all—know you as a customer?"

As Bobby talked the settled, sullen hostility on the girl's face slowly changed into a sort of bewildered fear. As indeed Bobby had hoped might be the result of the long harangue just delivered and the object he had had in mind. For he had reasoned that if he struck at the security she had felt in secrecy, and showed her how much he knew, then it was possible she would break down. And so it happened, for now she said with fear:

"You knew all that all the time?"

"Oh, yes, and much more as well," Bobby told her smilingly, "but I'm not certain yet what you've done with the Vermeer painting."

"It's where it was all the time till he took it away," she said then. "Under the sheet covering the river god statue in the picture gallery."

CHAPTER XXXV

NARRATIVE

It was clavering who reacted first to this intelligence. The form his reaction took was a stifled yell, a quick turn, and the beginning of a wild rush towards the house. But it was checked by an angry roar from Bobby, a roar calculated to put into the shade for ever any roaring by any bull of Bashan that ever was.

"None of that," Bobby ordered. "You stop here."

Clavering obeyed. It was, indeed, an obedience-compelling roar that Bobby had emitted. Clavering said:

"There's nothing there. I've looked."

"So have I," said Bobby. He turned again to Mrs. Hardman and, producing once more his brandy flask, poured out a liberal allowance he put to her lips. "Drink this," he said. "It'll do you good. I expect the doctor won't be long. Drink it up," he urged, and she obeyed. It brought colour back to her cheeks, and it loosened her tongue as well, a result possibly not wholly unhoped for by Bobby, who said persuasively: "I think you would be wise to tell us all about it. I know most of it, but I would like to hear your side."

"Oh, all right," she said. "I suppose I may as well."

"From the beginning," Bobby said, and warned her: "Only, mind, the truth. I know enough to be able to check what you say. How long have you been masquerading like this?"

"Ever since I married him," she answered. All the time she referred to Major Hardman by the pronoun, never once using his name. It was as though she did not dare to use it. "It was his idea," she went on. "I mean, to do it as a regular thing for a purpose. I had before sometimes just for fun. That's what he said it was for at first, just fun. But then he began to get me to do things, and then, when there were questions, he said I had a twin brother, and if they tried to find him they couldn't, because, of course, there wasn't one. When the police came, though, I had to show up as Frank, but they hadn't anything to go on, they could only ask questions, and they never guessed. But they kept on coming, and we knew they were bound to find out sooner or later. He—said we would have to close for a time, so we shut down, and came here to be out of the way till it was safe to begin again, and it was partly because of the Nonpareil sale that he thought of here. Because in sales at these big, old country houses there are things you can pick up; and even if it's only junk, and sold as junk, you can often get a good profit if you can say it came from somewhere like Nonpareil and do a sales talk about valuables forgotten or overlooked in attics and muniment rooms."

"A common trick," Clavering commented, "only the Antique Dealers Association hoof you out if they get to know—and they generally do."

"We never tried to join," she explained simply. "We knew it wouldn't be any good. When it was the Nonpareil view day I went dressed up as Frank. He—stopped away because someone might have known him, and he wanted to be able to prove he wasn't there, and didn't know anything about what his nephew—me—might have done. I saw the Betty Anson girl looking at a picture, and I thought it looked good, though I didn't know. I told her it wasn't worth anything, but

170

she went to speak to the auctioneer's man, and I didn't want him to show it anyone, so I hid it in the picture gallery behind the dust sheet covering one of the statues. It was the only place I could think of. It was no good trying to take it away, the men were watching. When I got home I told—him—and he was very excited, and he said I must get hold of it somehow, and it must be me, because it wouldn't do for him to show. But next day, when I went, it wasn't there any more. Someone had moved it, and when I told—him—he was so furious I thought he would kill me, and he did hit me—it was the first time—and it was then I made up my mind to leave him."

"A pity you didn't, then and there," Bobby said. "Why didn't you?"

"I was afraid," she answered. "Besides, he said he was sorry." She paused, thinking, remembering perhaps. She said slowly, half to herself: "Somehow it's hard to leave your man." She went on: "I couldn't find out what had become of it, and when the sale began I watched and watched and waited, but it never came up. Afterwards we heard about a dealer having bought up a job lot of odds and ends left over, and how he said there was an old picture on wood might be the one a young gent had been asking about, and he could have it for a fiver if he still wanted it. So I put on my boy's clothes and went to ask. The dealer said he had it, and I thought it might be the same. But he wanted the money on the spot, and I hadn't brought enough with me, and I said £5 was too much. Always—he—used to say the more badly you wanted a thing, the more careful you must be not to show it, and never be too ready to pay the first price asked. So I wasn't."

"One of the better known tricks of the trade," commented Clavering. "I mean, of course, the first principle of all successful buying."

Taking no notice of this comment, she continued:

"I asked him to let me see it, but he wouldn't, he said it was put away, and it was near closing time, and he would like to see my money first. When I got home and told—him—he was most awfully angry. He gave me such a push I fell down, and he kicked me. He said why couldn't I have pawned something to make up the money even if I had been too big a fool to take enough with me, and I got angry, too, and he hit me again. It was too late to do anything then, and he said I must be there first thing in the morning, but in the night there was an air raid, and when I got there, there had been a bomb, and there was nothing left of the shop or anything, and the dealer had been killed, too. He—was angrier than ever, and he said it was all my fault, and I had lost a great fortune. He got drunk that night, and he knocked me about so I was in bed nearly a week, and I made up my mind again to leave him, only I didn't know how, and I knew he wouldn't let me if he could help it, and I had no money. I thought I would make sure the picture had really been destroyed, and I went to look. There wasn't anything left at all, because there had been a fire as well as the bomb, and there was nothing, only ashes. But I talked to some of the neighbours, and some of them were saying had the dealer left any relatives, because no one had ever heard of any, and he had money in the savings bank, so they didn't know who would get it. And one of them said there was some of the stuff he bought at Nonpareil still there, but another woman said it was only junk, and most likely not worth the trouble of fetching, especially now when it was so difficult to get about. That made me think there might be just a chance that the real reason why he wouldn't let me see the picture when I asked was that he had left it at Nonpareil, only he hadn't wanted to say so. I didn't say anything at home, but I waited till—he—was away for a few days; and I got an order to view, and I went to Nonpareil, and I found it there, put away in the cellar with the rest of the odds and ends the dealer man had bought up. I still didn't say anything, but I took it and hid it again where I had put it before in the picture gallery, and I never said a word, but I liked to think of it there when he wanted it so much and thrashed me for what he called being such a fool and losing the chance of getting it. But it was there all the time, and I could tell him any time I wanted to, only I never did. But it was nice to feel I knew and—he—didn't. Then I began to think I would take it away and sell it myself, and get the money, and then I could leave him, go right away somewhere, where he wouldn't know, and couldn't find me. A nice private hotel where they were all classy people and no one would ever think of looking for me, and no work to do either, just sit about all day. Once when we were both in London, I went into Mr. Tails's place in Mayfair because I knew they wouldn't ask too many questions, or want to know too much. I knew they were that sort when there was the chance of a good bargain. I didn't think they would know who I was—I was being Frank, of course —but they did. I don't think they much believed me, they thought it was most likely only a try on, but they were excited all the same."

"I know," Clavering interposed, "they didn't believe enough to keep it to themselves, but they did believe enough to start them talking."

"I suppose so," Mrs. Hardman agreed. "It made more talk than I wanted or expected, and—he—heard, and so—he—knew it was what I said started it all. I had to pretend I had only gone to Mr. Tails's place because I had been hearing talk, too, and I wanted to try to find out if there was anything in it. He—wanted to know who I had heard talking, and I had to say someone, so I said it was Ned Doors—the man they call Lovey. Ned and I had worked together before and Ned used to say when I was tired of—him—why shouldn't we join up? Only Ned said that to every one, and didn't mean it much to anyone, except for a week or two. I told him I was in a bit of a fix because of not wanting—him—to know who had really told me or he would be jealous mad. So I got Ned to pretend it was him had heard about the junk left in the Nonpareil cellar and the chance there was of the lost picture being there. Ned was ready enough to agree when I said if it was there it would be worth money, and he could claim half. What I really most wanted was for someone else to know about it in case—he—got suspecting I had known all along, because then I was afraid he would beat me up or kill me, but he couldn't, not if there were others in it, too. But I didn't know till afterwards that Ned had a twin brother just come back from America after being in gaol there a long time over a hold up. Ned took his brother with him when they went to Nonpareil, and—he—was more furiouser than ever I had seen him at there being two more to share. It was his job all along, he said, and he wasn't going to have anyone else butting in, and I said he couldn't help it, because they were in, and he said he would find a way, and it made me frightened the way he said it, but he never guessed it was all through me they were in—Ned and his brother. There was no trouble getting into Nonpareil. The caretaker left the door open sometimes when he was cleaning, so it was easy to make an impression of the lock and a key to fit. I hoped they wouldn't find the picture. I thought they would look in the cellar, and when it wasn't there I thought they would give up. But they found it. In the picture gallery where I had it behind the dust sheet over the river god group. At least, it was Ned's brother found it, but Ned was in London and didn't know. And he never did, not till I told him after I had taken it from where—he—had it hidden in our drawing-room at home. I had to have someone to help, and first of all I thought I would ask Betty Anson, because she saw it first, and would know about it and she's a girl, too, and I thought she might be more likely to do what I wanted. But when I tried to get a word with her without anyone knowing, a man was there, and I had to run away. I thought it might be one of your policemen. After that I told Ned because I had to have someone to help, and he always said he wanted to be friends." She paused. She stared at Bobby with much of her old, sullen, resentful manner back again. She said: "If it hadn't been for you coming meddling—he—would never have known it was gone till Ned and I had got away. It's all through you what's happened now, and me being fool enough to let you out that time Ned had you fixed in the cellar, and he said you could rot there, you and one of your snoopers he knocked out when he saw him noseying around."

"Meaning me?" asked Clavering indignantly. "I'm not."

She went on unheedingly:

"It was only because I was afraid of all the fuss there would be, that's why I did it. I didn't care what happened to you, it was all the questioning I didn't w nt to have to face up to. When I told—him—he said

I had done right, and Lovey had been a fool to try it on, because it never made sense to mess up a cop if you could help it. But afterwards he was sorry, and so was I."

"But not me," said Bobby with some feeling, "not me at all."

"That's all I know," she said abruptly. "I can't tell you any more. Leave me alone."

CHAPTER XXXVI

DEDUCTION

BOBBY DID NOT try to persuade her to continue her story. For one thing he felt it would be useless to do so; indeed, undue pressure might even affect adversely any later tendency to talk. Probably, too, now that the effects of the brandy were wearing off, she had begun to realize that she was approaching dangerous ground. Besides, Bailey was now back, cycling up the drive from the entrance gates.

"Get through?" Bobby called to him as he dismounted. "You did? Good. Wait here now, will you? with this lady while the inspector and I get along back to the house."

"Lady? what lady?" Bailey asked, staring round. "That's the young gent I was telling you I seen dodging about round here." He stared again, and looked frankly bewildered. "Here, what's all this?" he demanded.

"Never mind that now," Bobby said. "If you can manage it, get Mrs. Hardman to your lodge till the doctor and the ambulance get here. They shouldn't be long. Get your wife to look after her. Mind, she is to be detained. Send one of my men to the hospital with her. Come on, Payne. You, too, Mr. Clavering. I'm not too easy about Tails, we've left him too long."

"Not to mention Mr. Parkinson being locked up," observed Payne, still a trifle uneasy about such autocratic behaviour, for of all the people in this country who have to watch their step, the police come first.

"I say," put in Clavering, still very bewildered, "is all that stuff about twins O.K., or were you just making it up as you went along to catch her out?"

"I don't try to catch people out," retorted Bobby, stiff and offended. "It's scientific theory, and you don't make up scientific theory—at least," he added, relaxing slightly, "you don't unless you're a swell scientist yourself."

"Do you think all that yarn of hers was true?" Clavering asked. "It was pretty tall in parts, wasn't it?"

"Yes, but it fitted in with what we knew already," Bobby answered. "I think it was true all right. You notice she stopped short when she began to think she might be incriminating herself. All she told us was about a more or less innocent attempt to trace a valuable picture. That's been the difficulty all along. Every suspicious or doubtful action could be explained as part of the rival search for the missing Vermeer. Difficult to make an arrest on a charge of murder when all your suspect need say is he was nosing round after a lost picture, and why not? Anything wrong in that? he asks, and there you are—stumped. Because you know it was certainly true of some of your suspects, and partly true about the actual murderer as well most likely. But as I see it now Mrs. Hardman gave us the key to the whole affair when she said Lovey Doors was away when the picture turned up, and only Hardman himself and Lovey's younger brother, Shut Doors knew about it."

"Why's that a key?" demanded Clavering, puzzled, and even Payne looked surprised.

Bobby, forgetting, in the absorption of his thought, the still imprisoned Parkinson, the injured Tails still waiting for help, came to a standstill, and began to talk, half to himself, half to them.

"Taking that as a starting point," he said, "and fitting it in with what we know, you can reconstruct the whole affair."

"Not me," said Clavering with emphasis.

"How?" asked Payne with interest.

"She told us," Bobby said, "about Hardman's fury and disappointment over two new-comers butting in to claim shares, and of his saying he would find a way out. As he did, for finally he got hold of the picture without anyone else knowing. What happened? The younger brother, Shut Doors, disappears with two bullets in his back. Miss Anson is induced to believe herself guilty, but there is subsidiary evidence pointing to a non-existent Frank Hardman who, however, had given proof of his existence by being thrown out of a public-house the evening of the murder. Looks as if Hardman had it all worked out, and then the shot Betty Anson fired gave him an opportunity to improvise he pounced on instantly. As I see it, he had made up his mind to get rid of Shut Doors before Shut had a chance to say anything to his brother Ned. I think it likely—or how did Betty Anson come into it?—that Hardman persuaded Shut the picture they found wasn't the right one, and that Miss Anson had it in her possession, waiting for a chance to dispose of it. Miss Anson was to be the bait to draw Shut into the forest, where he could be disposed of and his body hidden without anyone knowing anything about it. Shut would be told he must get the girl alone to bully the truth out of her, away from help. If it wasn't like that, how could Shut have known anything about her, when he was new to the district and had spent all his time at Nonpareil? Besides, we know from young

Claymore that someone else had been hanging about the Lonesome Barsley path at night, and Claymore had suspected who it was, and warned him to keep away or risk a thrashing. Naturally enough, when Miss Anson found a man following her again, she thought, as any girl would, that he was waylaying her for the usual reasons, not on account of a picture she had by that time forgotten all about. So when he tried to stop her she got scared, and let off her pistol shot that Hardman heard, and that gave him the inspiration for a really brilliant improvisation. At the moment he heard it he was on his way to meet Shut Doors, killing his intention, I feel certain. He happened to run across our man, Reed, and stopped to chat, because it's always a good idea to be friendly with the police if you can. Then they are sure you are respectable. When they heard the shot Miss Anson fired, Hardman evidently saw at once that it might give him the very opportunity he needed. That's shown by the way he at once spoke of it to Reed, to fix it in his mind, to provide an alibi. A shot had been fired, a killing was to be done, Reed was there to prove he hadn't fired the shot it would be taken for granted was the killer's. I think that shows a really remarkable quickness of mind on Hardman's part. It was when I began to realize that that I began to realize, too, how necessary it would be to have a complete case before acting. Hardman took care, too, to let Reed see him go back into the house. Of course he slipped out again at once to see what had really happened. He found Shut Doors, who told him, and told him how he had dodged Betty's shot by dropping to the ground. That would suggest to Hardman that he might be able to make Miss Anson believe her random shot had killed. If she could be got to believe that, why shouldn't the police, too? Hence his letter, unfortunately lost. I wonder if there's any chance of finding a rough copy at Tulips? We might with luck. And he made a mistake when he put two bullets into Shut's back, because Betty had only fired once. Though it's easy to take two immediately consecutive reports for one. And then I expect it's a murderer's instinct to make sure. Also the pistols were of different makes, though, no doubt, he had to chance that. The chief danger was that Betty might know quite well that her shot had not killed. She might have seen or spoken to Shut Doors afterwards, and seen he was all right. So Hardman provided other clues to point to the guilt of his Bunbury nephew, or else why the public-house scene earlier on?"

"Bunbury nephew?" interposed Payne, not catching the allusion.

"Oscar Wilde," explained Clavering. "Yes? Well?" he said to Bobby whose reconstruction of events he found fascinating.

"Hardman's next step was to go back to Nonpareil where he expected to find Lovey Doors. It was probably because he knew Lovey was coming back that night that Hardman had felt he must act before the two brothers got together. Hardman may even have feared that unless he got in first, they might get rid of him. I expect he told Lovey that his brother had been fooling with a girl in Wychwood, and that he was afraid there had been trouble, as he had heard pistol shots. They went to look, and Hardman would take care Shut was found. A slight hitch there. Shut was dying, not yet dead. That is shown by the fresh blood on the floor in the Nonpareil room. If Shut had been dead his wound wouldn't have bled, and probably they wouldn't have taken him there at all. He must have died almost at once, though. The medical evidence is that he couldn't have survived long. Then more complications. Jones and Parkinson came on the scene. We have to consider Jones's actions in the light of his real mission having been to see if he could find out anything about the rumoured Vermeer. He must have realized something queer was going on at Nonpareil, and he would naturally associate it with the Vermeer story. There was the patch of blood he and Parkinson had seen, and that Lovey and Hardman took such pains to get rid of. There was what happened in the picture gallery when Parkinson thought he saw the statues move—no doubt one or other of the Hardman-Doors combination trying to hide. Jones pooh poohed Parkinson's fears. Like Hardman, he did not intend there to be any more claimants than necessary for the Vermeer, with all it meant in cash and kudos. So he went back alone the next night, deliberately leaving Parkinson out, and hoping to get in touch with what he probably imagined was a rival Vermeer search party. Violence is so alien to the ideas of the respectable middle-class that he probably never even thought of personal danger. He must have interrupted Hardman and Lovey in the midst of their preparations for disposing of the dead body of Shut Doors. If he saw them with it, they would feel he had to be silenced. There can be no other reason for what they did. And we know Hardman was there that night, since there is the evidence of Bailey to show that someone, speaking like an educated man, returned the key he had previously given Jones. That can only have been Hardman. The key was returned to delay the search for Jones and the discovery of the body as long as possible. Hardman could not remove the picture till Lovey was out of the way. I daresay he got rid of him finally by egging him on against Miss Anson. However that may be, he certainly went back to Nonpareil next day, and when we arrived and he saw he was likely to be found he toppled over one of the busts from the picture gallery on our heads, more, I expect, to give himself an opportunity of escaping unseen than with any intention of killing—though I don't suppose he would have minded that result very much. Shut Doors's body must have been already removed. No doubt they hoped to get rid of it somewhere where it would never be found, and no one would know what had happened—except themselves. A man like Shut Doors can disappear without anyone wanting to ask why. Too many possible reasons. But it is difficult to conceal a dead body, and in the end they panicked, and simply dumped it in the canal. They would hope it would never be identified or connected with the death of Dr. Jones. And a pretty problem they left us with its double entwined thread of murder and lost painting that now Mrs. Hardman's story clears up."

He began to walk on towards the house. Clavering said:

"You've put it together all right, but isn't it all rather guessing?"

"I don't think so," Bobby said. "It all follows logically on what we know, and on what Mrs. Hardman told us. It fits the way truth does fit."

"An exercise in deduction," said Payne. "Classical I call it."

Bobby grinned. He was a bit excited himself, but he felt Payne's phrase was a good deal too pompous.

"An exercise in common sense," he suggested.

"That chap you saw trying to get through the Anson bungalow window, that would be Lovey Doors," Payne said. "Wouldn't it? Meaning to do in Miss Anson because he thought she had done in his brother?"

"I think so," Bobby agreed. "They were twins—identic twins, most likely, from their likeness to each other. There seems to have been a strong bond between them. Lovey believed Hardman's story, and meant to have his revenge. A good thing I was there, or we might have had another murder on our hands. Afterwards, Lovey still hung about, though keeping well out of the way, perhaps hoping for another chance to get at Betty. But I had put a man on watch. Very likely too, he was beginning to mistrust Hardman, and perhaps hoping to get to know something about the lost picture, or at any rate to get some cash out of it somehow. We know he got in touch with Tails the first time on the day of the commandeered taxi incident. Tails was ready to snatch at any chance. Lovey visited him again at his hotel, and from what Tails told you, Mr. Clavering, Lovey must have said he knew where the picture was and have promised to hand it over. Tails ought to have consulted us, but he didn't."

"Not likely," interrupted Clavering. "The last thing he would want."

"He told us his wallet had gone," Bobby continued. "Evidently he had the money in it to hand over to Lovey in exchange for the painting Lovey hadn't got. So Lovey knocked him out instead, took the wallet—probably there was a good fat sum in it—shoved Tails into the cupboard where we found him, and that was that."

They had rounded the corner of the house now, and come in full sight of the side door used by Bailey. A man was busy there, even frantically busy. It was Mr. Parkinson, and he was hammering away as if for dear life, driving in nail after nail through door and door-post so as to make opening it impossible.

"What on earth . . . ?" said Bobby, stopping and staring.

"He's gone mad," said Payne with conviction.

"Tell us how that fits in," said Clavering challengingly to Bobby. Parkinson heard them, and turned, and now he, too, stopped and stared—and his was even a bigger, wilder stare than Bobby's.

"You," he stammered, "you—I thought it was you, in there."

CHAPTER XXXVII

CONCLUSION

WITH A VIGOUR that sent Mr. Parkinson staggering backwards, Bobby snatched the hammer from him. He began an attack on the door, but Payne said "Let me," and, taking the hammer in his turn, started to withdraw the nails so energetically driven in but luckily more energetically than skilfully, so that the task of extracting them was easier than otherwise it might have been. With a baleful glare Bobby swung round on Parkinson, who said defensively:

"You locked me in, and I thought it was you, so it would serve you right if I did the same."

"Oh, you did, did you?" said Bobby, his glare more baleful even than before. "All right. You'll be charged with obstructing the police in the execution of their duty. Thought who was me?"

"I heard someone come in," Parkinson said, and repeated: "I thought it was you. If it wasn't you, who was it?"

Bobby did not answer. That was one thing he very badly wanted to know. He was asking himself what had happened? Had he been remiss in leaving Tails alone, especially considering Tails's still shaken and half-dazed condition. Yet the emergency had been real, and there had not seemed at the time any special risk in leaving him alone in the great empty house that had just been thoroughly searched. Nor could anyone have anticipated this last Parkinsonian folly. All the same, Bobby was uneasy, alarmed; and Payne, too, evidently felt much the same from the swift, fierce energy he was putting into wrenching out the nails, one after the other. He extracted the last one. The door opened. He and Bobby rushed through. Clavering followed, as did Parkinson, though more slowly. And when they reached the great hall where they had left Tails they found him still there, now, however, upright, exultant, revived and flushed with excitement, holding in reverent, outstretched hands an oblong wooden panel.

"The Vermeer," he shouted at them. "I've got it, I've got it," and he held it up, only barely visible in the dim half light. "Look," he cried. "Look."

At the moment Bobby was not interested in any picture, however great a masterpiece it might be, however wonderful. He said quickly: "There was someone here. Who was it? Where is he?"

"I don't know," Tails said, answering only the last question. "He was coming down the stairs, and he heard you, and he put this down and went up again, and I saw it." He paused, and said with a kind of greedy exaltation: "I've recovered the Vermeer; I've recovered the greatest picture ever painted. Look." He held it up. Flushed with triumph, excitement, joy, he said to Clavering, defeated Clavering, "I'll send you a ticket for the private view I'll fix up at our Mayfair place. Or I may show it somewhere else. The Royal Academy perhaps. They would appreciate the compliment. Or the National Gallery with someone really big to preside. The Prime Minister perhaps. Why not? What do you think? A unique occasion in the history of art. What do you say?"

The questions had been addressed to Clavering, but they went unanswered. Down the great stairway a man was coming, calmly, confidently, tranquilly. It was Major Hardman. He said:

"Ah, you've got it. Is it genuine, I wonder?"

He came on, still tranquil, still serene and confident, a man with no care in all the world, sure of his reception. But both Bobby and Payne noticed that he held his right hand in his coat pocket. They exchanged looks, and each knew what the other was thinking. Payne moved forward, and, as Hardman stepped from the lowest tread on to the floor of the hall, with one sudden expert and practised movement, Payne had both Hardman's arms held fast. Hardman made no attempt to resist. He said in a tone full of surprise and reproach:

"What's the matter? what are you doing?"

From that right hand coat pocket Payne dexterously produced a revolver, a little in the style of the conjurer and the rabbit.

"Is it loaded?" Bobby asked.

Payne released his grip on Hardman, who was looking a little less complacent now. Handling the weapon with extreme care, Payne gave it to Bobby who took it from him with equal care. Using a clean handkerchief as protection, he broke it open.

"Two chambers still loaded," he said, "two only, and there are four of us. Just as well perhaps. You have fired it recently, I think?" he said to Hardman.

"It's been fired," agreed Hardman, "at least I think so, but not by me. I heard firing just now. I wondered what it was, and went to see. I saw that revolver lying near a ditch in a field, and I picked it up. Someone must have dropped it. That's all I know."

"That means," Bobby said, "we shall find someone's finger-prints on it."

"Well, I'm afraid I've handled it a good deal," Hardman remarked apologetically. "I wasn't thinking about finger-prints."

"I found a bullet in a room upstairs, in the wall," Bobby said, unable to resist a certain admiration for the way in which Hardman, that expert in improvisation, was producing one excuse after another, fighting to the last. "We shall have to send that bullet and this thing to Wakefield to see if they are complementary. If so, I wonder how a shot fired outside in a field got into a wall indoors. By the way, how did that picture come to be in your possession?"

"I saw it upstairs," Hardman explained, still in the same airy fashion, even though now a certain suggestion of strain was creeping into his manner. "I wondered if it was the one there has been all the talk about. So I thought I had better bring it down here."

"Why are you here yourself?" Bobby asked.

"That," Hardman said with quiet dignity, "is a private matter. I would prefer not to discuss it. There were reasons, painful reasons. My unfortunate niece—however, with your permission we will leave it at that. I have tried to do my duty by the girl. Anyhow, I am glad to think the painting, which I understand is of some value, is in such good hands." Here he made a little bow to Mr. Tails, still lost in ecstatic wonder at his good fortune, still dreaming of the cash, the kudos, the publicity he foresaw. He was even dallying with the idea of trying to establish a claim to rightful ownership. He had as good a claim as any-one, hadn't he? Why not? And he was in possession. That was important, even very important. Hardman was continuing, with a little bow, this time, to Bobby: "So if you'll excuse me, I'll go on home. There are certain private matters, painful matters . . . if you want me at any time, you know where to find me."

Bobby said:

"I must ask you to come with me to headquarters. I am charging you with the murder of a man known as Shut Doors. I think this pistol will prove to be the one used in his murder. I suppose you hid it after the murder, but when I took away your other one, then you had to get this again. This pistol has been fired four times—six chambers and only two live cartridges left. One bullet from it I found in the wall of a room upstairs. A second bullet is in your wife's arm—or was, probably the doctor has got it out by now. Your finger-prints are there, too, on the window frame. I think that all adds up to proof. I shall also charge you with the murder of Dr. Clement Jones, or, alternatively, as an accessory, if the actual murderer was Lovey Doors. Probably you were equally in it. Where is Lovey Doors? And where are the two bullets unaccounted for? Are they in Lovey Doors's body when you thought he was getting away both with your wife and with the picture. Is that another murder to your account, and is his body lying out there in the fields where I think I saw him running and hiding a little while ago?"

But this was too much for Hardman, who understood, now, that Bobby knew practically the whole story. He tried to make one wild, desperate rush towards the door; but Payne was watching and ready, and Hardman found himself seized and held fast before he had taken a second stride. He snarled:

"You can't prove it."

"Where was Lovey Doors when you shot him?" Bobby insisted. "In the fields out there where I saw two men just now."

Hardman did not answer. He had become very pale for now that his attempt to bluff his way out by sheer impudence had failed so completely, he knew well there was no further hope. And, indeed, at his trial he made no attempt to defend himself, refusing to employ counsel, and even refusing to give any help to the counsel who was then assigned by the court to undertake his defence.

By this time the help Bobby had asked Bailey to 'phone for was beginning to arrive. Mrs. Hardman—the one time Frank—Frankie— was already on her way to hospital; and Bobby was glad to think that so far as he could see there would be no need to prosecute her, since there was no direct proof of complicity or guilty knowledge. Nor would she even be called on to give evidence, since a wife cannot be made to testify against a husband. In the custody of two constables Hardman began the first stage of his last journey. Tails, hugging the recovered Vermeer, said to Bobby:

"I want a car. I must get my picture into safety at once. You must let me have yours. It's most important to make sure of its safety."

"I'll see to that," Bobby told him.

"Oh, no, no," Tails told him smilingly, "that's my job. I daresay you hardly understand the world-wide interest all this is going to create. World-wide interest," he murmured again. "There are many arrangements I must make, but the picture itself must be my first care."

"I must ask you to come with us to headquarters, too," Bobby continued. "I want a full statement, if you don't mind. And I think I must take charge of the picture for the present."

"What? oh, nonsense," Tails exclaimed, not taking such a suggestion seriously. "It's in my possession, and it's staying there. I found it."

"If you will kindly hand it to Inspector Payne," Bobby said.

Payne stepped forward. There was almost a scuffle. There would have been a scuffle if Tails had not been so completely taken by surprise, so entirely outmatched. The picture passed into Payne's possession. Bobby led the way towards the door, Payne following with the picture. Tails came behind almost screaming in loud lamentation and protest.

No one paid him any attention except that the large arm of a large, newly-arrived constable held him at the rear of the procession.

When they were outside Clavering said to Payne:

"Put it down against the wall there, so we can all see it. It ought to be identified."

This seemed reasonable to Payne, who, indeed, for his own part, thought he would like a good look at a painting that had been the cause of so many happenings. Also Clavering's last word had been well chosen and appealed to official instincts. To Payne's and to Bobby's also. No one yet had had a clear view in good light, and it would be a disaster, they both felt, if they had got hold of the wrong picture. So Payne, Bobby nodding assent, did as suggested. They all stood to look. Even Tails was silent for the moment. Bobby said sharply to Clavering:

"Here, what are you doing?"

"Nothing," Clavering protested in tones of injured innocence as he replaced a small kodak in his pocket, "only taking a snap. Why not? No harm in that, is there?"

Bobby wasn't sure. Neither was he sure if he had any right to object to the taking of a photograph of the picture. He decided to let the incident pass. Besides, Tails was beginning again his loud protests, uttering the wildest threats, making fantastic promises, introducing the name of every influential personage who had ever been near his showroom. Bobby told him, sternly, to keep quiet. He could consult his lawyers if he wanted to. If he could establish his right either to the ownership or the custody of the picture, it would be handed over to him at once. No doubt there would be many claimants, Bobby said. The Tallebois family, for instance. They might argue that the sale had not been with intention, and was not valid. Possibly, probably, there would be other claimants, declaring themselves relatives of the dead dealer. Tails himself apparently. Finally, the Crown, as inheriting all goods of an intestate dying without heirs. And, in fact, this last claim seems certain to be established, and thus the picture will probably one day become the property of the nation, and one of the glories of the National Gallery. But not yet, for the case will be fought up to the House of Lords; and in the meantime an injunction has been obtained, forbidding public exhibition on the ground of diminution of value. In the meantime, until the Courts had decided, or official guardians could be appointed, Bobby explained that he considered it his duty to take charge—and if Mr. Tails didn't shut up and quick about it, he would be charged with obstruction, that umbrella of a charge that can cover almost anything, even though subsequently it has to be justified in open court. Tails subsided in sullen silence. Had opportunity but served, could wishes have turned themselves into deeds, there would have been another murder then and there, and Bobby would have been the victim. At headquarters

Tails was, however, in some slight degree pacified by being accorded the right and the satisfaction of seeing the picture deposited in safe keeping, and of superintending the operation.

"At any rate," he said moodily to Bobby when this operation was at last completed, "you can't stop me calling a press conference to-morrow and telling the full story. It's only me can give a really good, complete description of the picture. Clavering only had the merest glimpse. He won't be able to say much. I can give full details."

"Oh, yes, yes," Bobby agreed, and added carelessly: "You know he took a snap? Didn't you notice?"

"He did what?" Tails screamed, and this time he did really scream.

"A snap, a photo.," Bobby explained. "He's just rung up from London. Must have caught the afternoon express, quick work. He's given the *Evening Announcer* people an interview apparently, and they are bringing out a special edition. Oh, and he said he was having that snap he took enlarged for show at Solomon's place to-morrow. He said he would send you a special ticket, and his love to both of us—a cheeky young man," said Bobby severely. "I wish I had him in the force for a week or two."

But Tails was not listening. He had collapsed on the nearest chair.

"After all I've gone through," he said with tears in his voice, nor would he be comforted.

THE END